D0783217

UNVEILED

La Rhonda Crosby-Johnson

San Leandro, California

Copyright © 2019 by La Rhonda Crosby-Johnson.

All rights reserved. No part of this publication may be reproduced, distributed, or transmitted in any form or by any means, including photocopying, recording, or other electronic or mechanical methods, without the prior written permission of the publisher, except in the case of brief quotations embodied in critical reviews and certain other noncommercial uses permitted by copyright law. For permission requests, write to the publisher at the address below.

La Rhonda Crosby-Johnson
925 Narcissus Court
San Leandro, CA 94578

Publisher's Note: This is a work of fiction. Names, characters, places, and incidents are a product of the author's imagination. Locales and public names are sometimes used for atmospheric purposes. Any resemblance to actual people, living or dead, or to businesses, companies, events, institutions, or locales is completely coincidental.

Ordering Information: For information about bulk purchases, please contact La Rhonda Crosby-Johnson at larhondawrites@gmail.com.

Unveiled/La Rhonda Crosby-Johnson—First Edition.

Trade Paperback ISBN: 978-0-578-65269-6

Printed in the United States of America

Dedication

This book is dedicated to my parents, Irma Smith (1924-1978) and Johnny Smith (1931-2002), who raised me to believe I could do anything. I also dedicate this book to every little girl who has the courage to put on paper those things that live inside her.

Acknowledgements

Unveiled has truly been a labor of intense love. The great thing about it was that I didn't have to "labor" alone. It would take far too long to thank all those involved, so I'll name a few and trust the rest of you to know that I am forever grateful for all the love and support you have shown me during this journey. Thanks to any and everyone who listened to a portion of this story in its many forms over the years and encouraged me to stay the course. Just knowing you were there kept me company during the solitary experience of writing.

Special thanks to Walker, for being the first to tell me the first draft of Unveiled was a novel and I was a writer. Thanks to my husband for understanding my process, giving me the space needed to write (no matter what time of the day or night!), and for always loving me and believing in the success of this project. Baby, you're THE BEST! Thank you to my son, Raymar; all I do well, I do with you in mind. Thank you to Tina McElroy Ansa and My Sea Island Writers Retreat sisters. My life was forever changed on Sapelo Island. I truly understand what you meant, Tina, when you told us "hard writing makes easy reading." Thank you to Vicki Ward who published my first work of non-fiction and took me on my first book tour with the Seasoned Sistahs. Thank you to Erin Goseer Mitchell and my cousin Bernardine Broadous for your reading and feedback on the earliest drafts; what you see here is because you took the time to tell me what you thought. Thanks to the wonderful women who helped add style, fashion, and beauty to the pages of Unveiled. As you marvel at Rhonda Lattier's beautiful home or wardrobe, you are experiencing the knowledge and expertise of my sister, Karyn Smith, and dear friend, Mary Glenn. So glad y'all LOVE to shop! Thank you to the greatest book club in the world, Marcus Book Club. And with more love and appreciation than mere words can express, BIG Thanks to Blanche Richardson for EVERYTHING and for being the first editor of Unveiled. Love you, much! To Tira McDonald who with surgical precision took the baton and put her editing magic on these pages…thank you and thank you again!

And to you, the reader, THANK YOU for taking the time to read Unveiled and for making one of my biggest dreams come true.

Reviews are welcomed and appreciated. Please take a moment to leave a review on Amazon, Goodreads, and Apple Books. I'd love to know what you think.

Happy Reading,
La Rhonda Crosby-Johnson December 2, 2018

"But it is only after the deepest darkness that the greatest joy comes."

— Malcolm X

PROLOGUE

It was early. The sun had just made an appearance in the clear blue of the sky. The smell of the rich, dark coffee filled the elegant kitchen and added to the warmness of the chestnut-colored cabinetry and marble counter tops. The sleek, stainless steel appliances caught the light coming through the plantation shutters and gave the room a magical luminescence. Marie loved this time of day. The quiet and stillness allowed all her thoughts to march in order. She buttered a warm croissant; filled a small bowl with blueberries, sliced bananas, and strawberries; and took her coffee onto the patio. She sipped carefully from the delicate, sea-green porcelain cup and hoped not to burn her tongue in her haste to taste the strong French roast she loved.

Marie took her reading glasses from the pocket of her blue velvet housecoat and opened the *L'Ouverture Gazette*. Calling what went on in L'Ouverture, Louisiana news was stretching it a bit; but Marie hated not knowing what her colleagues and students were discussing during the day. She had finished her croissant by the time she got to the "Around Town" section of the newspaper. She laughed at a picture of one of her sorority sisters in a dress that did nothing to hide the bulges that had taken over the place where her waistline should have been when the headline of a small article in the lower left-hand portion of the newspaper caught her attention.

"It cannot be," Marie said aloud as she adjusted her glasses to try to get a better look at the small, grainy photograph accompanying the article. She read the article twice before reaching for the cordless phone that lay next to her fruit bowl. She dialed the number to the St. Vincent Sheriff's Department and took another sip of her coffee to still the shaking of her hands.

"May I speak with Sheriff Claude La Fontaine, please?" Marie spoke clearly into the headset. "Tell him it is Dr. Marie Morgan calling. I have information I think he'll find important."

CHAPTER ONE

Grief and the sickeningly sweet smell of too many flowers hung heavy in the warm air of the late August afternoon. Morgan felt the weight of tears shed and hearts breaking. She rubbed her hands down her black silk suit when she walked slowly toward the simple wooden coffin that held the body of her beloved baby brother, Winston. "*Half*-brother." She could almost imagine her mother, Marie, standing in front of her and uttering the word "*half*" as if it were some sort of disease. Morgan breathed deeply and pushed Marie's words from her mind as she exhaled. They had no place here.

Winston's mask-like, powdered face somehow belied the words "heart attack" that still echoed in her head. Morgan stepped away from the coffin and quickly brushed away her tears. She fled the church and barely heard the words of comfort tossed her way. Outside there would be air she could breathe without inhaling the pain of the mourners.

Morgan moved quickly once outside. Her legs felt somehow lighter than they had only moments before. She breathed deeply for the first time since she had received the news of Winston's death a week ago and headed for the sanctuary of her car. The tinkling melody of the car alarm signaled her safe haven. She slid onto the butter-soft, caramel-colored leather seat and found comfort in its warmth. She cranked up the car, rolled down the electric windows, and turned on the CD player. The soulful sound of Jill Scott's voice surrounded her as she watched the family file out of the church and head toward limousines with the words Garrett Bros. painted in gold across the rear doors and windows. Of course, it would be Garrett Bros. They were still the only mortuary in town that "knew how to do colored." Morgan had heard her maternal grandmother, Essie Baptiste, say that many times while she was growing up. Mama Essie, as everyone lovingly called her, had made everyone in the family vow to take her body to Garrett Bros. when her time came. Although it had been three years since Mama Essie passed, Morgan still felt her presence in this place. This thought alone eased the tension in her neck and removed the large knot that had taken up residence in the pit of her stomach.

Morgan fanned herself slowly with the funeral program, which created a pleasant albeit warm breeze. Winston's high school graduation picture grabbed her attention as she placed the program on the passenger seat of her car. At eighteen and dressed in his tuxedo, he still had the face of a little boy. Things had changed so suddenly Morgan thought as she eased her car into the funeral procession.

Weeks before Winston was to report to Grambling University on a football scholarship, his girlfriend, Tanya, told him she was four months pregnant. Winston stayed in St. Vincent, married Tanya, and took a job driving a delivery truck for a local market. They named their son, William. Winston continued his training after he promised Morgan he would make good on his scholarship "one day." Now six years later, he laid dead of a heart attack at the age of twenty-four.

The gravesite ceremony was sad; final. Morgan felt goose bumps rise on her arms, despite the wet heat of the afternoon. Her stomach churned as she cast her eyes downward away from the flailing arms of the mourners encircling the freshly dug grave. Morgan clinched her teeth and willed herself not to cry. She feared if she started she might never stop. Irene, Winston's mother, had to be carried away by relatives and friends as she kicked, screamed, and threw herself at the coffin to stop it from being lowered into the ground. Family and friends tried unsuccessfully to quiet and soothe her before getting her seated in the back of the Garrett Bros. limousine. Morgan was drained and suddenly felt the reality of Winston's death like a weight tied around her heart. She decided to forego the traditional funeral repast at Irene's and instead went straight home after leaving the cemetery.

"Mama! Mama!" Morgan called as she entered the living room of her mother's home. The hardwood floors and rich mahogany wainscoting gleamed in the shadows of the early evening. The silver tea service shone brilliantly atop the highly polished buffet and was only rivaled by the matching silver candelabras that stood guard on each side. Morgan smiled as she wondered whose house had all the extra dust that was forbidden in Marie's home. She spied a note leaned against a crystal vase filled with white tulips on the dining room table.

Lisa, I hope you have not exhausted yourself completely with the day's events. I am giving a lecture at the university, followed by a reception sponsored by the Deltas. I'll be late. Your uncle Raymond wants you to call him.

- Mama

Lisa. Here was another reminder that she was no longer in New Orleans. No one there knew the "L" in L. Morgan Franklin stood for Lisa. For that matter, no one there knew much about the Rockhurst district of L'Ouverture, Louisiana.

L'Ouverture would barely be called a city by her more sophisticated and glitzier sister, New Orleans. It was a city where the smell of salt water and magnolias mingled together in the always too wet and too sticky air. Gumbo filled with spicy homemade sausages, crawfish the size of your fist, and crabmeat so sweet you thought you'd bitten into a praline, could be found in your best-dining establishments and clapboard shacks on the highway that divided the city into four districts: Rockhurst to the east, St. Augustine to the north, La Fitte to the west, and St. Vincent to the south.

The tongues of L'Ouverture's 4,950 residents couldn't decide whether France or the West Indies should dominate the language, so they mixed them together like jambalaya, often making sounds that those not born to the region didn't recognize as English. While many of L'Ouverture's youth headed for New Orleans and other big cities once they finished high school or just gave up, those who stayed were of the opinion that L'Ouverture's natural beauty and easy way of life made up for what it lacked in sophistication. On Saturday nights at Queenie's Jook Joint in St. Vincent, you could still find some of the old timers who claimed to be direct descendants of L'Ouverture's Founding Fathers.

Depending on which old timers were doing the talking, there were some Founding Mothers thrown in too. Like many southern cities, L'Ouverture's history came from the mouths and minds of the elders instead of official documents. Most could agree the first Black settlers of L'Ouverture arrived somewhere between 1811 and 1820 from the West Indies with Demarquis Rouge, a Frenchman of great wealth. He brought with him a man some said was the son of his father's favorite concubine, Francois De La Rockmonde, who claimed to have been a part of Toussaint L'Ouverture's Haitian Revolution. These African, West Indian people found the lush, humid area familiar and to their liking.

While Louisiana was a slave state, slavery looked different in L'Ouverture than in other parts of Louisiana in the early days. Many local legends said it was because of the mist that rolled up from the swamps in the middle of the night and mixed up the minds of slaves and slaveholders. Other tales said God had just smiled more when He put his breath to the small patch of land that would be called L'Ouverture and took some of the meanness out of the French who strived to turn L'Ouverture into their own playground. They made the rules as they went along. Demarquis Rouge had only one thing on his mind when he arrived in the new world— pleasure. He was not going to let a little incongruity like the color of skin get in his way.

The lines between slave and free were often fuzzy, particularly as wealthy Frenchmen made homes and families with their women, often of mixed race. Demarquis Rouge died after three months in what was to later be called La Rouge. No one seems to remember how, but before long De La Rockmonde was seen as the leader of this new land among both white and Black. So proud of his time, real or imagined with the great leader of the Haitian Revolution, Toussaint L'Ouverture, De La Rockmonde named the small enclave L'Ouverture.

The sights and sounds and somewhat better weather of New Orleans began to draw L'Ouverture's French gentry away from their swamp oasis. By 1822, L'Ouverture's Rockhurst and St. Vincent districts had joined America's small number of all-Black settlements. Francois De La Rockmonde died during an outbreak of yellow fever in 1825. His wife, Marshaleen De La Rockmonde, moved away from St. Vincent and founded the Rockhurst district in his honor. While it may not have been a part of any thought-out plan, French and other white settlers went about their business in the St. Augustine and La Fitte districts and left their darker brothers and sisters to fend for themselves in St. Vincent and Rockhurst. L'Ouverture had its share of racial tension and animosity softened only at times by the fact a rich white banker in La Fitte could probably find many of the colored mill workers in St. Vincent in his tangled family tree.

As time passed, the happy-go-lucky days of Demarquis Rouge's pleasurable playground gave way to the drawing of harsh color lines, hatred, and violence. Over the years, folks learned how to stay in their respective places.

Morgan's friends and colleagues in New Orleans had no idea until her junior year in college she had been Lisa Morgan. It had been that year she found out Dr. Russell Morgan was not her father. She had needed a copy of her birth certificate to include in her application for study abroad. Rather than bother her mother, she had written the county clerk's office for a copy. She was more than a little confused when she received it and saw the name *Alexander Franklin* printed on the line above the word "father." She thought it was a mistake, until she reviewed the rest of the document and discovered all the other information applied to her. She brought the birth certificate home with her when she visited for Christmas that year.

"Lisa, we thought it would be best if you never knew." *This was all Marie Baptiste Morgan would say as the color disappeared from her smooth café au lait cheeks.*

"Lisa, I am your father. This doesn't change anything. I love you, Lee-Lee," Russell Morgan had uttered around the lump that formed in his throat. His sapphire ring flashed in the light from the fireplace, as he mopped his cinnamon-colored brow. Despite her anger, she had smiled at the use of his special nickname for her.

"Who is Alexander Franklin?" she had asked as their eyes suddenly found interest in the pattern of the Oriental rug. The question sent Marie crying from the room. Russell left the room to follow her with a glance toward Lisa that conveyed how sorry he was she was in pain. Lisa's question had gone unanswered.

For years, she attempted to get answers from her parents and for years her father's evasiveness and her mother's anger were her only answers. Finally, Morgan found it easier not to ask. Months prior to graduating from college, she'd filed the necessary documents to have her name legally changed. She had packed *Lisa Morgan* away in a place that belonged only in L'Ouverture. L. Morgan Franklin headed to Harvard Law School. She spent her days and her roommate would say, most of her nights, engrossed in law reviews, journals, and probably every important U.S. Supreme Court decision since the turn of the century. She clerked for influential judges, interned at a legal aid office, and still found time to be an editor on the Harvard Law Review. It was no surprise she finished in the top five percent of her class and was being seriously courted by law firms from California to New York. After graduation, Morgan spent a year in London at a prestigious international law firm before returning to Louisiana and accepting a position with McDouglas,

Bradshaw & Newman in New Orleans, one of the south's leading corporate law firms.

Dr. Russell Morgan had been diagnosed with liver cancer during Morgan's first year with the law firm. She had rushed home to be with him and spent her days and nights seated beside his bed. The night before her father died, she held his small, paper-thin hand and prayed silently as she listened to the sounds of his labored breathing. He whispered how much he loved her and how proud she had made him. He had begged her to forgive him for not telling her about Alexander Franklin. She had covered his face in kisses as she cried and declared nothing else mattered except him getting better. He had smiled a smile that said they both knew that would not happen and told her the only thing he would ever get a chance to tell her about Alexander Franklin; the only thing Marie had ever told him. "Lee-Lee, he's a bad man. He hurt your mother. I only wanted to protect you both. I never meant to hurt you." He squeezed her hand and she was reminded of the strong hand she had held so many times as a little girl—his little girl.

A brilliant light shone in his eyes and a smile effortlessly took over his mouth just before he whispered his last, "Daddy loves you, Lee-Lee." Then with a suddenness that seemed to take the air from the room, he closed his eyes for the last time.

Morgan had grown up in two worlds; each world welcomed her with open arms. The Black upper-middle class world of her father, Dr. Russell Morgan, a Meharry Medical College alum, was filled with lawyers, doctors, and Black politicians. Dinners with family and friends from this world were held in grand dining rooms with crystal chandeliers, linen napkins, and tablecloths. This world was filled with piano and ballet lessons, museums, travel, and debutante balls. Her mother, Marie Baptiste Morgan, had grown up differently. She had grown up in the heart of the St. Vincent district, where Black folks didn't mind cursing each other out over a lively game of dominoes or throwing scalding water on a cheating husband.

While Morgan moved easily between Rockhurst's Black elite and St. Vincent's down-home folks, and found comfort in both, Marie had viewed them as warring opponents. After graduating from Tulane University, she had married Russell and joined him in his world. Marie was glad to leave her earlier days behind. As she studied for her master's degree in English, again at her beloved Tulane, she worked nights at a local diner to pay for charm school classes. She took speech classes and ridded her tongue of the memory of words spoken while running barefoot along St. Vincent's dusty roads. By the time she received her doctorate in sociology, Marie's world was replete with a grand home (or estate as they called big houses with front yards the size of parks) in the Rockhurst district; a handsome, smart, and well-respected husband; and the finer things in life that helped her forget the many nights she'd gone hungry as a child. Marie visited her mother only once in a while and no longer thought of herself as having lived any other way.

Russell insisted Morgan spend equal amounts of time with both Marie's family in St. Vincent and his family in Rockhurst. While the Morgan family had been prominent in L'Ouverture for generations, Russell's parents had taught him his good fortune had come on the backs of less fortunate Black people; Black people who had sacrificed, struggled, and died so he might have a chance at a better life.

Russell had always been fascinated by the stories of the Morgans told by his grandparents, great uncles, and great aunts at family gatherings. He could listen for hours as "the old folks" told stories of their childhoods and recounted the journey of the African in America. The Morgan clan were said to be a proud people who maintained personal dignity even during slavery. Many of his ancestors had fought in wars with the hope America would be a better place for their children. His paternal grandmother, Pearl, even had a picture of her great uncle who was a sailor in the Continental Navy. These stories always made Russell feel a certain sense of pride and a connection to the things and people around him. With his love of science, medicine seemed a natural fit for Russell. Becoming a doctor was his way of doing meaningful work like the great men and women of his family.

Marie's mother, Essie Baptiste, reminded Russell of these people his mother and father often spoke about with reverence and appreciation. Essie had always been kind and loving toward him. He could count on her to have a hot bowl of something delicious, wise words when he needed counsel, or a joke that would make him laugh until his sides ached. When Marie stopped visiting her mother altogether, Russell began taking Morgan to see Mama Essie every Saturday after her ballet lessons. Morgan adored her Mama Essie. Where Marie was often critical and cold toward her, Mama Essie always had a hug and kind words. It was to Mama Essie who Morgan took her childhood traumas and teenage crises. Mama Essie's encouragement, love, support, and common-sense advice had made her more than a grandmother. She became Morgan's trusted confidante and friend. Morgan had been devastated when she passed.

Morgan kicked off her black eel skin pumps and carried them in her hand into her mother's study. She called her uncle Raymond, Marie's only brother, and was soon laughing at his jokes. Some of the day's sadness was finally lifting. Before ending her call, she promised to see him for dinner the next day.

CHAPTER TWO

B y the next evening, Morgan felt relaxed and
refreshed by the cooler breeze that came through the car
window as she headed to her uncle Raymond's for dinner. A
smile spread across her face as she pulled up in front of the large
white frame house that held so many of her fondest memories.
The large wooden porch swing painted dark green to match the
shutters and trim swayed slightly as she pulled onto the driveway
behind her uncle's old faded, blue Chevy pickup. She stepped
onto the front porch and laughed as she reached for the doorbell.
Above the doorbell was the wooden plaque she had made during
vacation bible school when she was seven. The words "Door
Bell" carved in her neatest seven-year-old script.

Lisa had rushed home to show the plaque to her father.
She had discovered he was still at the hospital, and had
reluctantly decided to show her mother. Later that afternoon, her
Uncle Raymond had stopped by and found her crying on the
back porch. The plaque had been discarded in the yard. Marie
had called it "ridiculous and crude" and refused to have it
anywhere near her front door. Lisa could still remember the look
on Marie's face when she had held up what Lisa had considered

her masterpiece. Marie's turned up nose and twisted mouth gave her the look of someone who had smelled something rotten. She had held the plaque between her thumb and index finger and away from her body as if it would bite.

Marie had uttered through clinched teeth. "This thing looks like something you would find on some backwoods shack, Lisa. It is hardly fit for the trash heap. There is no way I will allow you to put that thing near our front door for all to see. You should've taken the knitting class. You might have been able to make yourself a decent scarf."

The next day, Uncle Raymond had picked Lisa up from vacation bible school and drove her straight to his house where the plaque had been protected with a clear varnish and hung proudly above his doorbell.

Morgan entered the house and was met by the sound of her uncle Raymond's "Come on back" greeting and the mouth-watering aroma of his prime rib. Her stomach began to grumble in anticipation as she moved quickly down the hall toward the kitchen. He rubbed his hands on the towel he always kept near the sink, hugged her, and gave her the message that her cousin Lonnie Jean would be working late at the hospital. Morgan made herself busy in the kitchen as Raymond finished dinner. This kitchen felt like an old friend. She had spent many hours in this kitchen, first with Mama Essie and later with Uncle Raymond and Tee Tee Corrie. She and Lonnie Jean made their first attempts at cooking in this room: A Mother's Day breakfast of French toast, sausage, and eggs for Mama Essie. Mama Essie had eaten the food, brought to her on a tray with a rose in a small vase, as if it had been prepared by the finest chef in Paris. Anthony, Lonnie Jean's ten-year-old son and Morgan's godson, was having dinner at a friend's house. There was no need to delay supper. Soon they settled at the large kitchen table.

"You get back out to see Irene and Carl?" Raymond Baptiste asked as he poured gravy over a mountain of the creamiest mashed potatoes Morgan had ever seen.

"No. I thought they could probably use some rest," Morgan answered as she slowly chewed the prime rib and savored its flavor. She sighed and allowed the taste of her uncle's food to heal all the hurt places in her spirit.

"Nothing like your Uncle Raymond's prime rib, huh, Little Girl?" Raymond smiled at his niece as his light brown eyes showed his delight.

"As Mama Essie would say, 'nothing this side of heaven.' I wish you would open the restaurant again." Morgan said quickly and took another bite of the prime rib. She looked sheepishly across the table at her uncle. His smooth caramel skin reminded her of the warm butterscotch syrup on top of his bread pudding. Gray strands of hair had begun to stake their claim to his head of thick, wavy hair.

Raymond shook off the comment and put a large spoonful of sweet peas with baby carrots swimming in butter on Morgan's plate. His thick gold wedding band flashed brightly and caught the remainder of the day's sunshine coming through the kitchen window. Raymond had always loved to cook. When he left the army, he returned to St. Vincent to marry his high-school sweetheart, Coretta Granger. It was no surprise when he used his G. I. Bill and opened Ray and Corrie's Kitchen the following year.

The restaurant was clean and simple, like the people who ate there, with food that rivaled many of Louisiana's finest restaurants. On any given day, you could find a Black janitor from St. Vincent agreeing with a white mill worker from La Fitte that Corrie had the best pecan pie in the world; while doctors and lawyers from both Rockhurst and St. Augustine argued over their preferences for Raymond's gumbo or jambalaya. Together Raymond and Corrie made a life for themselves; raised a daughter, Lonnie Jean; and ran Ray and Corrie's Kitchen for almost thirty years. Raymond often said they'd shared a love that "was warm like flannel and smooth like silk."

In the spring of 2000, Corrie complained of stomach trouble. It was cancer. The doctors had operated and removed over half of her stomach and spleen. Radiation and chemotherapy had followed. The treatments left her frail, scared, and bald. Just as she began to take a turn for the better, doctors discovered a new growth in her uterus which quickly spread to her ovaries. This time, Corrie refused more surgery and debilitating treatments. She hid her pain in the solace of Raymond's embrace and Lonnie Jean's smiles. By fall of the same year, she was gone. The dinner following the funeral was, of course, held at Ray and Corrie's Kitchen. L'Ouverture's citizens, Black and white, crammed into the restaurant to eat mountains of dirty rice, crawfish stew, pecan pie, and banana pudding while they talked of the good times they'd spent with Ray and Corrie over the years. After playing the song he loved to play for Corrie on the jukebox, Percy Sledge's "When a Man Loves a Woman," Raymond locked up the restaurant and never opened the doors again.

"Shame 'bout Winston," Raymond said and moved the conversation away from the restaurant. He filled a large bowl with Morgan's favorite dessert: blueberry dumplings topped with his famous vanilla-bourbon whipped cream.

"It's hard to believe he's gone," A huge blueberry dumpling sat on the edge her spoon. Raymond wiped the corner of his mouth on his napkin and cleared his throat. Morgan recognized the sound and braced herself. Her uncle Raymond only cleared his throat before he had to say something he thought would be difficult for the listener to hear. "Knew it would be hard on you. Didn't want you workin' yourself up even more," he spoke slowly as he poured himself a cup of coffee. "That's why I ain't said nothing before now."

"Said anything about what?" Morgan felt her pleasant evening slipping away like the whipped topping melting over her warm blueberry dumplings.

"A friend of Lonnie Jean's was working the night they brought Winston into the hospital. She said he'd been shot," Raymond began, his eyes begged for her forgiveness. "Lonnie Jean gets to work the next day and Garrett Bros. already come and picked up the body."

"Mama never said anything about this." Morgan felt dazed.

"Your mama don't live on this side of town no more, Little Girl." He wished there was something he could do to erase the sadness that had returned to his niece's eyes.

"Has anyone gone to the police with this?" Morgan questioned while she pushed her dessert away. She looked into her uncle's eyes while her own filled with tears.

"That's where things take a peculiar turn. Lonnie Jean say all reports say heart attack. When Carl get wind of the shooting story, he take it straight to the sheriff. Sheriff say, the reports said Winston died of a heart attack; damn shame but it ain't a crime. He sent Carl on his way."

"Uncle Raymond, are you telling me someone killed Winston?" Morgan's eyes searched her uncle's face as if she would find the answer there. When he remained silent, she asked, "Uncle Raymond, do you think someone murdered Winn?"

"Think so, Little Girl. You remember Whitey Peters, Eddie and Earthalene Peters' boy? Well, he a deputy sheriff now. He been looking around, but so far ain't come up with nothing. Seem to me, something going on and Winston got himself caught right in the middle of it." Raymond stood and began to clear the table.

Unlike Raymond's dinner, the thought of Winn being killed was difficult to digest and left a sick knowing in the pit of Morgan's stomach. She helped him clean up the kitchen and rode with him to pick Anthony up from his friend's house. Anthony's non- stop chatter on the way back home and Raymond's questions about New Orleans and her work took her mind off Winn's death and the questions that were forming about his possible murder.

The mood became almost festive once Lonnie Jean made it home. They all enjoyed a lively game of Scrabble and Anthony's laughter at the crazy words Raymond tried to use to win. The house filled with music when Morgan and Lonnie Jean turned on

Raymond's old console stereo and danced to records they hadn't heard since high school. Morgan allowed her family to push thoughts of heart attacks, gunshot wounds, and police cover-ups out of her mind for the moment. Uncle Raymond and Anthony long gone to bed, Morgan and Lonnie Jean said their goodbyes sometime after midnight with hugs and kisses. Driving home, Morgan barely heard the plaintive sounds of Maxwell from her car's stereo because the conversation she'd had with her uncle Raymond replayed itself over and over in her head. She wiped away tears, as the thought of someone murdering her brother refused to leave her mind. Before she knew it, she was pulling her car onto her mother's circular driveway on what her uncle Raymond called "the other side of town."

"Well, Raymond finally let you get away," Marie said, as her daughter entered the room and kissed her cheek. Marie placed the book she was reading on her lap and took off her reading glasses. Her sitting room was dark. A small reading light provided the only light and cast ghostly shadows on the pale, yellow walls. She stretched slightly on the chaise lounge and enjoyed the rough feel of the brocade fabric against her silk pajamas.

Morgan did not need light to know this room, one of her favorite rooms in the house. Rich, creamy, off-white carpet, delicately held the white and gold, antique Queen Anne writing desk and chair. The pale, yellow walls gave added color to the rich, lemon- yellow silk draperies and chaise lounge. White china vases filled with snow white roses and lilies gave the room a sweet, soft scent that was powerful without being overwhelming. White silk brocade covered wing chairs adorned the corners of the room. The richness of the brocade fabric matched that of Marie's chaise lounge and added the feeling of elegance to the space. Morgan and her father had nicknamed it the Lemon Pie Room.

"You smell like blueberries," Marie commented as her sharp pointed nose wrinkled slightly showing her distaste. Despite the expression on her face, Morgan could not deny her mother's beauty. Morgan remembered watching the 1959 version of the film *Imitation of Life* with Mama Essie when she was about six years old and wondered how her mother had gotten into the television set. Marie's resemblance to the actress, Susan Kohner, who had played the grown-up Sarah Jane was uncanny.

"Uncle Raymond made blueberry dumplings." Morgan sat on the end of the chaise lounge. "I have not eaten that, well since…since I was at Uncle Raymond's last."

"The way Raymond loves to cook *and* eat, it's a wonder he isn't as big as a house," Marie grunted in response as she thought of her brother who did not appear to have gained a pound since high school. "How are Lonnie Jean and Anthony?"

"They're good. Lonnie Jean had to work late, so she missed dinner. Anthony had dinner at his friend's house, so it was just Uncle Raymond and me for dinner. We went to pick Anthony up later and I couldn't believe how big he's gotten."

"Children do that, Lisa." Marie's voice indicated boredom with the conversation. "At least, Lonnie Jean had enough sense to put him in school over here. He attends Mercer Academy. It is one of Rockhurst's finest elementary schools. I hear he is very bright." "Lonnie Jean's off tomorrow so we can spend some time together." Morgan smiled for the first time since she came into the room and thought ahead to the day planned with her favorite cousin.

"How long are you planning to stay here, Lisa?"

"Just until Sunday. I have to return to work Monday morning. I wish I could stay longer and spend some more time with Irene and Carl. Winn's death has been really hard on them. I can't even begin to imagine the pain Tanya and William must feel."

"Things happen, Lisa. No need to put your life on hold." The chill in Marie's voice raised goose bumps on Morgan's arms. She clinched her jaws with the anger she always felt whenever Marie spoke of Winn.

"Mama, why didn't you tell me there was talk Winn was shot and killed?" Morgan returned the conversation to the topic she wished to discuss.

"I should have known better than to let you go over to Raymond's alone. He's prone to senseless gossip, just like the rest of them over there." Her voice rose in pitch and volume. Morgan knew that tone. She had struck a nerve. "I did not see any need to go into all that, Lisa. Winston is dead. How he died does not matter."

"I cannot believe you just said that. Mama, my *brother* may have been murdered. That matters," Morgan yelled and jumped to her feet; her rage filled the room. She moved toward the window as far away from Marie as possible. "Lonnie Jean said her friend told her Winn was shot five times. Five times, Mama! That means someone *wanted* Winn dead."

"Stop being dramatic, Lisa. Who would want Winston dead? It was probably just a case of being in the wrong place at the wrong time." Marie regained control of her voice. "You know how they live out there. It was probably one of those drive-by shootings that kill one of them every Saturday night."

"You are too much, Mama." Morgan shook her head in disbelief. "At least your drive- by theory is an improvement over the heart attack lie."

"Lisa, that's quite enough," Marie warned. "I am still your mother and you will watch your tone."

"Yes, ma'am," Morgan said and sighed in response. She was suddenly exhausted. "It's just that Winn never got a chance. I cannot stop thinking how none of this would have happened if he had just been able to get out of St. Vincent."

"Get some sleep, Lisa. You look miserable. You'll feel better in the morning," Marie said and lifted her book from her lap. She returned her reading glasses to her face effectively ending the conversation.

CHAPTER THREE

"D"amn girl. You musta robbed yourself a bank!"
exclaimed Mary Joyce Lyons, as Morgan got out of the
sleek, black BMW. She had purchased it brand new with the
money from her last year's bonus check.

"No, Mary Joyce. I just work," Morgan laughingly
responded and gave her twenty- two-year-old half-sister a hug.
She had Winn's deep-set dimples. Too many babies, in too few
years, had changed her once hourglass figure into a shape that
was now more comfortable in sweatpants and oversized tees than
the skintight jeans and midriff blouses she wore as a teenager.
"How're you doing?"

"How it look like I'm doin'?" Mary Joyce inhaled what
her nose told her was very expensive perfume. She stepped away
from Morgan and rubbed her tummy.

"I didn't know." Morgan noticed Mary Joyce's growing
belly for the first time. She turned away to keep Mary Joyce
from seeing the look of disappointment on her face. Mary Joyce
was already the mother of three boys who were all under the age
of five.

Mary Joyce read her sister's silence. "Everybody ain't perfect like you, big sister. Everybody cain't have a fancy lawyer job like you, so don't say shit to me. I hear enough of that from my mama and every damn body else who always got something to say to me 'bout my business." Mary Joyce's toasted almond complexion flushed red with anger.

"Speaking of career," Morgan said and left the sentence hanging between them in Mary Joyce's anger and the hot morning air. She looked Mary Joyce in the eyes and no longer attempted to mask her feelings.

"There you go with that again. Darrell just waiting on the right thing to come along," Mary Joyce responded to the question in Morgan's eyes about her husband. "Hard to get work out here; this ain't N'Orleans. I'll get back on at the cannery once the baby comes."

"While Darrell waits on the right thing." Morgan could not keep the bitterness out of her voice. "Where are Irene and Carl?"

"Mama in the house. Daddy had to get back to work. Mister Sam wouldn't give him no more time off. Can you believe that shit? Winn dead and all he can think about is who gone open up for him while he over in Rockhurst playing golf." Morgan shook her head and started walking toward the front steps.

"Hey, Lisa," Mary Joyce called as Morgan opened the screen door, "Good to see you, sis." She smiled. Morgan winked. All the angry words were forgotten. She stepped into the house—her other world.

Morgan could smell the pungent odor of cooking grease and the living smells of decades as soon as the screen door slapped closed behind her. Sunlight poured through the living room window. Morgan walked across the well-worn carpet and paused to look at the family pictures that covered the tables and mantel above the brick fireplace. She could hear the sounds of a TV talk show as she neared the kitchen.

"Morning," Morgan called as she entered the kitchen.

"Lord have mercy!" Irene cried and hoisted her bulk up from the olive-green vinyl and chrome chair. "I didn't hear you come in. Move them newspapers out that chair and sit on down. You want some breakfast, baby?"

"No thanks, Irene." The two women embraced. The too sweet smell of Dixie Peach hair oil and Jergen's lotion filled her nose. There was very little left of the woman who once had been known in St. Vincent as "quite a looker." Years of worry had dulled what were once shining brown eyes. Too many years of doing the job of two people had rounded her shoulders and put a bend in her back that made people forget she'd once stood tall at 5'7".

"So glad you could be here. Would'a meant a lot to Winn. He was some proud of his big sister, the N'Orleans lawyer," Irene gave Morgan's hand a squeeze.

"I was proud of him, too. Winn was my brother. There was no place else for me to be but here." Both women smiled through their pain at the mention of his name.

"How are Tanya and William?" Morgan asked as they sat down at the table. "I called for her a couple days ago, but Mary Joyce said she was sleeping."

"She havin' a tough time, Lisa. Her and William been out here since it happened. She gone to take William to school. He a child. He misses his friends. Did her good to get out of the house." Irene moved steaming grits around on her plate.

"You have a full house," Morgan commented, just at the moment Mary Joyce's three boys burst into the room. Despite the fact sleep was still crusty in the corners of their eyes and the bulge in the youngest boy's diaper suggested he was past changing time, they were happy as only young children could be. Morgan watched in amusement as they moved quickly around the kitchen and barely glanced at her or Irene. Eleven-month old Dejuan, bulging diaper in the air, bent over to grab a pot top from a low cabinet shelf. Morgan laughed as he proceeded to push it across the floor and make car sounds.

D. J., Mary Joyce's oldest son, who had just turned four years old, attempted to pull a cup of juice from the counter top before Irene's quick hands caught it. She handed the cup to him and quickly poured another cup for two-year-old DeMarcus before the scream he was preparing could leave his mouth. They scattered in three different directions and added their voices to that of the TV talk show host.

"You see your nephews?" Irene laughed and lifted DeJuan as he toddled by on legs new to walking. She called for the older two to come say good morning to their auntie Lisa. "Darrell, come get these boys out my kitchen. Darrell!" Irene called.

After what seemed like ten minutes and several more calls, the last being *"Darrell Lyons, bring yo' black ass out here and get these boys!"* Mary Joyce's husband entered the room. He looked as if he'd slept in the faded black shorts and t-shirt he wore. His bare feet made a sound like two pieces of sandpaper rubbing together as he moved across the kitchen's worn linoleum floor. He barked several times at the boys which caused them to disappear into the darkness of the backroom.

"Change the baby, Darrell. His diaper is more than soaked," Irene snapped and handed the squirming toddler to his father. She took her plate from the table and moved slowly toward the sink, the stiffness in her back showed in each step.

"Hey, Money," Darrell said as he simultaneously ignored Irene, placed DeJuan on the floor, and looked Morgan up and down. The sound of his voice brought images of a smoke-filled pool hall to mind. His stale cigarette breath warmed Morgan's cheek as he hugged her. The sharp smell of his unwashed body hung to his tall, lean frame. Morgan tried to hold her breath and not make a face.

"How are you doing, Darrell?" She hoped the answer was not already written all over her face.

"Be doing a hellava lot better if I was rollin' like you, Money," Darrell took a long look out the window at Morgan's parked car.

"Well just for now, Darrell. Roll yo' funky ass out my kitchen and get the boys cleaned up." Irene did nothing to hide the disgust written across her round, toffee- colored face. Darrell mumbled something, poured himself a cup of coffee, and left the kitchen. DeJuan crawled quickly behind him and back into the darkened room before the door shut. "That's one sorry excuse for a man. Lay around here all day drinking. Don't help Mary Joyce with them boys. Won't look for no job. Don't miss a single meal though. I done gone back to work at the school cafeteria to take some of the load off Carl. I swear if it wasn't for Mary Joyce and them boys, I'd put his Black ass out with the trash on Tuesday mornings."

"I just wanted you and Carl to know how sorry I am about Winn." Morgan opened her purse to get her checkbook.

"Lisa, you ain't got to do that. We making out all right." Morgan ignored her and wrote out a check.

"Good. Then this will help "all right" along." Morgan handed Irene the check. "Thank you, baby." Irene smiled with tears in her eyes. She put the check in the pocket of her cafeteria uniform.

"Irene, what happened to Winn?" Morgan asked as she and Irene began to clear away the breakfast dishes.

"You musta spent some time out to Raymond's. All that's just a lot of foolish talk, Lisa. Don't get yourself worked up behind it. Some things you just cain't explain. Been enough for me to keep mind and body together."

"Well, I think someone needs to start explaining about my brother's murder." She watched for a reaction on Irene's face. There was none.

"Baby, this is L'Ouverture, not N'Orleans. Don't do for Black folks in St. Vincent to ask no questions. 'Cause we don't get no answers." Irene sighed and turned her attention to filling the sink with dirty dishes.

Well, this might not be New Orleans, Morgan thought as she washed breakfast dishes, but she had made up her mind that she was going to ask some questions and get some answers.

Morgan helped Mary Joyce get the boys bathed and dressed after she finished with the breakfast dishes. Irene left for work, after she gave Mary Joyce instructions on things she wanted done before she came home that evening. Morgan couldn't get over how cute the boys were once they'd been cleaned. They'd taken Mary Joyce's light gray eyes and thick, tightly curled hair, while taking Darrell's only redeeming quality— his smile—or at least his smile before tobacco stains and irregular brushing took even that away. Morgan and Mary Joyce took the boys into the warmth of the backyard to play. Morgan sat on the bottom step of the porch watching her nephews chase each other around in circles. Mary Joyce wandered off into the wooded area behind the house.

"Do you still play?" Morgan asked. She left the door open to the old, detached kitchen Carl had converted to a work shed years ago. The smell of lemon oil mixed with the strong, musty closed-in smell of the room met her nose. Morgan cleared her throat.

"Your nephews don't leave me much time for playing the piano, Lisa." Mary Joyce's voice sounded far away even though Morgan could reach out and touch her. "You remember when my daddy brought this thing home?" Her fingers moved soundlessly across the yellowed keys of the old Baldwin upright, her polishing rag momentarily forgotten.

"We spent most of that summer stripping it down and refinishing it. I remember you wanted Carl to paint it yellow. That was your favorite color." Morgan sat on the dusty cushioned piano bench next to her sister. She had found the fabric for the cushion in an old scrap bag in Mama Essie's sewing room. She and Irene had used the yellow and blue flowered fabric to make the cushion, now faded with time and wear. "It sure was a mess when Carl brought it home."

"Yellow still my favorite color, but glad y'all talked me out of that. It was almost too pretty to touch when we got finished with it. I would sit for hours just looking at the wood. I'd never seen something so pretty and it was mine." Mary Joyce moved the soft rag in her hand across the top of the piano and worked the thick paste-like polish into the dark wood. "Daddy told Mama he found it at a church rummage sale over in St. Augustine. Know what he told me one time when he was out here listening to me play once?" Morgan shook her head and picked up a matching rag and began to wipe away her own circle of polish.

"He got it from a 'ho house' in La Fitte. Said he did some work for the woman that owned the place and when she got a new piano she let him have this one."

"Good thing he made up that story about the church rummage sale or you may never have been able to serenade us all summer," Morgan said and admired the richness of the wood that revealed itself after her polishing.

"I was pretty good, huh? Mama always wanted me to play church music, but I liked playing along to Daddy's old jazz and blues albums. Wanted my boys to play, but they just bang on the keys and fidget when I try to teach 'em. Darrell say his boys gotta play basketball. So, they can get rich enough to buy they daddy a big house and a car for everyday of the week." Mary Joyce rubbed her swelling belly. "She gone be different though. I'm gone teach her to play and let her play whatever she like."

"Or he," Morgan cautioned, just in case her sister was carrying another boy.

"Don't even think it, Lisa," Mary Joyce rolled her eyes. "No. It's a girl. I can feel it. Mama say I can have that little room off the washroom to fix up for her 'til me and Darrell get our own place. I already made some yellow curtains to go over that little window in there."

"A niece would be a nice change." She found herself hoping it was a girl for Mary Joyce's sake. "I know she'll play as well as her mama."

"I already asked Miss Cotton at church if she'd give her lessons when she get big enough. With lessons, she can be real good. Way better than me." Her soft gray eyes lit up and rivaled the light from the bare light bulb that swung over the piano.

"Maybe she can get good enough to play concerts and get the hell out of St. Vincent."

"I'm sure she'll be able to do whatever she sets her mind to," Morgan agreed in response. "You always did. You still can, you know?"

"There it is. I was wonderin' when you was gonna start in on me," Mary Joyce snapped, closed the lid of the piano, and stood up. "Where the hell am I goin' Lisa with three bad-ass boys, a lazy ass husband, and another baby on the way? They got jobs for folks like me at your fancy law office in New Orleans?"

"You know what," Morgan stood. "I didn't come out here to argue with you or to join in your little pity party, Mary Joyce. I'm just saying this doesn't have to be all there is to your life. You're young and smart. You don't like how things are going for you, you can change that."

"That's easy talk for you, Lisa. My pampered princess sister from Rockhurst. You ain't never had to go without; your fancy-ass mama made sure of that. Hell, I bet you had shit you didn't even want. You had all the chances, Lisa. You was allowed to have your dreams. Well out here in St. Vincent, the only dreams we know are nightmares and you standin' in mine."

"I wasn't trying to put you down, Mary Joyce." Morgan saw the tears clouding her sister's gray eyes. "I just want you to know it is never too late to dream a dream."

Morgan pressed a few twenties into Mary Joyce's hand as she hugged her and said goodbye. She'd stayed longer than she planned and would have to take the highway back to town to make it to lunch with Lonnie Jean on time.

"Mary Joyce would be better off running Darrell over with Carl's old truck," Lonnie Jean said. She laughed and looked at the menu.

"She's pregnant again. I just have a hard time understanding Mary Joyce." Morgan picked up her menu. "Is birth control against the law in St. Vincent?"

"Please," Lonnie Jean began and let out a long breath that turned the word into three syllables. "I wrote grants to fund three free family planning clinics. Got the money too. Had to return most of the money because we could only fill one day. They won't come in. I sent public health nurses out to them. They stand behind the screen door and look at them. Every year before school, I have to send health officers out there to threaten them with jail just to get them to bring the kids in for immunizations. Last year, L'Ouverture General got a van to go to the high schools to do sex education classes and give out condoms. That seems to be the only thing that has worked so far. They're having some of the same problems over in St. Augustine, but it's like the world moved on and left St. Vincent behind."

They took their time with the menu, sipped ginger tea, Morgan's favorite, and caught each other up with the latest happenings in their lives. Morgan encouraged Lonnie Jean to go out with a physical therapist who had been asking her out for several weeks. Lonnie Jean scolded Morgan for working too hard and told her she could stand to gain a few pounds. They laughed with the ease that comes from years of shared secrets and love that understands and accepts all faults.

"Lonnie Jean, what do you know about how Winn died?" Morgan asked after the waitress had taken their order. She pulled out a small notepad.

"Lisa, don't start nothing down here the rest of us can't live with," Lonnie Jean warned as Morgan began to flip through the notepad.

"Uncle Raymond said your friend was there when they brought Winn into emergency." Morgan ignored her cousin while she read from her notes. "Who was the attending physician?"

"Jesse Reynolds. He's from Houston or somewhere. He's only down here to work off his medical school bills. Don't understand the Black folks and scared of the crackers, but otherwise he's a pretty decent man. General's lucky to have him; he's a good doctor," Lonnie Jean said in exasperation. "Since you won't leave this alone, have a talk with Nora Hill. She was in surgery the night they brought Winston in and she's a friend of mine. Make sure she's still my friend, Lisa when you get through talking to her. Her shift starts at three."

"Who's handling the investigation?" Morgan wrote furiously in her notebook. "What investigation?" Lonnie Jean sipped her sweet tea.

"Winn's murder investigation?"

"Lisa, all the reports say Winn died of a heart attack. That doesn't leave anything to investigate."

"The attending physician has to report gunshot wounds to the authorities, Lonnie Jean, even in St. Vincent." Morgan's head began to ache at the thought.

"Lisa," Lonnie Jean started as the waitress placed a steaming bowl of oxtail soup in front of her with a platter of spicy cornbread that could easily feed a table of eight. Morgan had chosen the blackened red snapper, rice and peas, and collard greens. The waitress poured tall glasses of iced sweet tea for each of them and said she'd check back with them soon.

"I know. I know. This ain't N'Orleans," Morgan repeated the words Irene had spoken earlier. She closed her notebook and decided to enjoy her lunch and her cousin's company.

CHAPTER FOUR

"Chief, you remember that clerk over at General?" Arthur Lee DuPont asked as he quickly knocked and opened the door to the sheriff's office.

"Yeah, Arthur Lee, I remember her. Little Nancy," Sheriff Claude La Fontaine said. His thin lips were drawn up in what would have been a smile on any other face. "What about her?"

"She left a message for you. Said Morgan Franklin was over to the hospital yesterday afternoon asking that nurse, Nora Hill, questions about Carl and Irene's boy, Winston. Nancy said she overheard Nora say something about bullet wounds. Said some of the folks talking about what they *think* happened," Arthur Lee finished with the look of a dog that wants his belly scratched.

"Who the hell is he?"

"Ain't no he, suh. It's a she," Arthur Lee answered.

"Arthur Lee, you starting not to make sense, son. A woman named Morgan Franklin?" Sheriff La Fontaine's stomach began to tighten as it always did right before the burning acid poured into it. He would surely empty his newest bottle of Maalox today if this kept up.

Claude La Fontaine had only been in St. Vincent for a little over two years and he hated it more with each minute. He was on his way up, when some politician "friends" left him holding the bag on a fraud, corruption, and embezzlement scheme in Baton Rouge. He had escaped prison only because some very important people liked his wife, Hannah, and owed her very well-connected family some rather large favors. His "friends" banished him to L'Ouverture, they said, until "things cooled down some."

"What the hell kinda name is Morgan Franklin for a woman?" Sheriff Fontaine finally asked, while Arthur Lee stood looking at him. He would never understand these people.

"First name wasn't always Morgan, Chief. It was Lisa. She the daughter of Russell Morgan, that colored doctor everybody still talks about, and that fancy colored college professor live over in Rockhurst. She a big-time lawyer up in N'Orleans now. Guess she changed her name like some of them celebrities do. She come back from time to time to see her folks."

"What the hell a big-time N'Orleans lawyer doing asking questions about some boy had a heart attack?" Sheriff La

Fontaine asked. The confusion etched its way into the creases around his eyes.

"Probably 'cause he was her brother. Half-brother anyway. She the half-sister to Mary Joyce Lyons too. From what I hear, she ain't related to Irene's oldest boy, Carl Jr. though."

"What? Winston Banks got a fancy N'Orleans lawyer for a sister? You making less sense than normal, Arthur Lee. I thought you said she was the daughter of a colored doctor and professor?" His stomach churned with purpose now as he loosened the collar on his shirt.

"Well, that's where the story gets kinda tangled up, Chief. Story is that Lisa, Winston, and Mary Joyce all had the same Daddy. Doc Russell wasn't her real pa and Carl Banks ain't Winston or Mary Joyce's real pa, either," Arthur Lee hoped this information would take the confused look off of his boss' face.

"Well who the hell is they pa?" Sheriff La Fontaine scratched his head full of graying hair. He thought maybe he should just go home today, pack his things, and sail away on his fishing boat.

"Don't know that, Chief. Ain't never heard that part of the story."

"Look, I don't need nobody snoopin' round in St. Vincent trying to stir up trouble. Who can I talk to about this

Morgan or Lisa or whatever the hell her name is?" Sheriff La Fontaine threw the now empty Maalox bottle into the wastebasket. He stuffed a handful of Tums into his mouth, chewed fast, and hoped for immediate relief.

"Have to ride out to the swamps for that, Chief," Arthur Lee held a look of regret on his face.

"Why? Her pa livin' in the swamps?" Sheriff La Fontaine rubbed his chest. For a moment, he wondered if he was having a heart attack. He reached for a bottle of Bayer aspirin on the shelf behind his desk.

"Naw, suh," Arthur Lee stifled a chuckle, "The Witch lives out there."

"Witch? Arthur Lee, you sounding crazier by the minute, son. What the hell are you talking about?" The sheriff now felt a headache crawl into the space between his eyes and make itself comfortable.

"Get your hat, Chief. If it's any answers, they out in the swamp."

Celeste Du Maurier warmed her smooth, ebony hands near the roaring fire in the fireplace and sniffed the air. Someone was coming. Someone very bad. She sat in the straight-backed cane chair and braided her thick, silver-gray, waist-long hair into one large braid. She wound the braid around her head until it looked like a crown. The large gold hoops in her ears sparkled in the light of the fire. The only other light in the room came from the candles she had been burning for three days now. She had not eaten or drank during that time and sensed she would need her strength. This time, it will be bad, she thought as she pulled the emerald green shawl around her shoulders.

A little after 12:00 p.m., the teal blue and white cruiser marked St. Vincent Sheriff Department pulled off the dirt road leading into the swamp. The road soon turned to marsh as it headed into a yard filled with grasses and shrubs. The moss-covered cypress trees hid the bright noon day sun and cooled the swamp. It took Sheriff La Fontaine and Arthur Lee DuPont several minutes to find the wooden walkway that would take them across the swamp waters to the small, weathered shack at the end of the planks. The planks groaned and swayed beneath their weight and at times almost touched the water.

"Hey, Celeste. Celeste. You in there? It's Arthur Lee. Come on and open up," Arthur Lee called. His skin was covered in goose bumps as he looked into the dark, murky water. He had never liked this place. As a boy, his grandfather told him stories about these swamps. The swamps, he said, had been filled with

African slaves, run off from plantations all across the south. Arthur Lee could feel the muscles in his neck tighten as he remembered his grandfather's story about some slave catchers who had followed a group of runaways from Georgia into these swamps. The band of twenty men had never been seen again. Celeste was a descendent of those Africans. The area surrounding the swamps had once been alive with families full of happy, smiling children; laughter and love; safe from the hands of hateful white men. Celeste now lived alone with the nature of the swamp and the spirits of those Africans as her only company.

"Where else would I be?" Celeste asked from the shadows of the front door. Sheriff La Fontaine blinked his eyes and tried to stop his brain from registering that she seemed to just appear in the door. Arthur Lee jumped when he saw her.

"Damn it, Celeste. Why you all the time jumpin' out scaring folks? You like to give me a heart attack right here," Arthur Lee snapped, removed his hat, and wiped his sweat-drenched brow. "This here is Sheriff La Fontaine, Celeste. He took over after Billy Ray fell ill."

"I know who he is," Celeste said in a voice barely above a whisper.

Something he could not see splashed in the water and caused the sheriff to jump. He should never have let Arthur Lee drag him out here. All this talk about witches had given him the creeps.

"Chief need some information on Doc Russell and Marie's gal."

"Why you come here to ask me these questions, Arthur Lee?" She never took her eyes off the sheriff. His skin seemed to crawl under her gaze and he began to scratch the back of his neck.

"Chief needs to know who her pa was."

"You just said she was the doctor and Marie's gal. Ain't that your answer?" Celeste looked at Arthur Lee for the first time.

"Her *real* pa. Word is that it wasn't Doc Russell."

"Why you asking?" Celeste's nose wrinkled slightly. She could smell the sweat and fear of the sheriff.

"Look here. We askin' the questions," Sheriff La Fontaine snapped. Suddenly, his skin was unusually warm in the coolness of the swamp.

The door closed with a quiet thud. Arthur Lee would swear, later as he retold the story to the younger deputies, that he never saw Celeste's arm reach to close the door.

"Now you done made her mad," Arthur Lee moaned in response. "Chief, you cain't be talkin' to no witch like that. 'Specially one as powerful as Celeste."

"Witch my ass!" spat Sheriff La Fontaine as he scratched vigorously at his neck and turned to stomp away. The wooden walkway screeched under the force of his steps. "I can't believe I let you drag me out here to the damn swamp to talk to some crazy-ass- old woman living in a shack! I swear all of y'all nuts down here."

"She done put something on you, huh, Chief?" The sheriff put the car into gear and headed back up the dirt road that would lead them out of the swamp.

"Arthur Lee, shut up before I put something on you!" Sheriff La Fontaine yelled and banged his fist against the steering wheel as if that would make the car go faster over the unpaved road. "I don't want to hear no more of your talk about witches. Damn backwoods foolishness."

"You rubbed her the wrong way from the start. Ain't you seen how she was lookin' at you?" Arthur Lee shook his head and felt a bit of sympathy for his boss.

"I don't know why I listened to you in the first place. I must be losing my damn mind," Sheriff La Fontaine mumbled. The itching and burning of his skin was becoming unbearable. By the time they made it back into town, his neck, chest, and back were covered with a lumpy red rash that gave him the appearance of a raspberry. He took the rest of the day off and went to see his doctor.

Celeste made a cup of hot tea once her swamp was quiet again. The warm liquid felt good going down her throat. She laughed out loud as she blew the candles out. The smell of raspberries tickled her nose.

CHAPTER FIVE

"**M**organ, are you spending the night or moonlighting as the janitor?" Rhonda Lattier asked from the open doorway of Morgan's office. The sky outside the window served as a velvet black backdrop for the opulence of the office.

Morgan rubbed her eyes and looked at Rhonda. Her 5'9" height and made-for-the- runway body was elevated several inches taller by her three-inch stilettos. Today she was dressed in a St. John's knit suit in ruby red, one of her favorite colors. Rhonda was a partner at McDouglas, Bradshaw & Newman and the only female attorney she knew who dared to wear anything other than the blue, black, and neutrals of the legal profession. Many of her colleagues called her "The Peacock," but her legal expertise made it a loving moniker. Morgan admired her even more for her bold color choices. Most women with Rhonda's Hershey's chocolate complexion ran from the colors that were a staple in Rhonda's wardrobe.

"I just wanted to finish this brief before I went home. I have to be in court the day after tomorrow on the Craig Pharmaceutical hearing and I refuse to sleep with paperwork in my bed another night," Morgan said while she turned off her desk lamp. "Speaking of what's sleeping in your bed, whatever happened to that gorgeous center fielder you were dating?" Rhonda sat in the navy leather chair in front of Morgan's chrome and glass desk and crossed her silk stocking covered legs. They stretched out long and elegantly in front of her; her red Jimmy Choo lace-up pumps matched her suit perfectly.

Morgan laughed. "He was a wide receiver, Rhonda. Football honey, not baseball. That has been over for months. He calls from time to time. We just did not have enough in common."

"You're both beautiful, young, Black, educated, and rich. How much more in common do you need?" Rhonda laughingly asked. "Come on, let's go to the nearest happy hour. Hurricanes are on me."

"I'll pass." Morgan took her car keys out of her purse and slipped into the jacket of her charcoal gray suit. She did not possess the daring of her friend.

"Suit yourself, little sister." Rhonda stepped into the hallway and Morgan turned off the ceiling lights. "I'll have yours."

They chatted about the day's events and reviewed Morgan's strategy for the Craig hearing as they walked together to the garage. Morgan passed again on happy hour and waved when Rhonda passed her on her way out of the garage in her silver Porsche Carrera 4S.

Morgan rested her head against the seat's head rest and closed her eyes for a moment before she left the garage. She almost wished she had gone with Rhonda now. As Morgan eased the car onto the freeway and enjoyed the power of the BMW's engine, she glanced at the manila envelope on top of her briefcase. The envelope had been delivered by special courier just before she left. She hoped it held answers. She was losing patience rapidly and remaining hopeful was becoming a chore. It had been three months since she had watched the simple wooden coffin with her baby brother's body lowered into the ground and she was no closer to figuring out who had killed him.

Morgan smiled at her only neighbor as she exited the elevator. Her condominium was one of only two on the top floor of the building and gave her a spacious floor plan of 2,700 square feet. She was glad she had increased her budget to purchase the space. It had been a haven for her since she moved in last year. As she turned the key in her lock, she breathed deeply, exhaled the outside world, and prepared to retreat.

After she checked her answering machine for messages, took a quick look through her mail, and soaked in a hot bubble bath, Morgan slipped into her favorite white satin pajamas. She made herself an Asian chicken salad and filled her CD player with six of her favorite CDs before she opened the manila envelope. Morgan had previously received two similar envelopes since her return from St. Vincent. The newest envelope had been delivered by courier near the end of the day. She gasped when she opened the envelope. It was Winston's autopsy report, complete with photographs. Her stomach lurched and she fought to stop the wave of nausea which threatened to empty the contents of her stomach onto her steel-gray, ultra-suede sofa. She looked at the note. It was written on delicate, pink stationary. One simple sentence written in the center of the page read: ***It was not a heart attack.***

Morgan scanned the coroner's report until she got to the line that would answer her question. Cause of death: gunshot wound to the coronary artery. Morgan wiped tears from her face as the contents of the envelope began to sink in. In her hands was the proof Winston had been murdered. The reason for his murder was still a mystery. Everyone loved Winston. They always had. Lionel Pickens, the owner of the market where Winston worked, even had good things to say about him. Lionel was known for never having a kind word to say about anyone, white or Black. Someone in St. Vincent knew what was going on and wanted her to help.

Morgan allowed the sounds of Miles Davis' trumpet to settle her stomach along with the ginger ale she now sipped. The first envelope she received had come by courier to her office only three days after she returned to New Orleans. Inside it was three articles about St. Vincent's new sheriff, Claude La Fontaine. The first article had been neatly cut from the *L'Ouverture Gazette* announcing his arrival in L'Ouverture with his wife. There was a picture of him in his dress uniform receiving a congratulatory handshake from the outgoing sheriff. The second article was far from complimentary and came from a newspaper in Baton Rouge. It covered the story of Sheriff Claude La Fontaine who had been involved in the cover up of the racially motivated death of a young Black couple in Baton Rouge. The cover up allowed the killers, self-proclaimed white supremacists, to go free. The third article linked Claude La Fontaine to the misappropriation of funds and the receipt of illegal campaign contributions.

The second envelope had held a copy of a note Winston had written to a county clerk in the New York State Department of Health asking for information on Alexander Franklin. The clerk's response was stapled to the note and a computer printout listing all residents with the last name of Franklin in New York State.

Morgan left all three envelopes on the couch as she moved to the kitchen to put that morning's breakfast dishes and her dinner dishes into the dishwasher. She wondered if there was a connection between St. Vincent's new sheriff and Alexander Franklin. Did Winston think Alexander Franklin was in New York? Had he found him? Did any of this have anything to do with the fact her brother had been murdered? Morgan turned out the kitchen light and walked slowly down the hall to her bedroom. She needed to call her mother. She was about to hang up when Marie, her voice hoarse with sleep, answered.

"Is there anything wrong?" Marie asked as she noted the time on the clock. She had fallen asleep over some exams she was grading. It was after midnight. Lisa never called this late.

"Mama, I'm sorry to wake you. I thought you would still be up grading papers." "Well that was the idea when I sat down at the desk four hours ago. I think I dozed off for a minute. Lisa, what is it?"

Morgan hesitated. "I just wanted to know how Irene and Carl were getting along. I tried to call them this afternoon and the number was disconnected." At the last minute, something stopped Morgan from mentioning the envelopes or the information they held.

"Things appear to go from bad to worse over there. Mary Joyce went into preterm labor this morning. She delivered a girl, I think. Naturally, there are complications. As if that is not bad enough, that ignorant husband of hers was in a fight in some bar over there and broke a man's jaw. The authorities have him in custody."

"Oh no. Is the baby going to be all right?"

"Lisa, I have no idea. You'll have to speak with Lonnie Jean. I am sure she has more details. I saw Carl Jr. downtown this evening. I imagine he came to check on his parents."

"C. J. is home? Things must be serious."

"He probably just wants to make sure that husband of Mary Joyce's finds someplace else to live when he gets out of jail this time. Lonnie Jean said they found cuts and bruises on Mary Joyce when she was admitted to labor and delivery. Apparently, she had been beaten." Marie's voice filled with disgust.

"I will be there this weekend." Morgan made mental adjustments to her schedule. "There is nothing you can do here. I do not see any reason for you to worry yourself with their messes, Lisa. You know how they live." Marie yawned.

Morgan took a deep breath before responding and decided to ignore Marie's statement. "I will see you this weekend, Mama."

"Suit yourself, Lisa"

"Mama, do you have the number to the Empire Hotel?" C. J. usually stayed in a suite there when visiting St. Vincent.

There was no internet or cell service at Carl and Irene's and C. J. liked being able to stay in touch with his office.

"I hope you are not planning to bother him at this time of night."

"Good night, Mama," Morgan decided to end the conversation before she became even more annoyed with her mother.

"Good night, Lisa," Marie yawned again.

Morgan's next call was to Western Union to wire Irene and Carl some money. Then she called information for the number to the Empire Hotel in L'Ouverture, Louisiana.

"DuPont! DuPont! Boy, did you hear a word I just said?" Sheriff Claude La Fontaine finished the cherry cola with a loud slurp and put a spearmint Lifesaver in his mouth hoping to tone down the extra onions he'd had on his hamburger.

"Sorry, Chief," Arthur Lee apologized. His eyes were still focused on something behind Sheriff La Fontaine's head. The sheriff turned to see what had his deputy so distracted. "Don't look, Chief."

"Damn it, DuPont," Claude hissed and turned back toward his deputy. "Who the hell are you gawking at?"

"The guy in the suit sitting with C. J. Banks. Looks like law enforcement to me," Arthur Lee said in a hushed voice despite the noise in the busy diner.

"Banks?" Claude took a quick look over his shoulder before he turned back to face Arthur Lee whose face was now half hidden behind the *L'Ouverture Gazette* sports page."

"Yeah. He's Carl and Irene Banks' oldest boy. Their other son is that boy found dead over in St. Vincent a while back. Winston Banks. C. J. lives up in New York City now. Writes for a newspaper or something, I think. Don't look like that other guy is from around here. He's in law enforcement though. I can always tell," Arthur Lee said and hid his face behind the newspaper when C. J. glanced in his direction.

Claude raised his hand for the waitress to bring the check as he took another quick look at the two men at a table near the front door. Arthur Lee was right. The guy in the suit was definitely law enforcement, probably an agent. What the hell was he talking to this Banks fellow about, he wondered.

"What you think C. J. doing back here in St. Vincent so soon after his last visit, Chief? He don't usually come but a couple times a year and his visits to his folks ain't never this close together." Arthur Lee stood, put his hat on his head, and followed the sheriff toward the door.

Sheriff La Fontaine made sure to nod and tip his hat toward C. J. Banks as they passed his table. He didn't like the look in the man's eyes as he returned the nod. La Fontaine was sure he saw a challenge in the dark brown eyes that seemed to say, "I see you too." "Heard talk that folks over in St. Vincent ain't believing that boy died of no heart attack. Chief, you don't think C. J. down here trying to start up some trouble about his little brother's death, do you?" Arthur Lee asked once they were inside the cruiser. "Arthur Lee, I ain't got time to worry about what a bunch of niggers sitting around talking about in St. Vincent. They can talk all they want. A heart attack is a heart attack. Ain't gone have no trouble here from C. J. Banks or no-damn-body else," Claude snapped and felt the tightness roll up into a ball in his stomach. "Want you to drive out over there later this afternoon and put that word out. Let them talk about that. Now can you shut up and give me some peace and quiet?"

Arthur Lee continued the drive back to the sheriff's office in silence. He hoped C. J.'s visit to St. Vincent wouldn't become a concern of his. Somehow the goose bumps rising on the back of his neck told him otherwise.

CHAPTER SIX

All of Irene Banks' children had a man other than her husband as their father. Although her eldest son carried her husband's name, Carl Banks, Sr. Carl came from Brownsville, Tennessee to L'Ouverture, Louisiana in 1972. Irene was nearly four months pregnant when they met. They dated less than one month and got married. She had never tried to trick Carl into thinking the baby she carried was his. His kindness toward her would not allow that. All that mattered to Carl Banks, Sr. was that the pretty, brown-eyed girl with a smile that set the sun to shame answered "yes" when he asked her to marry him. He knew only the little Irene told him about C. J.'s biological father: He was a tall, good looking man she'd met during Mardi Gras the year she went to stay with a cousin of hers in New Orleans when she was eighteen. He was in the Navy and had bought her some cheap costume jewelry to remember him by before he sailed away.

The boyfriends Irene kept after the marriage did bother him, at first. *What did he expect?* He asked himself that question on those nights he sat up feeding Carl, Jr. and waited for Irene to come home. After all, she was a young, good looking woman, and he was almost fifteen years her senior. He poured love onto her she did not know how to receive and hoped one day his love would be returned. It took some time, but by the time C. J. was eight, Irene had settled down; their love had grown into the kind of love that was soft and sweet like hot cocoa on a rainy Saturday morning. Then she told him she was pregnant. Carl smiled and hoped there was something that looked like joy in his expression. She kissed him hard and wet on the lips and fixed his favorite dinner. After dinner, he took her and C. J. for ice cream. Later that night as he listened to her take her bath, he cried in the dark of their bedroom. The baby was not his. In his early twenties, Carl had suffered a spinal injury that left him with a slight limp. It also left him sterile. Ashamed and fearful he would lose Irene, Carl never told Irene about the injury or his sterility. Envelopes filled with money began to arrive one month after Winston was born. The envelopes were always left on the back porch with the same note: For the boy, A.F.

Two years later when Irene got pregnant again, Carl started to follow her. He'd seen her once when she came out of a hotel in St. Augustine followed by a very well-dressed white man with the strangest gray eyes he'd ever seen. They almost seemed silver in the fading light of the early evening. Even though she walked a few steps in front of him, he knew they'd been together and more than once. It was something about the way she held her body, almost as if not to fall back into his arms that had caused Carl to break down in the delivery truck as he drove away. When the baby—a girl—was born, the look on Irene's face when the doctor handed her the baby spoke the words neither of them had the courage to utter. The baby girl had the same strange gray eyes like Winston's and the man who had followed Irene out of the hotel that day. Irene took one look at Carl's smiling face as he reached for the baby and knew that he knew. She named the baby, Mary Joyce. The note changed after Mary Joyce was born. Now the notes read: For the boy and his sister, A.F.

The only thing Carl would let Irene tell him about Winston and Mary Joyce's father was that his name was Alexander Franklin. He did not want to know more. Carl had begged her to put his name on their birth certificates. He was their father, the only father they would ever know. The only father they needed to know. Irene did not have the heart to deny his tearful requests; however, she felt differently and told them the truth as soon as she thought they were old enough to   · understand. It made no difference to them. Alexander Franklin was just a name. Carl Banks, Sr. was "Daddy."

Carl and Irene settled into a comfortable life and raised three children in St. Vincent where hard times were as familiar as your next door neighbor. Somewhere between diaper changes and Pop Warner football, Irene had learned to love Carl with a love that ran deep and wide. Carl had begun to forget all about Alexander Franklin until the day he delivered a side of beef to a sprawling Rockhurst district estate. A beautiful little girl rushed past the man who opened the massive oak doors and onto the porch. The face of Winston and Mary Joyce stared back at Carl as she greeted him with a smile and a "Hello, sir."

"Pretty little girl you got there, Doc," Carl commented as Dr. Russell Morgan signed for the meat.

"Don't let that face fool you. She's as stubborn as a mule," Russell responded, then laughed, as he watched his daughter ride her pink bicycle in the circular driveway. "Bring the truck around to the kitchen entrance and I'll help you get that meat inside." "You must be having quite a Fourth of July celebration. You got half a cow out there."

Carl looked back at the child; her ponytails flew behind her as she sped by as fast as her eight-year-old legs would allow.

"Knowing my wife, half of Rockhurst will be here," Russell said with a smile. "You have a family, Carl?" Russell asked. He had read his name from the patch on his tan work shirt.

"Yes, sir. A wife and three kids. Got two boys and a little girl," Carl answered. His eyes filled with the love he felt for his family.

"Then you know how those girls can wrap you around their little fingers," Russell laughingly replied as the fathers nodded in agreement and understanding. "Happy Fourth of July, Carl." Russell slipped a $20 bill into his hand.

Carl never mentioned the little girl with the face of his two youngest children to Irene. Over the years, he made lots of deliveries to the Morgan home. The doctor was always friendly. His wife was just the opposite. *She thinks she's better than me.* Carl thought when his deliveries brought Marie Morgan to the door. The white-looking ones in Rockhurst always treated him like that. As if the Black in him would somehow expose their carefully crafted self-deception. Carl had never intended to mention the little girl on the pink bicycle, Lisa, her father had called her, to anyone. Almost four years to the date of first seeing her, all that changed.

"Your son has lost a lot of blood." The boyish looking, pink-faced doctor began. "I'm afraid he's going to need a transfusion." The words sank in slowly and hit hard as Carl felt Irene go limp in his arms before righting herself. His heart sank. His son could die tonight. He could see it in the watery blue eyes of the young doctor.

Eight-year-old Winn had been riding in the back of a pickup truck with his neighbors and friends when the crash occurred. They were thrown 13 feet from the truck. Winn's three

friends, nine-year-old Hugh Loggins and his thirteen-year-old
twin brothers, Lyle and Kyle, had been killed instantly.

"It seems Winston has a very rare blood type. Neither
you nor your wife is a match. Neither is his older brother." The
doctor looked away. The look said he knew why.

"What about Mary Joyce?" Irene asked, her face
streaked with tears.

"Her records show she had rheumatic fever as a baby.
There's been some kidney damage. She can't donate," the young
doctor stated as if reciting from a very boring textbook. "To be
absolutely honest with you, transfusion might not do any good.
Winston has some very serious internal injuries. We'll make him
as comfortable as we can, but I'm not hopeful. I'm sorry." He
patted Carl's shoulder as if he had practiced the gesture in
"How to Tell Parents Their Child is Dying 101" and walked
away.

The next thing Carl remembered was he was sitting in
the living room of Dr. and Mrs. Russell Morgan.

In his usual gentle and calm manner, Carl presented his
belief the Morgans' daughter had the same father as his son. He
explained the last thing he wanted to do was cause them any
trouble, but he was desperate to save his child's life. Carl
became nervous as he watched Marie Morgan's very attractive
face harden into a crimson mask. Her almond-shaped, dark

amber-colored eyes seemed to smolder as her body stiffened. The room grew hot with her anger. He noticed only sadness in the dark brown eyes of Dr. Morgan. He knew the look. He often saw it in his own eyes when people commented on how much Winn or Mary Joyce acted like "their daddy." They meant him. He knew differently. He knew what the doctor knew.

"How dare you?!" Marie hissed and then stood. "How dare you come into my home and insinuate such things?!"

"Marie, stop it," Russell said quietly. "She must never know, Mr. Banks. Never."

Marie glared at Carl as she stormed from the room giving him a look that twisted his insides and somehow chilled him in the warm room. Russell Morgan went to wake Lisa. Once Lisa was dressed, he only said she was needed to help a sick little boy and she would have to be very brave.

Russell offered no explanations at the hospital as his daughter's blood matched that of the dying boy. He sat with Lisa during the transfusion and told her how proud he was of her and what a brave and generous girl she was. She smiled at him and told him it only hurt when the needle went in.

Carl remembered being touched as Russell came over to wish him, Irene, and their son well. He had even gone in to see Winston and talk to the doctor. He assured them everything possible was being done for their son.

"I hope my blood helps your little boy get better," Lisa said. She had smiled at them as her father led her toward the bank of elevators. It was Mary Joyce's smile. For the first time that evening, Carl Banks, Sr. cried.

Winston slowly recovered. Russell and Carl developed a relationship that extended beyond service man and patron. He visited Carl and Irene whenever he was visiting patients near their home. He brought Lisa to play with the Banks children. Although he would never tell Lisa the children she played with were actually her siblings, he thought it important they have a relationship. Marie, naturally, was ignorant of these visits and of Lisa's relationship with Winston and Mary Joyce Banks. Both Russell and Carl were amazed the children looked so much alike and did not seem to notice. They wondered silently if this would change as they grew; if it would bring questions neither was prepared to answer. As if in silent agreement, they never uttered the name Alexander Franklin.

"Lisa, chile what you doin' back down here?" Carl asked as he opened the door for Morgan early Saturday morning.

"Mama told me about Mary Joyce. How's the baby?" She gave him a big hug and followed him to the kitchen.

"She the littlest thing I ever seen in my life, but she a fighter," Carl poured himself and Morgan a cup of coffee. "Irene been at the hospital the whole time. This wearin' her down, Lisa. Don't know how much more of this she can take. When I talked to her last night, she said them doctors was goin' to let Mary Joyce come home today. Don't know when they gone let the baby come home."

Morgan opened the refrigerator, took out a slab of bacon and four eggs. "Where are the boys?" She filled a pot with water and salt for the grits.

"Darrell's ma been keepin' them since Mary Joyce went into the hospital. She a good woman. Feelin' pretty bad about the way Darrell been actin'. Say she gone help out more with the boys." Carl sipped his coffee and watched as Morgan started making breakfast. The sweet, smoky smell of bacon soon filled the kitchen. "Junior come home day before yesterday. Hadn't been for him, I mighta broke that nigga's neck when that doctor told me about all them bruises on my girl. Me and Irene keepin' a roof over his head, and he beatin' our daughter. He lucky to be in jail and not laid out on a slab out to Garrett Bros."

"You can't blame yourself for that, Carl. Mary Joyce is a grown woman," Morgan whisked eggs and milk together in a bowl.

"Thanks for saying that and I know you right, but it don't help me none to know I was feedin' that nigga and he was beatin' my daughter," Carl grumbled, and then sipped his coffee. "Thanks for the money you been sendin' too. I'll see you get it back once I catch up on some things. We done got a little behind." He did not look at Morgan when she placed the plate of bacon, scrambled eggs, and grits in front of him. She buttered toast and brought it to the table along with her plate.

"I will not take any money from you or Irene. It was not a loan. It was a gift," Morgan said and took a bite of the bacon. She hardly ate bacon anymore and the sweet, salty taste of the hot pork almost made her sigh aloud. "How are Tanya and William?"

"Went back home for a while, but I think it was too hard on her being in they place without Winn. She stayin' with her sister over in La Fitte. William miss his daddy, but he doin' all right. He was here with us till all this happen with Mary Joyce." Carl shook his head over the run of bad luck his family was experiencing. "Damn shame what they done to my boy, Lisa."

Morgan almost choked on her coffee. "Carl, then you don't believe the story about the heart attack?"

"Hell, no! Wasn't a damn thing wrong with Winston's heart. I heard the rumors same as everybody else. Somebody killed my boy, Lisa. I just been quiet about it, 'cause it upset Irene so. Figured it was more important to get her through that than stir up trouble. I mentioned it to Junior, though," Carl put some of Irene's homemade apple jelly on his second piece of toast.

"I knew something was going on when Mama told me she'd seen him downtown," Morgan said and sipped her coffee. "What does C. J. say about all of this?"

"You know Junior. He don't say much 'til he got somethin' to say. Did a lot of writin' in one of them little notebooks he keep on him. Made some calls and took off for a few days. Then he come back. He up to something but won't say what yet. I just told him to be careful. We done lost enough already. Don't think we could stand to lose no more." "Carl, don't worry about C. J. He can take care of himself." Morgan placed a forkful of scrambled eggs and grits into her mouth. Carl Banks, Jr. was a writer for a New York newspaper. His 6'3" bronze frame held what appeared to be 240 pounds of pure muscle and often caused him to be mistaken for a boxer.

"He seen to it that Mary Joyce pressed charges against that devil Darrell. Don't know what he said to her, but she signed the papers to have him locked up. Look like he gone do some real time this time around," Carl said. He sighed and sounded relieved. "Seem like he was mixed up in some robberies up in St. Augustine and God only knows what else."

"Good." Morgan hoped this would give Mary Joyce the time she needed to make some different choices for herself and her children. They both turned as they heard footsteps in the hall. Irene entered the kitchen.

"Honey, where's Mary Joyce?" Carl quickly rose and guided Irene to one of the kitchen chairs.

"She wouldn't leave the baby," Irene said. She patted Morgan's knee and gave Carl a weak smile as he kissed her forehead. "I told her we'd come back for her later this evening."

"Let me get you some breakfast," Carl moved toward the stove.

"How is Mary Joyce?" Morgan asked. She brought Irene a cup of hot coffee.

"She's worn out, Lisa. She so weak and tired; she can hardly stand. This baby liked to took her on away from here. The doctors say she ain't givin' her insides a chance to heal up right. I been tryin' to tell Mary Joyce she was havin' these babies too close to one 'nother. They done told her the next one just might kill her," Irene stated. She reached for the pint of Half & Half on the table and poured some into her coffee. "Lord forgive me, but I'm prayin' there won't be no next one."

"What about the baby?" Morgan asked. "When will she be able to come home?" "Her name's Penny," Irene said, her voice went soft. "I ain't never seen a baby so little in all my life. She barely big as a penny herself. Her lungs ain't very strong they say. Something wrong with her heart too. The doctors say they might be able to fix her heart if she get strong enough for the operation. They givin' her some kind of medicine for her lungs. She got a rough road ahead, but something tell me she gonna make it through."

"I'm going to call a specialist I know in New Orleans. I'll make sure Penny gets what she needs to get well." Morgan said.

"We cain't afford no special doctor, Lisa," Carl replied and dropped his head.

"I know that, Carl; but I can. I'll need to get some information from Lonnie Jean." "Chile, you done more than enough already. We can take care of this ourselves," Irene insisted. The pain in her husband's eyes turned the taste of the coffee in her mouth bitter.

"Irene and Carl, I do not mean any disrespect, but I am not asking for your permission," Morgan stated in a voice she usually reserved for the courtroom. "Penny is my niece. She sounds like a very sick little girl. She will not be able to get well here at General."

"Ain't no need in arguing with that girl, Reenie. "She 'bout as stubborn as the Doc was." The thought brought a smile to his weary face.

"Carl's right," Morgan said. She winked at him and grabbed her purse from the chair near the kitchen door. "Now finish your breakfast. I'm going to see Lonnie Jean." Morgan kissed Irene and Carl and left the house.

CHAPTER SEVEN

"Lisa! Lisa!" Whitey Peters called and ran toward Morgan as she walked toward the hospital entrance.

"Whitey!" Morgan smiled as she was picked up off her feet and swung around by 6'6" Deputy Sheriff Matthew "Whitey" Peters.

They had called Matthew Peters by this nickname as long as Morgan could remember. Whitey had the whitest skin of any Black man Morgan had ever seen. Instead of adding color, his blue-green eyes and sandy hair only amplified his paleness.

"Girl, what you doing back in our little town?" He teased and placed her back on her feet. "A big New Orleans lawyer like yourself."

"Just checking on the family," Morgan said and smiled. She was glad to see her old friend.

"I sure do hate the bad time Mister Carl and Miss Irene having lately. First Winn and now Mary Joyce and her poor little baby girl. Heard you was in town for the funeral."

"I still cannot believe he's gone." Morgan's eyes held tears that threatened to fall. "But it's good to see you. What are you doing at the hospital, Mr. Deputy?"

"Had to bring in a couple of knuckleheads got to fighting over at Queenie's and cut each other up some." Whitey glanced at his watch. "Shoot."

"What's the matter?"

"I'm late for a meeting with Sheriff La Fontaine. He gone have my ass for sure." "I'll be here until Monday," Morgan said as Whitey kissed her cheek. "Let's have lunch.

"Sounds good," Whitey called over his shoulder as he rushed toward his cruiser. "If I still have a job, I'm off tomorrow. Call me. I'm in the book."

Morgan entered the hospital registration area and was shown to the L'Ouverture General Hospital Intensive Care Unit. The dim lighting, old computers, and scarcity of staff reinforced her decision to get Penny out of here. If asked, Morgan would swear the waiting room's old vinyl couches and cracking plastic chairs and tables had been there when she volunteered one summer as a teenager. She shook her head as she made her way down the dimly lit hallway and remembered an article Marie sent her several years ago on the new medical center in Rockhurst. It housed a large medical library named after her father. Marie had been certain to highlight the words, "*made possible by a generous donation from his widow, Dr. Marie Morgan.*" Morgan asked an aide who was delivering lunch trays where she could find Lonnie Jean. She pointed to a room at the end of the hall. Morgan knocked and entered.

"Hey, Mary Joyce. Look who's here," Lonnie Jean said while she glanced at Mary Joyce and hugged Morgan.

"Hey, sis," Mary Joyce greeted her from a chair near the incubator. Her voice was weak and dark circles ringed her light gray eyes.

"Hey, sis," Morgan said and bent down to hug her.

"The doctor say she need an operation on her heart." Mary Joyce turned her attention back to the small baby in the incubator. "But she too little right now."

"She'll be fine." Morgan ignored the look that said otherwise in Lonnie Jean's eyes. "You look like you could use some rest, though."

"Mama came to get me this morning. I cain't leave her here all by herself, Lisa. She ain't got nobody but me." Tears slid down Mary Joyce's cheeks. "I guess they told you 'bout Darrell, huh?"

"Don't you worry about Darrell right now. You visit with Penny while I step outside and talk to Lonnie Jean. Then, I'm taking you home to get some rest."

"Thank God you came," Lonnie Jean said as soon as they had stepped out of the room. "She'll listen to you. She kicked a fit when Irene tried to take her home this morning. We had to give her something to calm her down."

"She looks like she's ready to fall out."

"Mary Joyce isn't well, Lisa. It was a hard labor. Then they had to do a C-section. This makes her second one. She lost quite a bit of blood. I tried to get her admitted to Rockhurst Medical Center, but they aren't too welcoming to L'Ouverture's uninsured. She's got to rest." Lonnie Jean's jaw tightened as she continued, "Sometimes I get so sick of watching this over and over again. They keep having baby after baby after baby until somebody or everybody dies."

"I checked with the chief of staff at Rockhurst this morning. She said their neonatal isn't set up for a baby as sick as Penny." Morgan felt tears forming in her eyes.

"Probably because they don't get babies as sick as Penny over there." Lonnie Jean didn't attempt to hide her bitterness. She'd watched too many babies suffer and die in St. Vincent.

"I'm getting Penny out of here," Morgan stated firmly and regained her composure. "I called a friend of mine from New Orleans. He is on his way here now and is ordering a transfer. She needs a chance and I don't think General has one big enough for her."

"Getting her out of here will be the only chance she's got, Lisa. We're doing the best we can, but she's just too sick," Lonnie Jean said in agreement. "Who's your friend?"

"Dr. Maurice LaShurr. He's the best in the area for neonatology. He's also a pediatric surgeon who specializes in cardiology."

"First of all, counselor. How did you end up with a friend who's a doctor? Second of all, cousin, he's more than the best in the area. He's probably one of the best in the country. I went to a seminar he did in Atlanta three years ago. Some of his recommendations on neonatology are responsible for what you see here. Before that, General didn't even have a neonatal intensive care unit. Babies and adults were all in the same unit. How do you know Dr. LaShurr?" Lonnie Jean asked unable to keep the look of curiosity off her face. Maurice LaShurr was one of pediatric medicine's most brilliant doctors and definitely its most handsome and eligible bachelor.

"His father started a professional exchange program for Black physicians and attorneys, if you can believe that. Doctors had to mentor law students and attorneys mentored med students. Maurice's father was one of my mentors. I do some volunteer work for him from time to time," Morgan explained.

"I see," Lonnie Jean winked at Morgan.

"Lonnie Jean, don't start. We're just friends." Morgan was all too familiar with her cousin's matchmaking look.

"How soon do you think he'll get here?" Lonnie Jean filed the conversation about just how friendly her cousin and Dr. LaShurr really were away for a later time.

In answer to her question, the elevator doors opened and out walked Dr. Maurice LaShurr and General's Chief of Staff, Dr. Preston Andrews. Lonnie Jean had just recently seen a photo of Dr. Maurice LaShurr in a medical journal. She hoped the photographer had a day job because he obviously had failed to capture the essence of this man. He was more handsome than she remembered him from the conference. There was no mistaking his athletic build, even in the light wool black slacks and what was obviously a shirt that had been designed to fit only him. While there was no mistaking his brilliance as a physician, he could have easily fit in as a wide receiver on any team. His 6'3" frame elegantly held what appeared to be 210 pounds of perfectly toned muscle. His cocoa brown skin made you think of melting chocolate and his intense dark brown eyes were framed by soft black lashes that would have easily made another man look feminine. On Maurice LaShurr, they just added to what magazines called sex appeal.

"Nurse Samuels," Dr. Andrews called out and nodded his head toward Lonnie Jean. "This is Dr. Maurice LaShurr. He's here to exam the Lyons baby. She's to be transferred to Rivers C. Medical Center in New Orleans. Will you order an ambulance?"

"Nice to meet you," Maurice said in greeting and extended his hand to Lonnie Jean without the airs most doctors used.

"Nice to meet you too, doctor," Lonnie Jean said. She smiled in return and shook his hand.

"Maurice, this is my cousin. Lonnie Jean Samuels," Morgan made the proper introductions.

"I'll get that ambulance, Dr. LaShurr and an attendant to accompany you," Lonnie Jean said. She was already on her way to prepare for Penny's transfer.

"Mary Joyce. Out," Dr. Andrews ordered. He pushed the door open and walked into the room. His disrespect and disregard for the young mother was evident in his tone and written on the frown between his bushy and unkempt eyebrows. He had no time for the hysterics she'd shown when her mother tried to take her home. He had an appointment with a bowling ball and visions of a championship for his team. Morgan and Maurice followed.

"Excuse me, Dr. Andrews," Maurice said. He stepped between his colleague and the young mother to prevent a volatile situation from erupting. Then he continued, "Mrs. Lyons. I'm Dr. LaShurr."

"Hello," Mary Joyce replied to his greeting but looked confused.

"It's all right, Mary Joyce. He's a friend of mine," Morgan said. She placed her arm around her sister's shoulders. "I think he can help Penny get better."

"If you won't be needing me anymore. I have patients to see," Dr. Andrews rudely stated and loudly cleared his throat. The expression on his face showed his obvious distaste for the young Black doctor.

"Thank you, Dr. Andrews," Maurice said to Dr. Andrews' rapidly retreating back. He was already reading through Penny's chart. He then moved to a small sink to wash his hands and put on the latex gloves that were on a table near the incubator.

"Mrs. Lyons," Maurice said after a few minutes in which his entire attention had been focused on examining Penny. "May I call you Mary Joyce?"

"You might as well. Everybody else do," Mary Joyce answered as she had never been asked for permission before.

"Mary Joyce, I want to take your baby to a hospital in New Orleans where we have doctors who are really good at helping babies when they are as sick as your daughter. Unless we help her real soon I'm afraid she won't get any better." Maurice's voice was gentle and soothing, but firm.

"To N'Orleans?" Mary Joyce's body withdrew into itself frightened at the thought. She looked as if he had just asked to take her baby to Mars. "I don't have no money for no fancy doctors in N'Orleans. She gone have to get better right here. All my other babies was born right here. Well, except for Darrell Jr. We call him D. J. He come out in the backseat of Darrell's Mama's car."

"Other children?" Maurice looked at Morgan.

"She has three boys. The oldest just turned four," Morgan explained.

Maurice knelt on one knee in front of Mary Joyce's chair and said, "Listen, Mary Joyce. Your daughter is very small and not very strong. We have medicine that can make her stronger so she can have an operation to fix the problem with her heart."

"Mary Joyce, please listen to him. It's the best thing for Penny," Morgan pleaded. "You sure you can make her better?" Mary Joyce was unsure about the doctor or anything he had just explained, but she trusted her big sister.

"I won't lie to you, Mary Joyce. I'm not sure of that. But I am sure she won't get any better if she stays here."

Once Maurice left the hospital with Penny and a nurse from General, Morgan drove Mary Joyce home. She bathed her, washed and braided her hair, and sat with her until she fell asleep. "Lonnie Jean says she is not well enough to travel yet,"

Morgan said and sat down at Irene's kitchen table. "Be sure she takes the medicine. There are iron pills and some antibiotics. Lonnie Jean said she will come out to see her in a few days. She should be able to go to New Orleans in a couple of weeks."

"Lisa, we can't thank you enough," Carl said as his eyes teared from relief and gratitude.

"Don't thank me until Penny comes home," Morgan cautioned.

"Marie called looking for you," Irene said after she put a plate of red beans and rice in front of Morgan. "She wants you to call her. I didn't tell her you'd been out here all day, but I think she knows."

"Don't worry about Mama." Morgan took a forkful of the beans and rice into her mouth. Her eyes rolled with pleasure. "Irene, don't tell Uncle Raymond; but, you make the best red beans and rice in the world. You could make a fortune with these in New Orleans."

"The smile on your face is fortune enough for me." Irene heaped another generous helping on Morgan's plate and stood. "I'm gone lie down for a while." She kissed Carl on top of his balding head and left the kitchen.

"Junior want you to call him over at The Empire. He tried to wait around here for you, but had to get to an appointment of some sort," Carl said once he could no longer hear Irene's footsteps in the hallway. "Said he got some information for you."

"Thank you." Morgan looked at her plate of food and not at Carl.

"Lisa, now I don't know what you up to but I know I don't want nothin' happenin' to you. I couldn't live with that and it would kill Irene sho'nuff." Carl's tone was stern; it forced her to look at him. "Now I know you been askin' around about what happen to Winn. If I know, then the folks that don't like questions know too. Whoever killed Winn is dangerous, Lisa. Look here. I know how you felt about Winn, but won't nothin' bring him back, baby. It ain't worth the risk of you gettin' yourself hurt. Or worse. You hear what I'm sayin' to you?"

"I'll be fine, Carl." Morgan hoped the look on her face reassured him. She buttered a huge cornbread muffin. The words "or worse" echoed in her head. "Anyway, you know what my daddy always said…'risk nothing, get nothing.'"

CHAPTER EIGHT

Morgan decided to go see C. J. and headed to downtown L'Ouverture. She couldn't believe how little the town had changed since she moved away. The small, in-need-of-repair wood framed houses that filled most of the St. Vincent district gave the impression time had stopped somewhere in the late 1940s. Morgan lowered the volume on the public radio station talk show, as she glanced at overgrown yards, broken down fences, peeled paint, and dilapidated front porches. She chuckled to herself at the somewhat larger, freshly whitewashed house at the end of the road, just before you reached the highway that led back to town.

Mrs. Raynal didn't let the obvious hopelessness and despair of St. Vincent have an effect on her. She had always been a proud woman. She and her two daughters had rebuilt their home with their own hands in the late 1950s following the lynching of her husband. The lynching had involved the burning of her husband's body in their front yard. The wooden shingles on the roof caught on fire and burned the house to the ground. While her yard did not have a proper lawn, there were clay flower pots filled with daffodils and daisies that lined the stone walkway and led to a bright blue front door. Morgan waved when she saw Mrs. Raynal come onto the porch with her knitting basket in hand and signaled as she made her way to the highway. An hour later, she was seated with C. J in his suite at The Empire Hotel.

The Empire Hotel sat squarely in the middle of Toussaint Square in downtown L'Ouverture. It was a stately white brick, three-story building with massive columns and a wide wrap-around veranda. In the 1700s, The Empire Hotel was the home of Frenchman Bertrand Guillaume and his mulatto wife, Desirée. Desirée had died in childbirth and left Guillaume with twin sons to raise. Grief and sorrow had forced his return to his beloved France and the house had remained boarded until purchased by a free man of color from Philadelphia in the late 1890s. After years of renovation, it was opened as The Empire Hotel in 1899 and brought the wealthiest of the nation's darker sons and daughters to its doorstep.

Morgan noticed with pleasure the elegance of the hotel's most recent remodel as she handed her keys to the young valet and entered the dazzling lobby. Her heels clicked on the polished, sand-colored marble floors as she made her way to the gleaming black marble front desk. Everywhere she looked there were vases of lilacs, peonies, lilies, and huge palms in gold urns. The hand-blown chandelier took her breath away. The violet, pink, yellow, and orange reflection from the crystals danced throughout the lobby. A smiling and gracious young woman, the slight wave in her hair spoke of her L'Ouverture genealogy, made the call to C. J.'s suite announcing her arrival.

"Well, at least I'm not the only one who thinks something is going on down here," Morgan said after she was comfortably seated in one of the cranberry-colored wing chairs in the living room of C. J.'s suite. Stacks of file folders were on the corner of the table. C. J. must've been hard at work for hours before she arrived.

C. J. shared his concerns about Winston's death and his voice cracked occasionally with emotion. She took a sip from the glass of sweet tea C. J. poured for her and removed her notepad from her oversized leather hobo bag. "Do you think Winn's death has anything to do with Alexander Franklin?" Morgan asked.

"Lisa, at this point I'm not sure what to think," C. J. said. He sighed and took a sip from a glass of red wine. C. J. continued, "I know Winn was looking for him. I gave an investigator friend of mine some stuff Winn had put together. The trail led to New York and went cold. Now you get this information about La Fontaine and the original coroner's report. I haven't had any luck getting my mama to talk about this

Franklin guy. I have never seen her shut down like she does when I mention his name."

"You would think he was the devil incarnate the way my mother acts. When I realized Winn and Mary Joyce were my brother and sister, I asked her about Alexander Franklin again." Morgan paused in recounting the story as the ancient argument rushed back. Gathering her bearings, Morgan continued, "She slapped me. The woman, who had never hit me in my entire life, looked me in the eyes and slapped me."

"Lisa, I'm sorry," C. J. responded. He could see the pain of the memory written across her face. "I made a call to the attorney general's office. I have enough to get the state police involved, but maybe my daddy is right. Maybe you should just let this go. I can include the information about Winn in the larger piece I'm doing. If we're lucky, his death might be able to prevent another one. Maybe that way we won't feel like our little brother died in vain. I got a bad feeling about all of this." C. J. glanced at her while he thumbed through the copies of the contents of Morgan's mysterious envelopes.

"At first it was just about finding out about our biological father. Winn and I were just curious. Mary Joyce never seemed to care one way or the other. If it was still about that, C. J., I could leave it alone. What real difference would it make? But it is about more than that now. It is about finding out who murdered our brother and why. I can't drop that. Can you?"

"Knowing won't change anything," C. J. said. He slid the blue accordion file across the table and emptied the remaining Bordeaux into his wine glass.

"I thought you wanted to know who killed our brother." Morgan attempted to wipe the burning sensation that indicated just how tired she was from her eyes with the back of her hand.

"I'm not talking about finding out who killed Winn. I'm talking about finding out about Alexander Franklin," C. J. said. He let the dark, red liquid pucker the sides of his mouth before he swallowed. "I was almost eleven years old when Mama told me Carl, Sr. wasn't my real father."

Morgan kicked off her shoes and folded her legs beneath her body in the chair. She watched C. J.'s face. There was a longing there that curled down the sides of his mouth and reminded Morgan of the way an infant's lips curl downward just before the tears begin.

"Actually, Mama didn't get a chance to tell me. I heard it for the first time when I was gathering bottles in the alley behind Queenie's Jook Joint one Sunday before church." He looked out the window instead of at Morgan. He did not want to see what might be reflected in her gray eyes that had darkened with nightfall. "Queenie had these two old guys she paid to do odd jobs for her around the place. They were pouring her homebrew into Mason Jars for the Sunday night crowd. They started talking about what a good- looking woman "Reenie" had been and how "that boy" looks just like his father. They said his name was Wade."

"What did Irene tell you about him?"

"At first she didn't want to say much. Said a father was the man who fed you and kept a roof over your head. When I was about thirteen or fourteen, I started asking her about him again. She told me his name is Wade Johnson. He had been in the Navy and he was from somewhere outside of Dallas. Said he had a wife and a family and that didn't leave room for us. She never saw him again after the night she told him she was pregnant. She said she sent a picture of me when I was born to his sister." C. J. smiled before he continued. "You know Mama. She said he is the one who missed out because I am the kind of son who makes parents thank God for making little boys. Lisa, all I'm trying to say is that anything you find out about Alexander Franklin won't make Doc any less your father. You understand that?" C. J.'s last statement sounded more like an order than a question.

Morgan nodded as she asked, "Whatever happened to him?"

"He was stabbed to death in a bar in Chicago when I was fifteen. One of his sisters sent Mama the newspaper article and a program from his funeral." C. J. took another sip of his wine before he continued. "She put it in my gym bag one morning. I found it when I dressed for gym that day. We never talked about it again."

C. J. picked up the file folder again. The look in his eyes told Morgan he was in this with her for the long haul. They spent the next three hours reviewing all the information and made notes about all the information they did not have. Morgan opened yet another folder. This one contained photographs. Her eyes, strained by the hours of scouring the fine print of documents and the poor resolution of photos, watered. She took a longer look at a photo that was even grainier than the others.

"Does that guy look familiar, Lisa?" C. J. asked as he shuffled through a stack of index cards. "His name is Dwayne Gibbins. Goes by the name Bingo."

Morgan took a closer look at a picture taken in a poorly lit parking lot. The man stood against a yellow emergency call box, his features all but obscured by the shadows and poor quality of the photo. Morgan stood and took the photos into the suite's kitchenette and hoped the overhead fluorescent light would help.

"This looks like it was taken at the university. I'm sure this is the faculty parking lot." Morgan held another photo up to the light. "You said his name is Gibbins?"

"Yeah. He's not registered as a student." C. J. anticipated her next question as he read from an index card. "He's known for hotwiring cars in Rockhurst and some petty theft in St. Vincent from time to time. Looks like he graduated to dealing and has a couple of gun charges. Shot a woman in a domestic dispute back in '95. His name also came up on one of the police reports a few days after Winn was killed."

"Okay. That's enough for now. Let's get something to eat," C. J. said and took the photos from Morgan looking into her reddened eyes. They ordered dinner: an open- faced crab sandwich, roasted red potatoes, and mixed green salad for Morgan; jambalaya for C. J. After they shared a generous bowl of banana pudding with banana rum sauce and whipped cream, they compared notes on their next steps then said their goodnights.

It was after midnight when Morgan opened the back door to her Uncle Raymond's house. She found Lonnie Jean in the dining room going through the day's mail.

"Good. You're up," Morgan said as she flopped down in a dining room chair across from Lonnie Jean. "Has Maurice called?"

"Well, hello Lonnie Jean. How come you not in bed, girl? I know you must be tired after working twelve days straight." Lonnie Jean playfully rolled her eyes at Morgan.

"Sorry." Morgan planted a quick kiss on her cousin's cheek. "How are you doing?" "About the same as you look. Exhausted. Yes, Dr. LaShurr called. He said Penny is already starting to respond to the medications that will speed up the development of her lungs. You may have saved your niece's life, Lisa."

"Not sure how much credit I can take, but I hope you're right. I'll check with him in the morning."

"I should hope so," Lonnie jean teased and raised her eyebrows. "Even if he is a doctor." As a nurse, she knew about the running feuds between the medical and legal professions.

"Will you stop?" Morgan said and playfully hit at her cousin. "I told you, he is only a friend."

"All unmarried friends have the potential to be more than friends. Especially, young, rich, attractive, intelligent, and unmarried friends," Lonnie Jean said. She laughed, then stood. "I'm going to bed."

"I know Winn was murdered," Morgan blurted out. Her words stopped Lonnie Jean's exit from the dining room.

"What do you mean, you *know*?" Lonnie Jean backed into the room.

"For the last couple of months somebody has been sending me information. First, I got some information about your new sheriff, Claude La Fontaine. Something about some mess he was into before he came here and then a picture of him at an awards ceremony. Then I got a copy of some correspondence between Winn and the New York State Department of Health. He thought Alexander Franklin was in New York for some reason. The last envelope I received was a copy of the original coroner's report and autopsy photos. The report stated Winn died as a result of gunshot wounds. There were pictures. It was no heart attack, Lonnie Jean."

"Who sent them?" Lonnie Jean asked as she returned to her seat at the dining room table.

"I have no idea. There is never a return address. I tried to get some information from the courier service. All they could tell me was the information was dropped off at one of their Louisiana offices. The names on the paperwork were different each time and the phone numbers were fake.

C. J.'s adding Winn's murder to the story he's been researching. I gave him copies of everything."

"Hold up, Nancy Drew." Concern creased Lonnie Jean's forehead. "Cous, this sounds dangerous. How is it all connected?"

"I don't even know if it is connected," Morgan said. "C. J.'s story is on the cover-ups of the murders of young Black men throughout the country and the role racism plays in the investigation and subsequent prosecution of the murderers. He said the information I've already given him on Winn is enough to open a state investigation into his murder."

"This doesn't just *sound* dangerous, it *is* dangerous. You forgetting this is L'Ouverture? Lisa, you could get hurt." Lonnie Jean put her hand to her throat. She looked more than worried now, she looked frightened.

"I'll be all right. Don't you go all soft on me." Morgan noticed the fear in her cousin's eyes.

"You promise me that if all this snooping around turns ugly, you'll stop." Lonnie Jean's stomach clenched around her worry.

"I promise." Morgan quickly looked away from Lonnie Jean's pleading eyes.

"You just lied to me. Didn't you?" Lonnie Jean knew her cousin well. Morgan nodded. "Then, promise to be careful."

"I promise." This time, Morgan looked Lonnie Jean in the eyes.

"Aunt Marie called all evening. She's pissed you haven't been home, although you know Aunt Marie would never just come right out and say that." Lonnie Jean changed the subject.

She knew in her heart there was nothing she could do or say to change her cousin's mind.

"Mama never comes right out and says anything. That's her problem. I'll go to church with her in the morning. That ought to pacify her."

"Good idea. She loves showing you off to all her friends at First Baptist of Rockhurst." Lonnie Jean nodded her head in agreement with her cousin. She rose again and hugged Morgan. "You just remember what I said. Be careful."

Morgan sat alone at the dining room table going over the day's events. The report from Maurice about Penny was good news. She would drive out to Irene and Carl's after lunch with Whitey tomorrow and give them the news. The meeting with C. J. gave her hope they might one day know what really happened to Winston; however, the unanswered questions about Alexander Franklin remained with her as she climbed the stairs and got ready for bed.

As Morgan turned off the lamp on the nightstand and saw the large red 1:03 a.m. on the alarm clock's LCD display, her mind drifted to the last conversation she had with her grandmother about Alexander Franklin.

"Mama Essie, they won't tell me anything," Lisa cried. Her head rested in Essie's lap.

"Lisa, wish it was something I could tell you, baby. But I don't know nothing to tell. By the time I found out about him, he had moved on," Mama Essie said and patted her back gently.

"Your mama was dating Russell at the same time she was foolin' with that Alexander. When she found out she was pregnant, they got married. When you was born, I took one look at them eyes and knew Russell wasn't your daddy. I'd heard about Alexander Franklin and everybody who knew anything about him talked about them eyes and how good looking he was. Everybody said his eyes was gray 'cause that's as close as the color gets to anything they'd ever seen before.

After Marie left home, I found a picture of him she had hid in a hole she made in the wall behind her dresser. And there was your eyes looking right back at me. Couldn't have been long before Russell knew the truth, but he loved your mama something awful. Me and Marie fought long and hard about it. I thought you should know the truth, but she was your mama.

When Russell started to bring you to see me regular, he begged me not to tell you. Said if I did, he'd stop bringing you to see me. I knew he was just scared Marie would find out. All he ever wanted to do was make that girl happy and take care of you.

I knew he'd do it too. I'd already lost Marie. I woulda died if I'd lost you too."

"Mama Essie, do you think he was a bad man? All Daddy ever said was he wanted to protect Mama and me from him. Why doesn't she want me to know? What doesn't she want me to know? Do you think he's here in L'Ouverture?" Lisa lifted her head and wiped her eyes.

"Baby, I don't know about none of that. What I do know is he couldn't be too bad a man because he had something to do with making you and ain't nothing at all bad about you. You listen to me, Lisa Evelene Morgan and listen good. Don't you let this mess of your mama's get you all mixed up. You got good things, real good things ahead for yourself. Don't you let your mama and no gray-eyed man named Alexander Franklin rob you of that, baby. Don't you dare let 'em."

CHAPTER NINE

"Lisa, I do not understand you," Marie said. She shook her head as she pulled her sleek, brand new 2004, desert silver Mercedes S500 into the garage. "You act as if the lifestyle your father and I created for you is not enough."

"Mama, I am not arguing with you today," Morgan said and waited for her mother to shut off the engine before she got out of the car.

"No one is arguing, Lisa. I am just trying to understand why you continue to involve yourself in the lives of those people. You are well aware of how they live out there. Anyone could have killed that boy." Marie opened the door that led into the house. "

Morgan's body tensed with anger. "Let me say this to you once, Mama. And then I will not have another conversation with you about it ever again. This means I will hear absolutely nothing you have to say on the subject again. So, let me help you understand. The reason I involve myself in the lives of *those people* as you call them, is because *those people* are *MY* people. Winston, Mary Joyce, and I have the same biological father; a man you and Irene refuse to talk about. And, in response to your assumption Winn was responsible for his own death because he was not allowed the privilege of growing up among Rockhurst's Black bourgeoisie, you are incorrect. Ignorantly incorrect."

Morgan turned and headed for the front door. Marie followed her and yelled something about not being talked to that way in her house. She stopped just short of the door slamming in her face. Marie cursed and threw a vase of lilies against the wall. A framed picture of her and a nine-year-old Lisa crashed to the floor and shattered the frame's glass. Marie kicked the fractured image of her and her daughter across the hardwood floor and stormed up the stairs to her room.

Morgan drove around for almost thirty minutes trying to calm herself down before her lunch with Whitey. Sometimes she could not believe her mother. She checked her face in the lighted vanity mirror before she got out of the car and walked the half a block to The Captain's Plate, a casual lunch spot on Rockhurst's pier. Morgan entered the restaurant and paused just inside the door to give her eyes a minute to adjust to the restaurant's dim lighting. There was Whitey at a booth near the back of the room. He waved at her. He looked very handsome in his brown pinstriped suit. His evenly lined hair let her know he had taken the time to get a haircut. The dark chocolate brown of his suit added a warm glow to his skin and gave it a bronze look that made his smile even brighter.

"Thought you went and stood me up, girl. Like you did for the eighth-grade dinner dance," Whitey teased in greeting. He stood and softly kissed her cheek.

"Boy, I had the chicken pox," Morgan said and laughed. "Will you ever get over that?"

"No." Whitey dropped his head feigning ultimate defeat.

"Whitey, you're still crazy." Morgan laughed. The tension from the morning with her mother drained away because of the laughter she shared with her old friend.

"You look good, Lisa. Everything must be working for you in N'Orleans." Whitey smiled and opened his menu.

"Thanks. You're looking good yourself," Morgan smiled. "Things are good. How about for you?"

"To tell you the truth, Lisa, things been better." Whitey lowered his voice. "What's the matter?" Morgan lowered her voice to match his.

"I'm leaving. Working for La Fontaine has been less than enjoyable for a brother. You know what I mean?"

"What do *you* mean?" Morgan was glad Whitey had brought up the subject she had come to talk about.

"He's one of those undercover racist crackers. He makes snide remarks about Black folks all the time. Messes over you on reports, passes you up for promotions, stuff like that. All the while grinning in the right Black faces and kissing the right

Black asses to keep the natives from getting restless. There were eight of us when he came. Just me and a little sister left. He turned her into a damn crossing guard and she's a college graduate. You remember Harry Albereau? He promoted him to detective over a brother, from Dillard, with a degree in criminal justice. That stupid white boy can't spell his name unless you give him the first letter." Whitey shook his head in disgust. "The brother left. Went to Chicago. Sued the department. They settled out of court and kept it real quiet. I think La Fontaine been in trouble somewhere before."

"Why do you think that?" Morgan resisted the urge to pull out her pen and pad. She made mental notes instead to keep the conversation as casual as possible.

"I was seeing this girl who used to work in the district attorney's office in Baton Rouge. She said La Fontaine was mixed up with some bad cops who got paid to do all kinds of stuff. Said he was known for destroying or planting evidence to suit them. Heard there was also some money missing and some phony testimony in some big case. She said he was the cause of some white boys getting off that killed a young Black couple. She got a cousin from St. Vincent that works here in the Medical Examiner's office. Nice girl. She runs errands for Celeste from time to time. Her and her cousin been keeping an eye on old Claude. She drops some info on me sometimes; helping a brother watch his back. Think La Fontaine's buddies must've sent him down here to let things cool off. He's been here a couple years. Every now and then, I hear him arguing on the phone with somebody about his cut or when are they gonna get him out of St. Vincent. This cat's bad news, Lisa." They stopped talking long enough to place their orders with Dina, their waitress and former classmate.

"What does he have to say about Winn?" Morgan asked after Dina placed a tall glass of sweet tea in front of her and a Sprite in front of Whitey.

"Said what they all saying. It wasn't no heart attack, Lisa."

"How do you know that, Whitey?" Morgan tried to sound as casual as possible over her pounding heart.

"I got on the scene after a few other deputies had arrived. There was blood everywhere—on Winn and inside the van. Arthur Lee Du Pont was in charge and rushed me off the scene so fast it made my head spin. Said the sheriff wanted me over on Chalet Road for some kind a domestic disturbance and thought I'd have a better chance calming things down over there. It was dark, but I could see the driver's side window was shattered and there were bullet holes along the side of the van. Nothing about that scene said "heart attack," Lisa. Then the next morning, La Fontaine puts me on loan to the La Fitte Sheriff's

Department to serve some eviction papers to some squatters who got themselves a lawyer. When I get back, Winn's buried and people talking about how sad it was about him being so young and having a heart attack." Whitey paused and took a long sip of his drink. He held an ice cube in his mouth before he continued. "The girl I'm seeing now, Pam, works at General in records. She saw an autopsy report that said Winn died of gunshot wounds. Said she saw some pictures too. I asked her to check it out for me. When she looked again there was a different report listing heart attack as the cause of death and the pictures was gone."

"Do you think Pam would talk to me?" Morgan's head spun with this new discovery. "I already told her you'd be calling. But call her at home. I'll give you her number. Things got weird at the hospital for her right after all this went down. I don't want my baby losing her job or nothing. Least till we get outta here." Whitey wrote the number on a small pad he pulled from his breast pocket. "You know what else Pam saw?" "What?" Morgan slipped the number into her suit jacket pocket.

"She saw Sheriff La Fontaine at the records room *before* the new autopsy report showed up. Caught her attention because that's something he usually sends Arthur Lee or one of us other deputies to do. She said she saw La Fontaine and some other guy she'd never seen before leaving the records office. Said they was both laughing and grinning with Nancy Hoover. She's the chief records custodian and a little too friendly with the sheriff, if you know what I'm saying," Whitey said. He smiled at Dina as she sat a large, steaming bowl of gumbo in front of Morgan and a plate of honey-garlic roasted crabs, mashed potatoes, and green beans in front of him. Dina refilled their glasses and promised to check on them in a while. They bowed their heads to say grace before Morgan asked Whitey another question.

"Whitey, how soon are you planning to leave St. Vincent?"

"Soon as possible. I'm waiting to hear from sheriff departments in Chicago, Atlanta, and Miami. Pam's leaving with me." Whitey's face beamed when he said her name.

"Sounds good." Morgan remembered her promise to Lonnie Jean to be careful and hoping her friend would be out of the way if things turned ugly. "Be sure I get an invitation to the wedding."

"Of course. All my rich attorney friends from N'Orleans will be invited," Whitey replied with a mock serious expression on his face.

They turned their conversation to the things old friends talk about when they have not seen each other for years and enjoyed the rest of their lunch together. They hugged at Whitey's car. Morgan refused to have him walk her to her car. She waved as Whitey honked the horn and passed her. She had just pushed

the button on her key ring to unlock her car door when Dina
came rushing down the sidewalk calling her name. She was
holding a small brown canvas tote bag.

"Hey, Lisa!" Dina called. "You left your bag."
Before Morgan could respond she had not left a bag, Dina said,
"Whitey said you left your bag." Their eyes locked long enough
for Morgan to know to take the bag. She thanked Dina. Dina
smiled and turned to hurry back to the restaurant. Morgan tossed
the bag onto the passenger's seat and got into her car.

Morgan entered the house and paused to listen for
sounds that would indicate her mother was home. She met only
quiet. *She's still angry*. Morgan thought as she passed through
the dining room. There was no note. She kicked off her shoes
and headed up the stairs. She was glad she would not have to
deal with Marie this afternoon. Morgan dropped her shoes to the
floor, tossed her jacket across the back of a chair, and sat down
on the end of the bed. She unzipped the canvas bag Dina had
handed her outside the restaurant; her imagination ran wild. She
was not prepared for what fell out of the bag. Morgan gasped,
covered her mouth, and dropped the plastic bag to the floor. She

took a deep breath before she reached to retrieve the bag. Her hands shook slightly as she placed the plastic bag, marked **Police Evidence**, in her lap. The bag contained an evidence document and the clothes Winston had worn when murdered. The shirt was covered in brown, dried blood. She could feel the stiffness of the dried blood through the bag's thick plastic and see the holes where the bullets had ripped through the fabric. The tan pants were also covered with blood. She held the plastic bag to her chest for a moment before she returned it to the canvas bag. She said a prayer thanking Whitey and asking God to protect him. She packed her overnight tote and left the house. She would call C. J. when she got home. Tomorrow, she would put the canvas bag in her safe deposit box along with the envelopes.

Marie gave a final wave to the few women still lingering in the church parking lot. Their "see you soons" and "call me, honeys" followed her to the car. The afternoon program at church had done little to lessen the sting of her argument with Lisa. She hoped she had lingered long enough for Lisa to have headed back to New Orleans. She was still too angry to face her; and the headache that was beginning at the nape of her neck, indicated she was not up for another argument. As she slid behind the wheel of her car, the automatic seat adjusted itself perfectly. She smiled in spite of herself because she loved this feature. She'd had the car for just over a month now and this had to be one of her favorite features. It was as if the car knew her and understood what she needed. With a gentle push of a button, classical music filled the car's custom-designed brilliant chrome and inlaid Italian wood interior. As she pulled out of the church's newly paved parking lot (newly paved thanks to her generous donation last year), she could not quiet the voices inside her head. The sick feeling she had in the pit of her stomach hours ago returned to join her growing headache. After all these years of living the life she had created for herself as Mrs. Russell Morgan and later as Dr. Marie Morgan, the demons of her past always seemed to find a way to sneak in like pesky cobwebs in a forgotten corner.

"Damn her," Marie cursed through clinched teeth and pressed harder on the accelerator. She found momentary relief in the way the Mercedes responded to her command and seemed to glide over the road. Why couldn't Lisa just leave well enough alone? Why was she always searching and digging as Marie struggled to bury and forget?

"Look like she gonna take her coloring after her daddy," said the copper-skinned smiling young nurse. Russell

had insisted she accompany Marie home from the hospital to assist her during her first days at home with the baby. The sparkling white nurse's uniform made the contrast between it and her skin even more dramatic. It was the nurse's comment that made Marie nauseous. The nurse cooed softly at the sleeping infant as she tucked the pink cashmere blanket tightly around her before she placed her in the bassinet next to Marie's large walnut four-poster bed. "She sure is a little beauty, just like her mama." The nurse smiled and hoped to undo the damage she saw in the young mother's face after her first comment.

"Take her out of here, please. I would like to get some rest," Marie said, unable or unwilling to keep the disgust out of her voice, and glared coldly at the nurse. Just like these ignorant Negroes to always mention color.

"Why she won't be no bother to you for hours, Mrs. Morgan." The nurse was surprised any mother would want to be separated from this wonderful little bundle for even a minute. "She all bathed and fed. Better to keep 'em close as possible to you when they little like this, my mama always say." The nurse smiled again.

"I do not recall asking you for the opinion of your mama. Now take her out of here," Marie snapped.

"Yes, ma'am, Mrs. Morgan. I'll get her over to the nursery right now." The nurse quickly moved toward the door with the sleeping baby as if both their lives depended on an immediate exit from Marie's room.

"Color. Color. Always color," Marie cried postpartum tears onto the pink linen pillow case.

It seemed color had been the cause of too many of her tears...

"Lawd, have mercy. Boy, what is your sister goin' on so about?" Essie Baptiste asked. She placed the bag of groceries on the kitchen table and kicked off her shoes, all in one easy motion. She had heard the cries of her nine-year-old daughter before she reached the back porch. She had already planned to whip Raymond, Jr. figuring he was the cause of his sister's distress.

"Oh, Mama, you know Marie," fourteen-year-old Raymond, Jr. responded. He didn't look up from his homework. "She been goin' on like this since them old gals of Miss Jean's went to pickin' at her on the way home from school."

"Raymond, I done told you to watch after yo' sister," Essie scolded. She wondered if she had enough energy left to hit

him in the back of his head, deal with her screaming daughter, and get dinner ready before Raymond, Sr. got home from work.

"Ain't that easy watchin' after Marie. She always runnin' somebody down with that old big mouth of hers," Raymond Jr. pleaded his case and hoped it would be enough to prevent the smack upside his head he could already see forming in the palm of his mother's right hand.

Essie took one look at his face, wiggled the tingling fingers of her right hand, and headed down the hall toward her screaming daughter.

Nine-year-old Marie Esther Baptiste lay kicking and screaming on her bed with not one tear in sight. Her mane of dark, soft curls made a tangled mess around her red face. She yelled even louder when her mother entered the room. Marie grabbed her pillow, placed it over her face, and acted as if she was smothering herself.

"From the way you carryin' on in here sounds like your day been harder than mine," Essie said. She sat down on the bed and wrestled the pillow away from Marie.

"I hate that old pig-face Barbara Jean and that old frog-eyed Mattie!" Marie screamed and jumped from the bed.

"Hate a powerful word, Marie. Ain't fit for nothing but the work of the devil." "Barbara Jean and Mattie with they old ugly, stinkin' selves is the work of the devil."

Marie cried hot, bitter tears now. Her usually pale cheeks were an angry crimson. "Baby, what did they do to make you carry on so and say such mean things?" Essie reached for her daughter. Marie pulled away from her as if Essie's hand was a red-hot poker.

"Why I got to be colored? Why cain't I be white like Barbara Jean and Mattie?" Marie's anger spat the words into Essie's face. "I'm white as they is. Whiter than Mattie 'cause she don't never wash her old ugly face." She held out her arms to offer as proof.

Essie sighed and her stomach tightened. She was too tired for this. Again.

"Marie, that's a question you gone have to ask the good Lawd if you make it to Glory. I ain't got no answer for that. I do know He know His business and He don't make no mistakes. He made you colored, so that's the right way for you to be."

"Ain't neither!" A dark green-blue vein in Marie's forehead pulsed. "If I was supposed to be colored, then I'd look like you and Junior. Even Daddy look more colored than me and everybody always sayin' how high yella he is."

"Marie Esther Baptiste," Essie yelled at her daughter, then stood. Her patience spent. "Now you listen here. I done heard enough of this foolish talk! You colored and that's all there is to it. Everybody colored got a different look to 'em and

yours just happened to look white. Ain't nothin' can be done
'bout that. Lawd, knows if it was, I'd make you black as night.
But lookin' white and bein' white is two different things. The
sooner you understand that the less grief you gone have. Now,
I'm tired and I ain't hearin' no more of it. March your little self
over to that basin and wash your face and braid your hair and
get on downstairs and get your lesson or you gone get some
color today. Black and blue 'cross your narrow behind."

Essie left the room giving Marie one final look that
moved her across the room to the basin filled with water. As she
dipped her face towel in the tepid water and looked into the
milky mirror over the basin she muttered to herself.

"Ain't gonna stay colored. You cain't do nothing about
being colored, Mama. But I can. And I'm gonna be as white as
Barbara Jean and Mattie. Maybe even whiter and ain't nothing
or nobody gone stop me."

The quiet of the house told Marie that Morgan was gone
before she peeked into her daughter's darkened bedroom.

"Good," Marie said aloud as she walked slowly down
the long hallway toward her room. She could never resist
admiring the silk fabric of the wallpaper or the beauty of the
gleaming mahogany woodwork. She'd fallen in love with this
house the first moment she'd seen it even though Russell had
insisted they move closer to the hospital. She'd have nothing but

the great house on the quiet, tree lined street. She'd spent a small fortune redecorating over the years and always got a great deal of pleasure from the envious looks and whispers of her friends when they visited.

Marie was glad for the peace and quiet she felt as she slipped beneath the cool, crisp sheets. She hadn't had a good night's sleep since Lisa had come home. She reached for the novel she'd started before Lisa's visit, but soon became bored with the author's rambling and wordy style.

"I should write a book," Marie spoke to the author's picture on the back cover of the book before she placed it on the nightstand. "Oh, if these walls could talk."

Russell stood in the doorway of Marie's sitting room and watched the heels of her shoes leave deep tracks in the soft, off white carpet. She cursed aloud, waved her hands, and threw books off her desk against the pale lemon-yellow walls. He moved forward and gently, but firmly took hold of her arm. His action saved one of the three hand- blown, crystal vases filled with tea roses and chrysanthemums from crashing against the gilded mirror over her desk.

"*Marie. Baby, stop this,*" *Russell spoke gently, eased the vase from her hand, and placed it on the desk.* "*You've worked yourself into a fit.*"

"*If I am having a fit, as you say, Russell, it is because of Lisa. Lisa Morgan. How dare she demand that we call her Morgan Franklin? Who in the hell does she think she is?*" *Marie spat the words at Russell, a scowl disfigured her usually beautiful face.*

"*She's asking for answers to questions, Marie. That's all. She's not trying to upset us. She just wants answers about who she is.*" *Russell could feel the heat coming off of his wife's body.*

Marie snatched her arm away and glared at Russell, her amber eyes blazed. "*Who she is? Who she is? She's who I say she is!*"

"*This has gone on too long, Marie; and now it's causing our little girl pain. Lisa deserves to know the truth.*" *Russell could feel his own anger heating up the back of his neck.*

"*What truth would that be, Russell?*" *What Marie had meant to sound like a laugh sounded more like the cry of a wounded animal.* "*You people kill me with your self-righteousness and romanticized quests for truth. Growing up in Rockhurst is all you know about the truth, Russell Morgan. Believe me, that truth had nothing to do with the truth of living in*

St. Vincent. Over there, that truth you all were so fond of could get you killed." Marie grabbed her purse from the floor where it had been knocked off the chair, left the room, and slammed the door behind her.

Marie jumped in her sleep. The slammed door in her dream had startled her awake. Her eyes flew open and stared into the darkness of her bedroom.

CHAPTER TEN

The phone rang three times before Morgan reached for it. The answering machine would take over on the fifth ring and she seriously contemplated allowing the device to do its job. She gave in on the fourth ring and answered.

"What are you still doing at home?" Rhonda's voice fought to be heard over Jay-Z's chant to brush the "Dirt off Your Shoulder."

"Lost track of time, I guess. I was trying to finish going through these applications for Penny's nanny. Gene stopped by with the background check information around 6:30 p.m." Morgan pulled the base of the phone closer to her and moved aside the stack of applications. "I come back to work in two weeks and I don't want to have to focus on this when I get back.

"Morgan, you're hiring a nanny, not the head of the C.I.A. Now, you promised, we'd have a night out, so get your ass down here. Those twins from Langley and Pierce are here and the cute one has been asking about you for the last hour." Rhonda took a sip from the third glass she'd held that night filled with a lemon drop martini and smiled at a very attractive man who looked like an Ashanti warrior who'd been dipped in extra dark chocolate.

"Rhonda, they're twins. They're both cute." Morgan quickly glanced at the 1906 limited edition brass Chelsea clock centered in the middle of her bedroom fireplace mantle. Marie had given her the clock when she graduated from law school and made sure each of the 200 guests at L'Ouverture's DuBois Estates Country Club knew it had been acquired at a private auction. Marie was equally proud of saying to anyone who would listen, that the clock had once sat on the desk of Edith Bolling Galt Wilson, the wife of President Woodrow Wilson, who was often called "The Secret President" for her rumored role in running the government while her husband recovered from a stroke. It was only 10:30 p.m. She had time to change and get there by 11:15 p.m. If she didn't, Rhonda would just call her the rest of the night.

"Exactly. And if you don't want me to cause a scandal by taking both of them home with me tonight, you better get down here in a hurry and stop me." Rhonda finished her drink. "Wear that sexy tangerine Yves Saint Laurent one-shoulder dress you spent a fortune on and never wear. It's got to be five brothers for every sister in here tonight," Rhonda said then quickly hung up. Morgan heard the click that ended the call before she could respond.

Rhonda's suggestion saved Morgan time going through her closet. She had been right. Morgan smiled at her statuesque and shapely reflection in the full-length mirror in her dressing room and slipped into a pair of brushed gold, strappy Jimmy Choo sandals with just enough heel to show off her long legs and let her dance until she was tired. A night out would be good for her. She'd spent the last several days in consultations with Penny's doctors. Maurice had proven to be a lifesaver. His expertise and support of her decision making relieved some of the stress she felt whenever she feared for Penny's wellness. Morgan spread a little sparkly gold lip gloss on her lips then placed it in the small evening bag along with her keys and wallet. Just thinking of Maurice made the prospect of dancing with the twins from Langley and Pierce dim in comparison. She shook her head to clear thoughts of Maurice away.

"Stay focused Morgan," she whispered as she turned off the light in her bedroom and headed toward the door.

"Well look at you," Dr. Maurice LaShurr greeted Morgan with a smile on his handsome face and entered the doorway of the neonatal intensive care unit at Rivers C. Franklin Medical Center. "You look like an old pro at that."

"You must be kidding," Morgan said and gently rocked her infant niece. Morgan had been visiting the hospital every day for the past two months. Penny was beginning to thrive and bond with Morgan. Morgan brought Mary Joyce to New Orleans as soon as she had been strong enough to make the trip so she could be with her baby. She offered to rent Mary Joyce an apartment close to the hospital so that she could help in the recovery of her daughter and bring the boys to visit and bond with their baby sister.

Mary Joyce hesitated to accept the offer and after only a week in New Orleans returned home on a Greyhound bus while Morgan was at the office. She said she had to check on her boys. Almost a week passed before Morgan heard from her again.

"Lisa, I cain't do all this," Mary Joyce cried into the phone. "Penny just too little and too sick. I cain't help her." *I cain't help myself.* Mary Joyce finished the sentence in her head.

"Mary Joyce, she's getting better. She needs you here. You're her mother. Get packed, I'm coming to get you and the boys. You can stay with me," Morgan said, irritated with her younger sister.

"Lisa, I ain't coming back. I cain't take care of her. You been hearing what that doctor friend of yours keep saying. She gone need more operations. What if she stay sick forever, Lisa? What I'm gonna do out here with a baby that sick?"

"You can't just walk away from her Mary Joyce. She needs you!" Morgan yelled into the phone. She barely recognized her own voice. "What will happen to her?"

"You the smart one. You figure it out," Mary Joyce slammed down the phone.

The next weekend, Morgan drove to St. Vincent to deliver papers she had drawn up that gave her custody of Penny Lyons and relinquished Mary Joyce and Darrell's parental rights.

"This ain't how we raised her, Lisa," Irene hissed as she paced the length of the living room. "Cain't talk no sense into her at all, she so busy feelin' sorry for herself."

"Mary Joyce know what's right. She just having a hard time doin' what's right," Carl said. The expression on his face was a mixture of sadness and disgust.

"Oh. She can see to do right by Darrell Lyons with his triflin' ass. Won't go see after her baby, but don't waste no time getting' out to the jailhouse," Irene fussed. She dropped down on the couch next to Morgan. The pain she felt was all tangled up in the anger. She dabbed the corner of her eyes with the hem of her apron. "What kinda mother does this? Cain't believe she gone give her baby away like some old toy she tired of playin' with," Irene yelled.

"We don't mean to put all this on you, Lisa. Know this the best thing for Penny and we sure appreciate all you doin'," Carl said. He put his arm around Irene's shoulders.

He picked up the folder Morgan had placed on the coffee table. Carl continued, "We'll make sure she get these papers and sign them."

Mary Joyce walked quietly in her bare feet, across the worn living room rug and picked up the heavy blue folder from the coffee table. She'd waited out back until she'd seen Lisa's car pull onto the main road before coming inside. She could hear the radio her father used to listen to baseball games coming from her parents' room. Irene had long since left for her part-time night job at a nearby nursing home. Mary Joyce wiped the tears from her eyes as she looked at the papers in her hands. Most of the words she didn't even understand, but she knew the power of the documents. These papers would take her little girl away from her. She pulled a blue ink pen from the pocket of her cutoff jeans and signed her name on the line over her printed name.

"Ain't nothin' I can do for her no way," Mary Joyce spoke to herself as she flipped through the documents and signed her name on several more lines. Lisa had obviously already been to the jail because Mary Joyce saw Darrell's signature above his name on the lines next to hers. She doubted he even cared.

"Be too hard on her growin' up out here anyway. Bein' the only girl with them bad ass little boys of mine. Lisa take her, she can grow up knowin' all these big words and how to act when she go someplace. Hell, Lisa take her she might have a chance to go someplace."

Mary Joyce knew her life had become a disappointment to Lisa and her parents. Her daddy was always telling her she just needed a little ambition. "Get some goals, baby. Goals'll take you somewhere." She'd had goals. She'd wanted to play the piano in night clubs in New Orleans like she'd seen in a movie once. She admitted her goals hadn't been as big as C. J.'s dreams of going to New York and becoming a famous newspaper man or to play football in the NFL like Winn. She never liked school enough to even think about doing something like Lisa and becoming a lawyer, but she had goals.

Mary Joyce shook her head at her childish memories of wanting to marry a rich boy from Rockhurst, drive a fancy car, and live in a big house like Lisa's Mama. She could've done it, too. She was pretty enough. Boys all over L'Ouverture told her she was pretty. She should have listened to Winn when he told her to stay away from Darrell Lyons. Winn said he was bad news because he always hung out behind Lawson Eddie's Fish Market drinking and gambling. Mary Joyce had thought Winn was just trying to boss her around. Darrell was fine and even though his car wasn't new, he had one. That was more than she could say for most boys in St. Vincent. He told her he was going to buy her one of those fancy houses in Rockhurst one day and she could even have a cook and a maid. This had been all she needed to hear as a thirteen-year-old to convince herself she was in love with the seventeen-year-old boy with the pretty smile and the not-so-raggedy car. Yes, she could believe her prince charming might just be hidden somewhere behind the sweet, wet kisses and adolescent charm of the boy who liked drinking and gambling behind Lawson Eddie's Fish Market.

Mary Joyce finished signing the papers and told herself to forget how much she had hoped for a little girl when she found out she was pregnant again. She hadn't cared how the nurses at the clinic rolled their eyes at her when she came through the door with her belly already straining the fabric of one of Darrell's t-shirts. She could hear them whispering about her being stupid, and not having enough sense to keep her husband off her as she placed the plastic cup, warm with her urine, inside the cabinet that opened into the lab from the restroom. What did they know about her? They had their fancy jobs and healthy babies. Mary Joyce wiped away new tears as she remembered how disappointed Darrell had been when the nurse looked onto the ultrasound screen and announced her three boys were about to have a little sister. On the ride home, she'd tried to convince him how nice it would be to have a little girl; how pretty she'd look and how much fun he could have spoiling her. She had wanted to name her Lisette. She thought the name sounded fancy like the rich girls who lived in Rockhurst. Darrell had laughed at the name and said it sounded like some stuck-up white girl's name. Darrell had called her Penny because he felt she'd come to take the last pennies out of his pocket.

"You be a good girl for your Auntie Lisa, Penny," Mary Joyce said. She wiped the tears from her face, laid the papers on top of the blue folder, and left the room.

CHAPTER ELEVEN

"I keep telling her she's in the wrong profession, Dr. LaShurr," the nurse commented. She gently took a sleeping Penny from Morgan's arms.

"You are great for my ego, Elaine. I must see about getting you a raise," Morgan said. She laughed and followed Maurice into the hallway.

"I didn't expect to see you here this late. It's almost 10 o'clock," Maurice said as he glanced at his watch.

"I always come to say good night. Why are you here so late?"

"I wanted to check in on a little boy I operated on yesterday. His grandmother's been really worried. She can't get here every day because she's taking care of some other grandchildren. I just wanted to reassure her."

"Maurice, I cannot thank you enough for all you have done for my niece," Morgan said while they walked toward the bank of elevators.

"Sure, you can. Have dinner with me tomorrow night," he said smiling.

It was a few moments before Morgan was able to answer. The intensity in his eyes caught her off guard. "Sure. I'll be here until around 7 o'clock. How about 7:30? Is Arnaud's all right?"

"Sounds great if you're treating," Maurice teased and then pushed the elevator button. Arnaud's was one of the finest and most beloved restaurants in the French Quarter.

"Sure thing." Morgan stepped inside the elevator and pushed the garage button. As he reached across her to push the button to the doctor's parking garage, she smiled to herself as she caught the fragrance of his spicy cologne and had to stop herself from inhaling too deeply.

"She's doing well, isn't she?" Morgan never felt quite sure from one day to the next. "She is doing very well. You are part of the reason for that. Another couple of months and I think she will be strong enough for surgery. What you have done for her is huge, Morgan. And I am not just talking about getting her transferred out of General. I am talking about rocking her to sleep every night. Good old-fashioned love goes a long way."

"She's my family," Morgan said when she exited the elevator. Maurice found himself smiling long after the elevator doors closed.

Morgan was glad most of her day had been spent in court. It kept her from getting nervous about having dinner with Maurice. She still couldn't figure out why just thinking about sitting down to eat with him made her pulse race. She'd skipped going back to the office after court like she usually did and headed home to take a leisurely bath. If you could be in love with a room, Morgan was in love with her master bath. The Lagos blue quartz counter tops surrounded the square, silver double sinks and Kohler faucets in a sea of shimmering blue. The wall color was a pale aqua blue with white trim that always made her think of the rich vanilla icing Uncle Raymond used to frost his coconut layer cake. The jetted corner spa tub and seamless shower surrounded by turquoise glass rivaled those found in the finest spas.

As she dressed, she hummed softly to herself. She grabbed her purse, looked at her watch, and punched in the four digits on the alarm's keypad. She had just enough time to head back over to the hospital to tuck Penny in for the night.

Maurice stood as Morgan entered the restaurant, smiled, and waved her over to the best table in the place. "Calm down, brother," he whispered to himself as she made her way toward their table. The granny apple green blouse with a single ruffle down the front and the camel colored slacks hugged her hips just right. The butterflies in his stomach that had taken flight when he'd handed his car keys to the valet had now grown to the size of bald eagles. He could not believe that the palms of his hands were sweating. This had not happened since his first slow dance in junior high school.

"Good to see you, Morgan." Maurice was unsure of whether he should shake her hand or embrace her. He pulled her chair out for her instead. "You look nice."

"Thank you. So do you," Morgan said. She hoped the look she was giving him was not too brazen. She diverted her glance to the chair he pulled out for her and sat down.

"It's not often I get to see you without your white coat or surgical scrubs." She wondered how she could have missed his broad shoulders and exquisitely muscled forearms. The black cashmere pullover sweater made it impossible to miss tonight.

Maurice caught the look in her eyes, felt his cheeks warm, and realized he was blushing. Morgan picked up a menu. "The food here is fantastic. I hope you're hungry."

"Oh, I am." Morgan hoped he could not hear her heart pounding.

"Then let's order. If you're in the mood, the Shrimp Creole is wonderful." Maurice looked over his raised menu.

"I'll take your word for it." Morgan placed her menu on the table as Maurice waved the waitress over to the table.

"You know why they named her Penny?" Morgan asked, after she swallowed the most delicious spoonful of Shrimp Creole. "Because Darrell said she'd come to take the pennies from his pockets."

Maurice finished the last of the seafood gumbo and carefully moved his plate of the infamous Arnaud crab cakes in front of him. He waited for the tears to leave Morgan's eyes. "People do the best they can, Morgan. Don't be too hard on Mary Joyce. From what I saw of her while she was here, she doesn't have much more to give that little girl."

"I know you are right. But it is still hard for me to swallow sometimes. Mary Joyce never seemed to want much for herself and it looks like she has succeeded in getting just that. Instead of spending time here with her daughter, who remains in the NICU, she's visiting Darrell in jail. The same Darrell who beat her butt into an early labor. That's the reason Penny's there in the first place."

"Well, I'm just glad you were able to help. Penny is very lucky to have you for an aunt," Maurice said. Morgan found the sound of his voice soothing. "Morgan, I have to change the subject for a minute. I can't hold it any longer. How is it we've been friends for over three years and I didn't know a thing about Rockhurst or St. Vincent or the fact that the "L" in your name stands for Lisa?"

"Sometimes there are things you just don't get around to sharing, I guess. Then when you think about it, it doesn't seem to matter as much."

"I could understand if you were ashamed of your background, but I don't get the feeling that's the case."

"It's not," Morgan stated simply and made the most of her last bit of Shrimp Creole. "I guess I have my father to thank for that. He always made me feel really special. Even when he was very busy, he'd find a way to spend time with me. It could have been him reading to me at bedtime or showing up to drive me home from school. He used to take me on his rounds when I was little. I think he dreamed I'd follow in his footsteps and become a doctor. Even after I found out he was not my biological father nothing changed in our relationship. Russell Morgan was a very special man."

"Dr. Russell Morgan. I still can't believe you grew up in the same house with the world-famous Dr. Russ, as we called him. He's probably responsible for half of the Black physicians in this country. He made us believe it was possible." Admiration filled Maurice's voice. "When I was in college, I read everything he ever wrote. Although he didn't always get credit for it, he was way ahead of his time; particularly as it relates to the care of premature infants. When I was in med school, I worked nights at a mortuary just so I could pay to go to his conferences and seminars. At the time, I had no idea one day I'd sit in a fancy restaurant having dinner with his beautiful daughter."

"Thanks for inviting me to take you out to dinner," Morgan teased. "I didn't realize how much I miss getting out. The last couple of months I haven't seen anything except the inside of neonatal intensive care, courtrooms, and my office. There is hardly any time left to do anything for myself."

"Then as Penny's doctor, I insist you remedy that immediately." Maurice's dark brown eyes sparkled. "Come with me to my parents' place at the lake tomorrow. They are celebrating their fortieth wedding anniversary with a weekend long event. I can only go up for the day. Come with me. I know they would love to see you. It's beautiful there this time of year and the event is casual so you'll have a chance to relax. Yes is the only answer, I'll accept. As Penny's doctor, of course."

"Well as Penny's doctor, you know I was planning on spending the day with her tomorrow." Morgan took a sip of her pinot noir wine.

"Morgan, she'll be fine. We can stop by before leaving in the morning and I'll take you straight to her when we get back so you can rock her to sleep." Maurice's eyes pleaded and conveyed more than his words. "Doctor's orders."

"I guess trying to come up with another reason for not going would be a waste of time, huh?" Morgan began to like the idea of spending a day at the lake.

"So, smart. You should have been a doctor." Maurice laughed as they reached for the dessert menus. After careful thought, Morgan decided on the Crème Brûlée, while Maurice chose the Chocolate Toffee Bombe. The waitress took one look at how easily they laughed together and brought extra plates because she knew they'd want to share. She was right.

Morgan thought of thousands of brilliant, clear diamonds spread out on aquamarine velvet as she looked at the afternoon sun reflecting off the lake. This had been such a good idea. The gathering of over sixty people was comfortable and fun with everyone celebrating, not only Maurice's parents' anniversary, but the joy of being alive at this moment in such a beautiful place. The stress of the last few months was washed away by the peace of the late spring day. Maurice and Morgan excused themselves after a lunch of jambalaya, dirty rice, shrimp creole, crawfish, tomato and cucumber salad, okra stew, cornbread, and

pecan pie. They promised to return in time to see his parents cut
the five-tier wedding cake and take their second "first dance."

They walked in the woods surrounding the lake, enjoyed
its beauty, the quiet, and each other's company.

"Morgan, you ever think about getting married? Starting
a family?" Maurice asked as they sat under the shade of a
Cypress tree.

"Sometimes," Morgan admitted. "I figure I'm only
twenty-eight. I have time. Now, I have Penny so the family part
seems to have taken care of itself. What about you?"

"I already did." Maurice looked into Morgan's eyes and
noticed how their clear gray now reflected the lush greens and
rich browns of their surroundings.

"Excuse me?" Morgan took her attention from the
wildflowers and focused it completely on Maurice.

"I was married. My wife's name was Michelle. We had a
son." The sound of a distant waterfall played like soft music in
the background. "It's like you said last night. When I was going
to tell you, it just didn't seem to matter."

"Well guess what, Dr. LaShurr. It matters now.
Confession time."

Maurice smiled at her. He could not seem to stop
smiling at her. "I was nineteen, a sophomore at Stanford
majoring in Human Biology, on the Dean's List, the whole

works. The son of Drs. Mason and Della LaShurr of New Orleans and my seventeen- year-old girlfriend was a senior in high school and pregnant."

Maurice's words came slowly as he mulled each one over in his mind before he spoke. It was so important she understood. "Her parents insisted we get married right away. My father was enraged. He thought she made up the whole thing to trap me. My mother wanted to avoid any scandal. She didn't want anything to distract me from my studies. We were married on Michelle's eighteenth birthday, two days after she graduated from high school. My father's friend, who is a judge, performed the ceremony in our living room. She joined me at school and started working in the campus bookstore. Michelle wanted to be a music teacher. We made plans for her to start school as soon as the baby was old enough. He was born during Christmas break." Maurice paused.

His eyes were filled with tears. Morgan reached out and took his hand. It trembled slightly in hers. She could feel his heart breaking.

"I came home early from class one day. I wanted to surprise her. It had been really hard on her away from her family and taking care of the baby all by herself. He was about four months old. I found her in bed with one of my professors." Maurice looked away and wiped a tear that had fallen onto his cheek. "Needless to say, things got pretty bad between us. She took the baby and went home. I didn't visit. My parents made sure our son had what he needed and I was grateful for their generosity. I hate to admit but I didn't see him much. When he was almost two years old, I got a call from my mother saying I needed to come home immediately."

"Maurice, you don't have to go on if it hurts too much." Morgan watched as the pain took the usual sparkle from his dark brown eyes. "It's okay."

"I need to tell you this." Maurice squeezed Morgan's hand. "His name was Trenton. He drowned in the bathtub. Michelle's mother found her naked and beside the tub rocking his lifeless body in her arms. They ruled it accidental, but I always wondered. Michelle never recovered and they committed her to a mental health facility in Massachusetts. I went to see her as often as I could, but most of the time it was easier to stay away. I don't think she ever recognized me. She committed suicide last year."

Maurice took Morgan by the hand and helped her to her feet. He held her hand as they walked back toward the party. Their silence said everything.

CHAPTER TWELVE

"Well, well, well," Rhonda greeted Morgan on Monday morning. She came into Morgan's office holding an oversized, black coffee mug with the words–**NO IS A COMPLETE ANSWER**–written in gigantic, white block letters. She was dressed in a brilliant lime green pants suit. In grand "Peacock" fashion, she had chosen to accessorize the suit with a lemon-yellow silk blouse and shoes that cost enough to pay an average-sized family's grocery bill for a month. Her dark brown hair was styled in a dramatic French roll. Beautiful, creamy pearl studs the size of marbles graced her ears and complimented the matching three-strand pearl necklace around her neck. Morgan thought she looked as if she had just stepped off a Paris runway instead of out of the partners' Monday morning meeting. "Newman wants to see you at 10:30 a.m. to go over the Morris Bell brief. It looks like he wants you to take Jerry Randall's place on the team. You are in the big leagues now, girlfriend."

"Close the door," Morgan said, her eyes grew big. The Morris Bell Case was one of McDouglas, Bradshaw &

Newman's largest accounts. It was well over $500 million dollars. "Are you sure?"

"Morgan, do I ever say anything without being totally sure? I just left the partners' meeting." Rhonda placed a manila file folder on Morgan's already cluttered desk. The woman must have been here since before dawn, Rhonda thought. It was only ten minutes to eight o'clock and her desk already looked as if she had completed an entire day's work.

"This is a huge chance for them to really see me at my best," Morgan said almost to herself as she opened the file.

"Please. They know your best or you would not be taking over for Randall." Rhonda sat down in one of the leather chairs in front of Morgan's chrome and glass desk.

"How is Jerry?" He was one of the forty attorneys employed by the firm. This morning, her secretary had brought her information she needed for an afternoon meeting, her morning cup of Earl Grey tea with cream and lemon, and news of Jerry's car crash over the weekend.

"He's got one hell of a hangover to go with his broken ankle," Rhonda reported. "His wife has a concussion and had to have surgery for some internal injuries. She is going to be fine. Especially, after she divorces Jerry's alcoholic ass and takes half of his money." Rhonda laughed and took a sip from her mug.

"You are awful. Maybe Jerry will finally get some help." Morgan shook her head. "Whatever." Rhonda was finished with that conversation. "Now, I want to hear about the weekend at the lake with that fine ass Dr. LaShurr. And hurry up because I have work to do."

"First of all, it was not the weekend. It was for part of the day on Saturday. And there's not much to tell. I spent the day with an old friend."

"Morgan, now you're getting on my nerves." Rhonda rolled her eyes. "I have been at that hospital with you. I have seen the way the brother looks at you with those big, dreamy bedroom eyes. All I am saying is you better take them damn "old friend" glasses off and put on some "my man" glasses or I might just have to swoop down on The Doctor myself."

"Rhonda, you have a great day." Morgan opened the folder and reached for a leather- bound journal on the shelf nearest her desk. She needed to concentrate and talking about Maurice might make that difficult. Rhonda would have to wait until after her meeting with Newman to hear about her day at the lake.

"Well, counselor, I *do* have work to do. Later." Rhonda laughed as she left Morgan's office.

"Mama, I will not have this conversation if you are going to yell," Morgan said. She held the phone away from her ear. She had been expecting this call all week. A week ago, C. J. had sent her a copy of his newspaper article. It had opened an investigation into Winn's murder. The investigation would be handled by state police instead of the St. Vincent Sheriff's Department because of their alleged involvement.

"Lisa, just leave things alone!" Marie screamed. Her voice had reached unprecedented levels in volume and pitch. "Because of the trouble you stirred up, Carl was fired. The people you claim to care so much about are now in worse shape because of you."

Morgan did not understand where Marie's anger came from but she could not help but flinch at her mother's venomous words. Irene had called her a couple of days ago to tell her Sam Austin had told Carl he no longer needed him. Carl had worked for him for over twenty years. The only thing that had eased her terrible feelings of guilt was the thankfulness Carl and Irene expressed at the work she had done to get Winn's murder investigated. C. J.'s article had been carried in newspapers across the country and there was even talk of a book deal. Carl and Irene could not contain their pride. C.

C.J. had a number of TV interviews lined up and had been asked to go to Washington,

D.C. in a few weeks to speak to a committee on racially motivated hate crimes. Carl and Irene wanted the truth, no matter what it cost them.

"I cannot believe you. I did not kill Winn, Mama. Someone else did. I just want to know who killed my brother. Why can't you seem to understand that?" Morgan snapped.

"I am leaving in a few days for a cruise to the Greek Isles with the university's alumni committee. I will be away for one month or more." Marie's voice was cold, her words crisp. Morgan was more than familiar with this tone. There would be no further conversation about Winston's murder.

"You couldn't have planned that better." Morgan's voice shook with rage.

"Lisa, what do you want from me?" Marie snapped before she was able to catch herself.

"What I have always wanted from you. Some consideration for someone other than yourself." Morgan moved the phone away from her ear again as Marie slammed down the receiver.

Morgan paced the length of the hallway between her home office and bedroom. She tried to walk the anger and frustration out of her system. Morgan did not need this tonight. She had to be in court early the next morning on the Morris Bell case. Morgan walked to her bedroom and opened her walk-in closet. She selected a simple-cut navy blue suit and a brand new cream-colored silk blouse and made a mental note to wear pearls. Pearls always made her look a bit older and more serious. A quick look in the mirror confirmed Rhonda had been right about the haircut.

Two days ago, Rhonda had persuaded her to cut her shoulder-length hair, usually worn in a casual bob. She had talked Morgan into Halle Berry's trademark pixie haircut. Morgan had to admit, the haircut elegantly highlighted her doe-shaped eyes and high cheekbones that were perfectly encased in her warm butterscotch-toned face. The look gave her sophistication and a little sass that Rhonda said she wore well. The phone rang again just as she poured lavender bath salts into the bubbling, steaming waters of her bath tub.

"Hello," she answered. She'd already made the decision to hang up if it was Marie. "Good work, Little Girl." The pride and warmth of her Uncle Raymond's voice reached through the phone and embraced her. "Your name wasn't mentioned, but I know C. J. couldn't have done that piece in the paper without you. How the hell did you two get that coroner's report and Winston's clothes?"

"As a super sleuth, I cannot reveal my sources." Morgan laughed. "It's about time you called. How was your hunting trip?"

"Great. Got some deer meat. Gonna barbeque. You oughta come on down in a couple weeks. When I got back, St. Vincent was buzzing with newspaper reporters and TV folks. The state police done took over the sheriff's office and La Fontaine's sweating bricks. I have a feeling we living in the last days of his reign of terror."

"Mama just called to yell at me. I guess she was storing it up all week. She tried to make me feel guilty about Carl getting fired, as if I did not already feel badly enough. Can you believe old Sam Austin?" Morgan lit the lavender and vanilla candles that encircled her tub.

"I believe anything these crackers do down here, Lisa. What I don't want to believe is your mother. She done outdid herself this time. I wouldn't hear none of her foolishness, so she ain't talking to me." Morgan did not ask for any details since she knew the history of her mother and uncle's relationship.

"She's leaving for the Greek Isles." Morgan tested the water's temperature and increased the flow of hot water into the tub.

"Lisa, your mama been running and hiding from something most of her life. Don't you let it bother you. It's just her way of handling things she can't control. No matter what happens, I just want you to know I'm proud of you. You oughta be proud of yourself too. Lonnie Jean's standing here wanting to talk to you, so I'll call you later, Little Girl. Remember, your Uncle Raymond loves you."

"Lisa, they transferred the attending physician, Dr. Reynolds, who was on duty the night they brought Winston in. Money miraculously appeared to send Nora to a seminar in D. C. that we've been begging to go to for the last three years. La Fontaine's girl, Nancy, suddenly decided to go back to school— in Houston. Everybody at the hospital is on pins and needles. Looks like they gonna hold the hearings in Baton Rouge. They subpoenaed the coroner and a couple clerks in medical records," Lonnie Jean spoke excitedly into the phone.

"C. J. said it would move fast. Did you get a subpoena?"

"No. The investigators questioned everybody who was in emergency that night. I was in labor and delivery that night, so I'm in the clear," Lonnie Jean assured as she heard the concern in her cousin's voice. "I'm okay. Don't worry about me. You got enough on your plate. How's Penny?"

"She is pretty amazing. You have to come up and see her. Maurice thinks he will be able to operate the first of the month. She's getting stronger every day and is simply gorgeous," Morgan smiled and turned off the water.

"Spoken like a true mother," Lonnie Jean teased. "Look, good luck with your big case in the morning. I'm off this weekend, so I think I'll take you up on your offer and come up.

Daddy and Mister Wayne are taking Anthony and some of his friends on a fishing trip, so I'll see you Saturday morning. I love you, Cous."

"I love you back." Morgan pushed the phone's END button and stripped away her clothes. She took a deep breath as she slid into the hot, bubbling water of the Jacuzzi tub and inhaled the relaxing fragrances of lavender and vanilla from the candles that burned around the room. It was not long before her conversation with Marie was forgotten.

CHAPTER THIRTEEN

The fourth envelope arrived three days before Penny's surgery. At first Morgan thought the envelope was empty. She shook it one last time and two small folded pieces of paper fell from the envelope onto her lap. The first was a copy of a birth certificate for Andrea Harriet Jones. Whoever she was she had been born on March 12, 1974 in Mt. Mercy, New York. Her mother's name was Gloria Jones. Her father was listed as John Jones. The second piece of paper was a handwritten note on the familiar, delicate, pink stationary. In the middle of the page was the simple sentence:

Andrea's parents are Geneva Hastings and Alexander Franklin.

Morgan tripped over the running shoes she had carelessly left in the middle of the hallway floor as she ran to the telephone to call C. J.

"Slow down, sis," C. J.'s voice rose over hers. "I don't understand what you're saying."

Morgan took a quick breath, sat down at her glass-topped breakfast room table, and then said, "C. J., I know why Winn was looking in New York. Alexander Franklin had a daughter, another daughter, I should say. She was in Mt. Mercy,

New York. Her name is Andrea Harriet Jones. She was born in
1974. Winn must have found something. He may have found
something that got him killed."

"Winn never mentioned much to me about the details of
what he was doing. He asked for some help from time to time,
but it never seemed to lead anywhere. Fax me a copy of the birth
certificate and the note and then put them with the rest of the
stuff in the safe deposit box. Let me see if I can find anything on
this Andrea Jones." Morgan ended her call with C. J. after a few
more minutes of updates and comparing notes.

Penny's surgery was only a few days away. In the last
month, she had placed St. Vincent and the unending questions
about Alexander Franklin on the back burner in order to confer
with doctors and spend time with Penny. Irene called a couple of
weeks ago to tell her they had two suspects in Winn's murder.
Two young white parolees from

Baton Rouge were being held: Josiah Clark and Lester
Lanier. They denied any involvement in Winn's murder. Morgan
expected that and thought it was just the usual denial of guilt
until she received a call from Whitey yesterday morning.

"Something ain't right about this, Lisa," Whitey said, his
voice a whisper even though he was calling from his apartment.
"First of all, this Lester Lanier is a thief. He has a rap sheet a
mile long and not one assault. He prides himself on stealing

without killing. He ain't never hurt nobody in his life. Why would he shoot a delivery man to death who didn't have but $17 and some change on him? Josiah Clark claims he was in Arkansas the night Winston was murdered. I followed up on that myself and his story checks out. Hate to bring you all this, Lisa. I know you all were hoping this was the end of it."

"It's not your fault, Whitey," Morgan said and sighed in resignation. "You keep me posted, okay? And be careful."

"Always, counselor. Always." Whitey ended the call and knew he would have to be more than careful.

Maurice entered the room quietly and pulled Penny's chart from the plastic holder near the door. He glanced at Morgan and smiled. She held Penny protectively on her chest. They were both sound asleep.

"Morgan. Morgan," Maurice whispered and gently shook her shoulder. She stirred before opening her eyes.

"What time is it?" Morgan asked and rose from the rocker to put Penny in the bassinet. "Late. Why don't you go on home and rest? Tomorrow's going to be a long day for both of you." Penny's surgery was scheduled for 8:00 a.m. His concern for Morgan caused him to frown. Despite the fact she had been asleep when he entered the room, the dark circles under her eyes said she had not gotten much rest lately. The tray he had brought her from the cafeteria hours ago was untouched.

"I just could not seem to leave her tonight. I think she knows something big is going to happen. She would not let me put her down after her last feeding. Carl and Irene are coming up in the morning. I called Mary Joyce again. She finally called back. She got back on at the cannery and said she can't take off from work." Morgan looked at her sleeping niece.

"You are enough for her, Morgan," Maurice said with a reassuring smile.

"I wish I could believe that. What will I tell her about Mary Joyce and Darrell? What do I say when she wants to know why she lives with her aunt and not her mommy and daddy like other little girls?" Morgan grabbed her jacket from the back of the chair.

"You'll tell her the truth. You'll tell her what she needs to know to grow up and feel good about herself. Now get out of here. I'll see you in the morning."

"Maurice, tell me again how she's going to be all right." Morgan slipped into her shoes and coat. "How she's going to grow up and be just like other children."

"Morgan, let's just get through tomorrow. All right?" Maurice was careful not to give her any false hope. They had talked about the procedure so much in the last month that he did not doubt that Morgan could perform the surgery herself. She knew Penny was strong enough for the surgery. He had been clear and honest about the risks. It had been painful for him to watch Morgan agonize over her decision to go ahead with the surgery. Maurice had made it clear Penny had no chance of survival without it.

He walked her to the elevator, kissed her cheek, and said he would call her when he got home. Morgan allowed herself to rest for a moment in his embrace. She was glad she had listened to both Lonnie Jean and Rhonda; otherwise, she may have gone on ignoring her feelings for Maurice. Lonnie Jean and Rhonda were convinced Maurice was good for her and never missed an opportunity to tell her. They had been right. Their relationship was moving slowly, yet growing deeply. He kissed her again quickly on the lips this time before the elevator doors closed.

Morgan drove home in silent prayer and felt a sense of calm as she opened the door to the condo. Lonnie Jean had fallen asleep on the couch; the old black and white movie on the television screen cast a soft, gray light in the otherwise darkened room.

"I must've dozed off," Lonnie Jean said and stretched as Morgan walked into the living room. "Want me to warm up something so you can eat?"

"No thanks. I couldn't eat anything. I keep telling myself she's going to be all right, but I'm so scared, Lonnie Jean." Morgan sat on the couch next to her cousin and placed her head in Lonnie Jean's lap. The tears began to fall instantly while Lonnie Jean's comforting hand patted her back.

"You got this. The best team of pediatric surgeons in the country will be in that operating room in the morning. There's nothing else you can do," Lonnie Jean whispered as Morgan cried. "Lisa, it's gonna be all right. Just have a little faith." She offered her own silent prayer and hoped she had just told her cousin the truth.

"I'm so glad you're here." Morgan sat up and took the tissue Lonnie Jean offered her. "You'd do the same for me, if it were Anthony going into surgery in the morning." When Lonnie Jean was sure Morgan had composed herself, she continued. "Carl called. Said he and Irene will be here first thing in the morning. Irene said she offered to work Mary Joyce's shift at the cannery so she could come, but Mary Joyce said it was no use coming all that way to see a baby who didn't belong to her anymore."

"Mary Joyce is full of it." Morgan was too tired to give Mary Joyce's comments any energy tonight. "She knows it's not even like that. Penny is still her daughter. I had to handle it legally for Penny's sake. I never told her she could not be a part of her life."

"You know that and so does everyone else with good sense. Oh yeah, Aunt Marie called. She said she would be praying for Penny and would call you tomorrow night. She sounded halfway concerned, Lisa. And a Mrs. Jones called. I took a message. It's over by the telephone."

"Mrs. Jones?" Morgan jumped up with more energy than she felt. She picked up the message. It was from Gloria Jones in Troy, New York.

"Lisa, who is she?" Lonnie Jean was confused by Morgan's reaction.

"She may be the woman who raised another one of Alexander Franklin's children. I'm hoping she knows something about him and is willing to talk. Lonnie Jean, can you do me a favor tomorrow?"

"Of course."

"Call C. J. and let him know about this message. Give him the phone number, but ask him not to call her until he hears from me." Morgan handed Lonnie Jean the note.

"You got it Nancy Drew." Lonnie Jean turned the television off as they headed to bed.

CHAPTER FOURTEEN

The promise of a bright, sunny day peaked at Morgan as she pulled open the curtains in her bedroom the next morning just after 6:00 a.m. She thanked God again for Lonnie Jean as she spotted her tea set on a teak wood tray on top of her dresser. She could hear Lonnie Jean singing in the shower down the hall. Pulling her bathrobe tightly around her, more for comfort than warmth, she poured the steaming tea from the pot into the cup. The spicy ginger tea tickled her nose as she held the handleless cup between the palms of her hands.

"You got this. It's gonna be all right," Morgan repeated the words Lonnie Jean had whispered to comfort her last night as she sipped the hot tea.

"You got this," Lonnie Jean said again once they were headed toward the hospital. The angelic voice of Yolanda Adams from the car's speakers reminded them the battle was not theirs, but the Lord's.

"Promise you'll keep telling me that." Morgan glanced at her cousin, who had insisted on driving, and turned up the volume on the car's stereo system.

"Promise." Lonnie Jean winked as she merged into the morning traffic.

Lonnie Jean made herself comfortable in the hospital waiting room as Maurice took Morgan to be with Penny for a few minutes before they prepped her for surgery.

An hour or so later, she waved to Carl and Irene as they stepped off the elevator. "How's she doing?" Irene asked. She gave Lonnie Jean a hug and settled herself onto one of the waiting room chairs. "Penny or Lisa?" Lonnie Jean asked.

"Both. This been some kinda strain on Lisa, I know."

"Was hoping to get here earlier, but Mary Joyce picked last night to stay out all night. Had to wait on Darrell's Mama to come get the boys," Carl grumbled.

"Don't worry about any of that. You and Irene are here now. Penny's doing fine and Lisa's doing the best she can right now. She should be back up here in a minute. She wanted to stay with Penny until they take her into surgery. I have to admit, I didn't think

Lisa was going to be able to handle all this, Penny being so sick and all, but she's doing a great job."

"When I took that first look at that baby, I knew God would have to make a way for her somehow. Lisa the only chance little Penny ever had, Lonnie Jean," Irene said as her eyes filled with tears and Carl took her hand. "I thank God every day for her."

"I'm going to get us some coffee. You all get comfortable. We're going to be here for a while," Lonnie Jean said and moved toward the hallway.

Rhonda brought lunch at noon. Carl took a few bites of a roast beef sandwich, while Irene sipped occasionally from her Styrofoam cup filled with sweet tea and ignored her chicken salad sandwich. Lonnie Jean did not do much better and picked at a delicious Cobb salad she wouldn't have been able to resist under different circumstances. Morgan's crab sandwich remained wrapped. She took a few sips from the chocolate shake she usually devoured in minutes. Rhonda's attempts to distract them with local gossip and stories from the office failed. No one could take their minds off of what was going on upstairs in Operating Room 3.

It was three o'clock in the afternoon when the elevator doors opened and Maurice walked toward the waiting family. Lonnie Jean took one look at his face and knew something was wrong. She moved quickly to Morgan's side as Maurice approached.

"We were able to repair the blood vessels in her heart that were left unconnected because she was so premature," Maurice spoke slowly and allowed time for them to digest each word. "I'm afraid her lungs just aren't strong enough. They collapsed. We have her on a ventilator. We'll just have to wait and see how it goes the next twenty- four hours. We're giving her antibiotics now to prevent the possibility of pneumonia and infection."

Lonnie Jean put her arm around Morgan's waist as tears streamed down her face. Carl and Rhonda comforted a sobbing Irene.

"Maurice, tell me that she's going to be all right," Morgan pleaded and tried to control the feeling of hysteria she felt rising in her.

"Morgan, I can't tell you that. We've done all we can for her. Penny's a pretty sick little girl. Hopefully, we'll be able to take her off the ventilator sometime tomorrow afternoon. We'll know more then." Maurice wanted nothing more than to take her in his arms.

"Doctor, can we see her?" Carl asked, his arm was around Irene as she sobbed onto his chest.

"She's still in recovery, Mr. Banks." Maurice pulled his gaze away from Morgan's tear-streaked face. "I'll send a nurse for you as soon as it's okay." He reached out to take Morgan's hand. "Morgan, page me if you need me. I'm going upstairs to check on Penny now. And try not to worry."

Morgan could only nod. She felt no comfort in the touch of his hand. She allowed her body to fall into the waiting room chair. The stress of the last six months had waited for this moment to come crashing down on her. Her body almost ached with the fear Penny might not make it through the night.

"Morgan, don't you worry, girlfriend. You've been rubbing off on little Penny," Rhonda comforted. "She's going to make it through this. She's tough like her auntie."

"Your friend is right, Lisa," Carl said nodding. "Don't you dare start doubtin' now. All Penny got, all any of us got, is your hope. All your great, big, old wonderful hope." "I know you're all right. It just doesn't feel like that right now." Morgan wiped her eyes and stood. "I need some fresh air."

"Good idea," Lonnie Jean said quickly agreeing. "Rhonda, why don't you go for a walk with her? I'll take Carl and Irene back to her place so they can rest. I'll be back as soon as I can."

"Lisa, you call us if there's any change," Irene said as the elevator doors closed. Rhonda and Morgan opened the door to the waiting room courtyard and stepped outside. The warm, humid air brushed against Morgan's face like a soft, warm washcloth. It felt soothing after hours inside the air-conditioned hospital. Morgan and Rhonda walked in silence for a while. They barely noticed the new coat of shiny ebony paint on the wrought iron benches that lined the courtyard's brick patio. The hushed conversations of hospital personnel, patients, and visitors, who sat at the frosted glass topped tables, sounded like thousands of people whispering at once. Morgan stopped in front of the marble fountain in the center of the courtyard.

"I had no idea what I was doing when I started all this," Morgan said as she inhaled deeply and tilted her face toward the late afternoon sun. "I was so nervous after Mary Joyce sent the papers back. Like damn. Did I make a big mistake? Now I can't imagine my life without her, Rhonda." New tears began to fall.

"Well you don't have to because she's going to be all right," Rhonda said. She had no idea if her words were realistic or just filled with that great, big old hope Carl pleaded with Morgan to hold on to. "She's going to grow up with a rich-ass corporate attorney for an aunt. Morris Bell closed. You did it, girl. You won that shit. Norman Bradshaw cannot stop praising the work you did on that case, Morgan. The other partners are listening."

"Are you serious?" Work had been the farthest thing from Morgan's mind today. "Newman wanted me to let you know. He's ready to hand you another big case."

Rhonda smiled proudly. "And Jerry's in rehab."

"Really?" Morgan was numb from the day's events, but glad for the good news. "And his wife's filing for divorce." Rhonda had an "I-told-you-so" grin on her face. "Thanks for coming, Rhonda."

"Please. You're my girl. *Lisa*," Rhonda replied. She gave her a look that said, "You will tell me all about that."

"That's a long story for another day," Morgan knew that look. "Good, because I love long stories."

Morgan hugged her and then they headed back to the waiting room to wait for Lonnie Jean to return.

Morgan sipped cooling coffee from a vending machine cardboard cup and watched from the waiting room window as the New Orleans sun set. Rhonda had returned to the office for a meeting she'd been unable to reschedule and although she'd only been gone a couple of hours, Morgan felt her absence strongly. Waiting for Lonnie Jean to return from the neonatal intensive care unit, her thoughts were full of surgeries, ventilators, and fears Penny might not recover. Her prayers seemed to bounce back to her from the pale green walls. Morgan tossed the empty cup into a nearby trash can and turned her attention toward the television mounted on the wall in the corner. Maybe if she focused her attention on the fight breaking out on the stage of *The Jerry Springer Show*, the fear she felt crawling up the back of her neck would go away.

"Lisa, you can come up and see Penny now," Lonnie Jean said when the elevator doors opened. She held the door with her hand as Morgan stepped quickly inside. "She's had a rough day. I want you to prepare yourself."

Despite Lonnie Jean's warning on the elevator ride up to the neonatal intensive care unit, Morgan could not hold back her tears as she saw the maze of tubes leading from Penny's small body to the collection of machines and monitors in the room. The ventilator hummed just loud enough to remind Morgan it was breathing for her niece who was unable to perform this simple function on her own.

"Oh my God, Lonnie Jean. She looks so tired," Morgan's hushed voice seemed to echo throughout the cool room. "How can a baby look so tired?"

"She's been through a lot." Lonnie Jean offered a silent prayer of thanks that Penny was not back home at General and gently patted her cousin's back.

"She's got a long way back, honey. But that little girl right there is going to make it," Elaine said upon entering the room. She had come with Penny from St. Vincent General and had become so attached to her that Maurice had arranged for her to stay on at Rivers

C. Frederick Medical Center for the duration of Penny's stay. No matter what time of the day or night Morgan visited, Elaine was always there. For the first time, Morgan wondered if anyone was at home, in St. Vincent, waiting up for her. "Dr. LaShurr wanted me to tell you he'll be back up here in about an hour. He's downstairs checking on one of his other patients."

"He had a comfortable chair from the doctor's lounge brought up for you. It's over in the corner, since we knew it would take an Act of Congress and The National Guard to get you to leave here tonight. I brought your overnight bag. It's on the chair," Lonnie Jean said and looked knowingly at her cousin."

"You are the best cousin in the world," Morgan declared as they moved away from Penny's bedside to allow Elaine to do her job. They stood next to the window, near the chair that was going to be Morgan's bed until Penny was well.

"Well, that's a good thing, since I'm the only one you have. I called C. J. with your message. When I took Carl and Irene back to your place, he'd left a message on your answering machine. You were right. It seems Winn found y'all sister."

"Is he sure?"

"His message sounded pretty sure. You want me to call him back for you?"

Morgan nodded and said, "Let him know I'll call him tomorrow. He should go ahead and try to get in touch with this Andrea Jones."

"Lisa, all this is getting pretty crazy. Secret envelopes. Mysterious siblings. You think this Andrea Jones knew Alexander Franklin?"

"I don't know." Morgan let out a breath that ended in a sigh. She was too tired to give it much thought. "I just want to know what happened to Winn, that's all."

"I always wondered about something. Why did you change your name?" Lonnie Jean sat on the arm of the chair poised and anxious for her cousin's response.

"I was so mad at Mama for not telling me the truth and then not explaining herself. I really wanted her to hurt like I was hurting. I guess I thought if I changed my name to Franklin, it would force her to talk to me about Alexander Franklin. But then I realized it did not matter who my biological father was, I loved

Russell Morgan. He was my daddy. The name Morgan meant I was a part of him. Mama chose the name Lisa. She told me she named me after a model she had seen in a fashion magazine when she was a little girl. I remember her showing me the picture once when I was a little girl. I remember the look on her face when she looked at that model and wondered why she never looked at me like that. So, I got rid of it. I did not want anything that meant anything to her; even if it was just the name of some long-legged brunette model in an old magazine. It started out about her, but then became about me. I was confused about "Lisa" and who she was; but "Morgan," I understood completely." The lengthy explanation left Morgan spent.

Lonnie Jean hugged her cousin tightly and said, "I hope you get what you're looking for, Cous."

"Me, too." Although, Morgan wasn't quite sure what that was anymore.

CHAPTER FIFTEEN

Morgan spent almost every hour at the hospital over the next three weeks. Carl and Irene came and went. Lonnie Jean stayed with her for over a week and Rhonda was on a first name basis with more than one young, attractive doctor because of her constant visits to the hospital. Penny was off the ventilator, but remained in the neonatal intensive care unit. Maurice assured her daily Penny's progress was exactly what they expected. With some help from Rhonda and Lonnie Jean, Maurice had been successful in getting Morgan to move out of the NICU and back home. She returned to work with less than her usual vigor and focus, but it had been good to get back to what resembled a normal life. C. J. came for a weekend visit to check on her and Penny and to give her some additional information on Andrea Jones. Andrea Jones was dead. Her mother, Gloria Jones, now lived in Baton Rouge. C. J. arranged for Morgan to meet with her.

Morgan walked into the dimly lit restaurant. Her eyes took a minute to adjust to the candlelit ambiance of the room. A tuxedoed maître d' led her to a table dressed in the best linens, china, crystal, and silver.

"Miss Franklin?" A smartly dressed, cinnamon-colored woman asked when Morgan approached. Morgan could tell by her elegant style and manner that the woman was in her early sixties, but the absence of any wrinkles and her very fit body made it hard to believe. It was evident Mrs. Gloria Jones took extremely good care of herself. "I'm Andrea's mother. Gloria Jones."

Morgan gently clasped the outstretched, well-manicured hand in her own. She was unable to ignore the beautifully set two-carat diamond ring or jeweled Cartier wrist watch. Her simple apricot wool suit was obviously custom made.

"It is so nice to meet you. Thank you for agreeing to see me," Morgan said and seated herself.

"I took it upon myself to order a shrimp cocktail for you and some sweet tea. It was Andrea's favorite. I hope you don't mind." Gloria Jones sipped her tea.

"No. Not at all. I was sorry to hear about Andrea's passing. Was she your only child?" "No. We had a son. He drowned, while we were visiting relatives in South Carolina, when he was six years old. My husband, John, and I were devastated to say the least.

John, Jr. had come to us after I had suffered several miscarriages. It was an extremely difficult time for us."

Morgan sipped her tea and allowed Mrs. Jones to continue.

"It was John's idea to adopt Andrea. It was a favor for a friend of his," Gloria said as she enjoyed her shrimp cocktail.

"Who was his friend?"

"A woman by the name of Geneva Hastings. They dated in college and then went their separate ways. Geneva's way, I am afraid, led her to a life of fast and loose living. I think John always felt a little guilty about that, as if it had been his fault. You see, he ended the relationship when Geneva left school. He always helped her when she was in trouble. When she became pregnant, she came to us. John made sure she had the best medical care. She talked of keeping the baby and settling down. Geneva was excited about making a new life for herself with the father of the baby. But things changed," Gloria paused the telling of her story. She finished her shrimp cocktail and took a long sip of her sweet tea before she continued. "The father, Alex, was married. Of course, he promised Geneva he would leave his wife and of course that never happened. By the time Andrea was born, he had disappeared and made it clear he had no room in his life for them. Geneva was heartbroken. Geneva stayed with us after the baby was born. Andrea was the most beautiful child I had ever seen and such a sweet baby. She always seemed happy and content. She had eyes like yours." After Gloria finished, she stared at Morgan without seeing her at all.

"Mrs. Jones, when did you and your husband adopt Andrea?" Morgan's question broke Mrs. Jones' apparent trance.

"One day I left the house to run some errands. John was at his office. When I came back, Geneva was gone. Andrea was sleeping in her bassinet. John was able to get social services to allow us to keep her until they located Geneva. After searching for her for several months, with still no trace of her, John talked to me about adopting Andrea. By then I loved that little girl so much, I probably would have lost my mind if Geneva had returned for her."

Morgan thought about Penny and completely understood Mrs. Jones' feelings about baby Andrea.

"Did you ever see Geneva Hastings again?" Morgan asked, as the waiter placed a crab salad in front of her. She wondered if it was another of Andrea's favorites.

"Yes." Gloria squeezed a slice of lemon over her grilled snapper. "She showed up, out of the blue, one Christmas when Andrea was almost five years old. She had gifts for Andrea. Even though Andrea was legally adopted by then, I was terrified Geneva had come back to take her away. It was soon obvious, we had nothing to fear. She had no room in her life for a little girl. She introduced herself to Andrea as Auntie Geneva and stayed and played with her for a few days. By New Year's, she was gone again."

"Did you or Mr. Jones ever tell Andrea about Geneva and Alexander Franklin being her parents?"

"John and I talked about it many times, Ms. Franklin," Gloria's voice cracked slightly with the emotion of the memory. Her eyes left Morgan's face and dropped onto her plate. "There never seemed to be a proper time. Before we could tell her, Geneva was killed."

"Killed?" Morgan gasped. She took a sip of water to force down the crouton now stuck in her throat. Gloria continued, "It had been years since we'd heard from Geneva. John opened the newspaper one morning and read an article about a woman who had been found murdered in a motel room. It was May of 1994. I remember it vividly because my women's group had held a luncheon to celebrate the election of Nelson Mandela as President of South Africa and I was looking for the write up in the morning newspaper. The motel was known to be frequented by prostitutes and the like. At first, she was a Jane Doe. Several days later someone came forward and identified the body. It was Geneva. After that, we saw no reason to tell Andrea. It all seemed like too much to place on her at once."

"Who identified the body?"

"The article stated it was one of the occupants of the motel." "Did they ever find out who murdered Geneva?"

"No. I doubt they looked very hard, dear." Gloria frowned. "We arranged for a private burial. It was the least we could do for her. She had given us so much: our beautiful daughter."

They talked more about Andrea as a child. Gloria listened intensely to Morgan talk about her upbringing in L'Ouverture and her life in New Orleans. Gloria ordered banana pudding and a café brûlot. Ordering for the first time that evening, Morgan decided on a slice of key lime pie.

"Mrs. Jones, how did Andrea die?" Morgan kept her voice soft.

"In a car accident. It happened the day after her graduation from Xavier on June 12, 1996. She was twenty-two years old. John's mother said she guessed the good Lord just did not see fit for our children to stay with us long. She said it was good we had loved them so well. I wondered how "good," the good Lord could be to take so much away from me." The pain Gloria felt cast a shadow upon her face.

"I am so sorry." Morgan wasn't just using the customary words, she meant them. She reached across the table and lightly touched Gloria's hand.

"Thank you, dear. It was a horrible shock to both of us. I don't know if John ever got over it. I received the call while talking to the caterers. We were planning a graduation celebration for her at our country club. She was a brilliant young woman. She dreamed of being a veterinarian. Beauty and brains, John always boasted. I fainted right there. The caterer had to revive me. He called John and we rushed to the hospital. Andrea and her boyfriend were both pronounced dead at the scene of the accident," Gloria's voice trembled. She took a sip of her coffee and hoped the hot liquid would melt the lump in her throat. "We all thought it was a horrible accident, until…"

"Until, what, Mrs. Jones?" Morgan gently urged after Gloria's long pause.

"The police report said Eric Smith, her boyfriend, had been drinking. Officers reported empty beer bottles in the car and said Eric reeked of alcohol. We, of course, were shocked, as were Eric's parents. Andrea and Eric did not run with that crowd. We had known him and his family since he and Andrea were in fourth grade. There had never been anything like this before. People told us that sometimes parents are the last to know." Gloria finished her banana pudding and touched the linen napkin to the corners of her mouth before she continued, "We allowed ourselves to believe that. Then the autopsy report indicated Eric was dead *before* the alcohol entered his system.

The beer bottles in the car did not have any fingerprints. Not even Eric's. This information led to an investigation and it was discovered someone had tampered with the car. The report said it was something to do with the brakes."

"Mrs. Jones, are you saying someone intentionally tried to kill Andrea's boyfriend?" "No." Gloria shook her head. "I'm sorry, Miss Franklin. I failed to mention they were driving Andrea's new car. It had been her graduation gift."

Morgan's breath caught in her chest, as if she had been struck with a heavy object. "Mrs. Jones, are you saying someone tampered with Andrea's car and killed her and her boyfriend?"

Gloria Jones nodded and reached for the item on the chair next to her and slid a leather-bound notebook toward Morgan. "When the police investigation uncovered nothing, we hired private investigators. This is the work they did. It turned up nothing. Turn to page thirty-seven."

The notebook seemed to grow warm in Morgan's hands as she looked at a photocopy of a handwritten note with what must have been the make and model of Andrea's graduation gift. Morgan was unable to make out most of the words, but there was no mistaking the initials, "AF" scribbled across the bottom of the page.

Under the copy of the note the investigator had written his own note: *found in the debris from the crash.*

Gloria read the question spreading across Morgan's face and waited for her to put her thoughts into words. "Do you know if Andrea was ever contacted by Alexander Franklin?" Morgan's head throbbed as she took in the information.

"There was never any reason to think so. We do not even know how Andrea would have known anything about Alexander Franklin."

"When I received Andrea's birth certificate there was a note included that said Andrea's parents were Geneva Hastings and Alexander Franklin. Obviously, someone else had this information. Do you think someone else may have told Andrea about her biological parents?"

"She never gave any indication she knew anything. I do not know what to think. It's possible someone could have told her. But, I have no idea who would have done such a thing." Gloria said. The coffee cup visibly shook in Gloria's hand. "My John passed away last summer. With his last breath, he asked if I thought Andrea may have known the truth. I couldn't answer the question, Miss Franklin. If she did, she must have thought us terrible to keep such a thing from her."

"Mrs. Jones, please do not upset yourself. We do not know what Andrea knew about Alexander Franklin or if she knew anything at all." Morgan hoped to sooth her. She thought the note was a clue that linked Alexander Franklin to the murders. Gloria seemed to relax as Morgan spoke. "May I have a copy of this report, Mrs. Jones?"

"You may have it, Miss Franklin. It was of no use to us. Maybe it can be of greater help to you."

Morgan called C. J. from her cell phone as she pulled the car onto Interstate 10 and headed back to New Orleans. Anita Baker's classic, "Rapture," provided a musical backdrop as she filled him in on her meeting with Gloria Jones. She promised to send a copy of the investigator's report to his office first thing in the morning. The hour and a half ride helped to clear her head. She had to go see Penny and then head to her office for a few hours to review the material her assistant had pulled together for a case she had been assigned earlier in the week. She tried to sort out everything Gloria Jones had told her and came up with only one conclusion: people who were in some way or another connected to Alexander Franklin were now dead.

"Stop it, Morgan. You're tripping. This is not about Alexander Franklin, this is about who killed Winn," she said aloud. She hoped the sound of her voice would calm the nervousness that was beginning to engulf her. Even as she spoke the words, she wondered if this were true.

Morgan pulled into the hospital garage. Her only thoughts were on spending the next couple of hours with Penny. She looked quickly at her watch and realized Maurice had probably already left for the night. She felt a little disappointed as she stepped off the elevator.

"How's my baby girl doing today?" Morgan asked Elaine as she headed toward Penny's room.

"She's good. Spoiled rotten just like every baby should be. Penny's got every nurse on the floor and half the doctors in the hospital wrapped around her little finger," Elaine said and laughed. "The question is, how are you?"

"Okay, I guess." Morgan sighed and suddenly felt tired. "Is Dr. LaShurr still around?" "No, he left about an hour ago," Elaine answered with a knowing smile on her face.

She reached into the pocket of her uniform smock. "He asked me to give you this message."

"Thank you." Morgan quickly took the note, headed toward Penny's room, and hoped Elaine had not seen the smile on her face.

"He had the same smile on his face, when he handed it to me," Elaine called after her.

CHAPTER SIXTEEN

"That must have been The Doctor," Rhonda said. She dragged out the last two words as if they were the title to a bestselling novel and placed her French, manicured finger between the pages of a leather- bound legal journal to save her place.

"We're going to have dinner at my place tonight," Morgan said while she looked at her watch and scribbled some more notes on the legal pad in front of her. It was already after 7:00 p.m. The city lights began to appear through the ceiling-to-floor windows behind her desk.

"Then I say let's call it quits." Rhonda slapped the book closed. "You've got the case won, Morgan. Perkins and his boys at Haget and Roche do not have a leg to stand on in the Geary case, honey. They'll settle. Geary will be thrilled *and* richer. You'll bill the maximum hours, get a nice bonus from the partners for another magnificent job, and take your beautiful, brilliant best friend out for dinner at her favorite, very expensive restaurant."

"You go ahead. I have to fax this addendum to Judge Walker before I leave. Thanks, Rhonda. I would have been here all night without your help."

"No need to thank me now, honey." Rhonda slipped into the turquoise blue leather mules she had kicked off when they started working hours ago. "Thank me in the morning when you wake up next to that fine ass doctor." She laughed, grabbed her purse, and closed the office door behind her.

An hour later, Morgan slipped into her jacket and quickly stuffed two bulging accordion folders into her briefcase. She couldn't ignore the butterflies that had taken over her stomach as she thought about the evening ahead with Maurice. Glancing at the clock on the wall, she scribbled a note for her secretary, hurriedly turned off the office lights, inhaled deeply to calm herself, and left the office smiling.

Morgan had taken a long, hot shower and slipped into her favorite sweatpants and a Dillard University sweatshirt when the doorbell rang.

"Hey there," Maurice greeted her with a smile and a bouquet of yellow roses and vibrant purple irises.

"Hey there, yourself. These are beautiful. Thank you," Morgan said. She took the flowers and kissed him softly on the lips.

"I must bring flowers more often." Maurice teased and placed his jacket on the pewter coat tree near the front door and followed her into the kitchen.

"Just bring you more often. You've been working pretty hard lately." Morgan poured him a glass of his favorite sauvignon blanc as he sat down at the marble kitchen counter. Morgan reached into a cupboard above the sink and brought out a beautiful copper vase for the flowers. After she filled it with water and placed the flowers in it, she returned her attention to Maurice.

"The AMA Conference is only three weeks away. Getting ready for that and finishing my article for *The Journal of Pediatrics* has kept me busy. You know how it is counselor." Maurice enjoyed his wine. He doubted he had ever seen a more beautiful woman.

"Have you heard anything about the director's position?" Morgan sat the vase on the counter amid take-out containers and sat down on the stool next to his. Maurice had applied and already completed several interviews for the position of Director of Pediatric Surgery at Rivers C. Frederick Medical Center.

"A third round of interviews begins Tuesday. There are five of us in the running. From what I hear, I stand a good chance, but you never know how these things will turn out. You ready for Perkins and his boys on Monday?"

Morgan smiled before answering. He always seemed to remember the details that many other men she had dated often ignored or forgot. "They do not stand a chance."

He held his wine glass up to salute her. "Is that The House of Thai I smell?" Maurice noticed the containers on the counter and the spicy aroma for the first time. "So, Ms. Franklin, you really are perfect?"

"Dr. LaShurr. Was there ever any doubt?" Morgan opened the containers and piled his favorites onto his plate.

"No. Not for me," Maurice replied, He clicked his chopsticks in anticipation. "Good." Morgan held a plump shrimp on the end of her chopsticks as Maurice opened his mouth. "Because I want you to know I do not have any doubts either. I know you would like things between us to move a little faster. There's just a lot going on in my life right now. This is the best I can do. Does that work for you?"

Maurice paused before answering and looked into Morgan's eyes. He could not believe he was in love with her. After Michelle, he thought it would be impossible to love anyone again. After a few failed relationships following that, he had promised himself he would be better off sticking to medicine and leaving love to those more fortunate than he. It was much easier on his heart. Medicine was something you could study, even perfect, to a degree. Love was unpredictable and messy. Morgan changed the way he felt about all that.

He slowly chewed the spicy chicken salad, glad she had gotten right to the point. The air needed clearing after the last time they were together several weeks ago and Maurice had been the only one on the couch ready to move to the bedroom. Morgan had asked him to leave. He had spent the rest of the evening being angry with himself and thought maybe he had read more into their relationship than was actually there. Maurice had seen Morgan the following morning at the hospital, gave her a distant nod, and mumbled good morning before he rushed down the hall away from her. Their limited time together over the next few weeks had created an awkward space between them. Maurice had been surprised she accepted his invitation for an evening together. He asked to go out for drinks. Morgan said she would rather spend a quiet evening at home and offered to pick up something for dinner. He felt hesitant as he accepted, but was now just thankful.

"Your best will always be enough for me, Morgan," Maurice's tone was serious; his eyes stared at her intensely. "I didn't mean to ask for more than that."

"Oh, no," Morgan said to lighten the mood just a bit, a seductive grin on her face. "I like that you asked. I just want some things cleared out of the way before I answer. That's all."

"So, counselor, are you going on record that I may ask again?" Maurice teased. He felt a lightness that did not come from the wine.

"Most definitely, doctor. Most definitely." Morgan threw a saucy wink his way as she spooned pad thai noodles onto his plate.

They were well into their second video and the pralines and cream ice cream when Maurice's phone vibrated against his belt. Snuggled in his arms, Morgan felt it. She felt his body stiffen as he listened and sat up.

"Morgan, put on your shoes. It's Penny."

"The waiting and not knowing is what I cannot stand," Morgan said. She paced as she glanced again at her watch.

"Morgan, can I get you anything?" Elaine asked. "Dr. LaShurr will come and let you know what's going on as soon as he can. Try not to worry. Dr. LaShurr and his team are the best." As if on cue, Maurice entered his office. Morgan froze. She was unable to read the face she called his "doctor face" and her heart pounded.

"Morgan, there's some leakage from the vessels we repaired and Penny is showing signs of a bacterial infection. Her blood pressure is dangerously low. We are treating the infection with antibiotics, but she needs surgery to stop the bleeding and repair the blood vessels. I have to operate tonight." Maurice tried to keep the urgency he felt in the pit of his stomach out of his voice.

"Tonight? Maurice, is she strong enough for this? You said yourself she is still pretty weak. She's not even breathing entirely on her own yet. Can you give her something that will stop the bleeding?" Morgan's words rushed out and matched the vicious pounding of her heart. She resumed her pacing.

Maurice reached out and took her in his arms. He could feel her body trembling. Her fear turned her light gray eyes a dark charcoal color. "She's already been given something to slow the bleeding. She's not responding. If she were stronger I'd say give the medicine a little more time, but that's not the case. If I don't get this bleeding stopped, we'll lose her. Morgan, she'll die before morning."

"Oh, my God." Morgan covered her mouth with both hands to stop the scream that quickly filled her throat and worked its way into her mouth. She pulled away from him. Hot, frightened tears filled her eyes. "Maurice, I cannot lose her. Please don't let her die. Go ahead. Do the surgery." Morgan turned away.

Maurice glanced at Elaine, mouthed the words, "take care of her for me" and left the office.

"Come on, honey," Elaine said and took a now sobbing Morgan in her arms. "Let's get your face washed. I don't want Penny to see you looking like this when she wakes up. Morgan, the doctors are going to do all they can for Penny, but you got to believe she's gonna make it. You just keep your mind on all the hugs and kisses you'll be giving her when she wakes up. I'll call Rhonda to come and sit with you while Dr. LaShurr takes care of our little princess."

Morgan wiped her tears and allowed herself to be led into the bathroom in Maurice's office. She tried to smile at Elaine and appreciated her words of comfort even though her mind had fastened itself around the thought she might never see Penny awake again.

"Rhonda, this is taking too long," Morgan said. She moved from her place on the loveseat in Maurice's office and went to stand near the window. "What time is it?"

"Just about thirty-one seconds later than it was the last time you asked me. Morgan, sit down. You already owe this hospital enough money. You want to pay for wearing out the carpet in The Doctor's office too?" Rhonda asked. She patted the seat next to her.

Instead of sitting next to Rhonda, Morgan sat in a straight-backed leather chair across from her friend and gave a look that said "you're right and I'm glad you're here." When Rhonda had received the call from Elaine, she rushed immediately to the hospital from a benefit dinner she was attending for a group of African American law students. Rhonda's father, Roman Lattier, was the chairman of the committee and a nationally renowned criminal defense attorney. He sponsored the black-tie fundraising event each year. Even after three hours of waiting in Maurice's office, Rhonda was stunning. The elegant black crêpe Carolina Herrera strapless evening gown seemed especially made for her curvaceous body. A necklace of blood-red marquis cut rubies separated by brilliant yellow, round cut diamonds adorned her neck. Her earrings dropped nearly to her bare shoulders and displayed the same ruby-diamond-ruby pattern as her necklace.

"Sorry to pull you away from the dinner. You look fantastic."

"Please. It's the same dinner every year. The only thing that changes is my dress. I have to talk to Daddy about doing something to bring some life to that event. I was thinking about a casino night or costume ball. He thanked you publicly for all your help developing the new mentoring project and I quote, 'your ongoing commitment to the young, Black legal minds of America.' You are his hero, you know?" Rhonda laughed. "Yeah, right. Your father was a tremendous help to me. I know I would have never passed the bar on my first try without all those weekends he spent helping those of us in the program that year prepare. I'm just trying to give a little back. Make the road a little easier for somebody else."

"His newest girl toy was there. In a slinky, sequined fire-engine-red dress." Rhonda rolled her eyes beneath natural lashes paid for by the hundreds. "A cheap, off-the-rack slinky, sequined fire-engine-red dress to be exact. You should have seen the look on the faces of that old, Black, rich, country club set when she came in on Daddy's arm. And did I mention the three tons of synthetic gold ringlets piled on top of her head and the green contacts? Her store-bought breasts were prominently displayed to the dismay of every saggy breasted woman in the place and to the pleasure of every drooling man. I must admit the diamond and pearl earrings she was wearing were incredible. They were big enough to choke three or four horses simultaneously. They must have been a gift from my father because they were real. Where does he get them? 1-800-RENT-A-HO?" Rhonda laughed at her own joke.

"Did you behave?" Morgan questioned her friend.

"Before or after I spilled hot cream of asparagus soup in her lap?" Rhonda answered with a straight face.

"You didn't?" Morgan's eyes grew wide with the possibility. "Rhonda, please tell me you did not pour hot soup on the woman."

"I didn't, but it sure was tempting," Rhonda laughed. "Did you call Mr. and Mrs. Banks?"

"The phone is disconnected again." Morgan was worried about Carl and Irene. She looked at her watch for what seemed the thousandth time. "I called my Uncle Raymond. He said he would drive out and tell them."

"And what about Miss Marie?" Rhonda knew there had been more tension than usual between her friend and her mother.

"I can't take my mama, tonight. I'll call her in the morning." The thought of talking to Marie about Penny made Morgan even more anxious.

The door to the office opened. Morgan and Rhonda sprang to their feet as if they had been ejected from their seats.

"Morgan, Penny is going to be okay. We repaired the damage to the blood vessels and the bleeding is stopped. She's still sedated, but it looks like she'll recover just fine," Maurice answered the question on her face. He watched her body relax. "I want you to meet Dr. Wayne Pierre and Dr. Natalie Faison. They assisted in Penny's surgery. This is Morgan Franklin, Penny's aunt, and her friend, Rhonda Lattier.

Morgan and Rhonda shook hands with the doctors.

"You have a tough little girl there, Miss Franklin," Dr. Pierre said. He moved his eyes away from Rhonda and back to Morgan with great effort.

"She has a long recovery ahead, but she is going to be just fine. Before you know it, you will have to run to keep up with her," Dr. Faison assured her.

"What about her lungs and the infection?" Morgan asked, not quite ready to celebrate. "Her lungs are as well as can be expected for what she's been through. We put her back on the ventilator for the night so she won't have to work so hard to breathe. So far, she's responding well to the antibiotics and her blood pressure is within normal limits," Maurice stated. He glanced at his colleagues who confirmed his report with silent nods.

"Thank you all so much," Morgan said. She gave Rhonda's hand a squeeze and let out a breath she didn't realize she was holding.

"You are so welcome," Dr. Faison said and carried the conversation now for Dr. Pierre who had given up on trying *not* to look at Rhonda. "You can come up and see her in a couple of hours."

Maurice took Morgan in his arms and held her close after Dr. Faison and Dr. Pierre left the office. "Baby, it's all right now. Penny's going to be okay." He wiped tears of relief from her eyes.

"Well, looks like everything is under control here. I am going to see if I can find somebody to help me use the rest of the hours I have left on this dress. By the way Dr. Pierre was examining me, I think it is still working in my favor," Rhonda said and moved her hands over her hips to smooth wrinkles no one could see.

"Rhonda, thank you so much for coming. I would not have made it through these last few hours without you." Morgan moved from Maurice's arms to give Rhonda a big hug. "Sure, you would have. Just not as well." Rhonda winked. "Doc, will you take care of my girl for me?"

"It will be my pleasure, Ms. Lattier…my pleasure." Maurice held Morgan tightly in his arms.

CHAPTER SEVENTEEN

Morgan lay across the foot of her bed as the sultry voice of Lalah Hathaway filled the room. She loved this time of morning. The light raindrops hitting her window added to the peacefulness of her Saturday morning. Penny was doing great and she had decided to take a little time for herself this morning instead of having breakfast in the hospital cafeteria. Maurice was away in Washington, D.C. at the American Medical Association conference and so for the first time in months, Morgan had a chance to spend some uninterrupted hours alone. She stretched and opened the encyclopedia-sized document she received from C. J. on John and Gloria Jones, Geneva Hastings, and the deaths of Andrea Jones and Eric Smith. She sipped her tea and settled onto the soft mountain of pillows on her bed. The report from C. J.'s friend was very thorough Morgan thought as she read page after page of his detailed investigation into the deaths. C. J.'s notes in the margins and a note written to John and Gloria Jones by the investigator indicated both thought the deaths were suspicious and somehow connected to Alexander Franklin.

The phone rang and momentarily broke her concentration. Morgan pushed the **TALK** button on the phone as she turned yet another page of the report. A young woman's voice, screaming and crying, caused her to sit straight up in the bed. The report slid to the floor with a thud onto the thick carpet. At first, she thought it was Mary Joyce. Then she recognized the voice as Pam's, Whitey's fiancée.

"Pam, you have to calm down. I can't understand what you're saying," Morgan repeated several times. She grew frustrated and a bit more frightened each time. "What did Whitey find?"

"No, Lisa!" Pam screamed into the phone. "They can't *find* Whitey!" "Who can't find Whitey? Pam, what do you mean?"

"Lisa, he's missing," Pam yelled out sobbing. "We were supposed to go to a jeweler in La Fitte to look at engagement rings and he never showed up. When I called the station, Arthur Lee said he hadn't come into work that day. I called him and there was no answer. I went over to his apartment because I thought maybe he overslept or something. The place looked like a hurricane had gone through it. Tables were turned over, and his clothes were everywhere. His dresser drawers and kitchen drawers were emptied out onto the floor. He said if something like this happened for me to call you. Sheriff La Fontaine is acting like Whitey left on vacation or something. He didn't even send anybody over to dust for fingerprints or anything 'til I went to the station acting a fool. Lisa, what's goin' on? What's happened to my Whitey?"

"Pam, I don't know what's going on." Morgan's mind rushed past one horrible possibility after the next. "Try not to worry. Whitey knows how to take care of himself. Let me make a few calls." She pressed the **END** button on the phone, hoped for the best, but somehow knew it would be the worst.

Morgan had just dozed off when the phone awakened her. She looked at her watch and saw it was 7:30 p.m. Hoping it might be someone returning her call about Whitey, she reached for the phone and was shocked when she heard Marie's voice.

"Whitey Peters is dead," Marie said in response to Morgan's hello.

"What?" Morgan yelled as she hit her knee on the nightstand when she swung her legs out of the bed. "Dead?"

"They found his body out by the old Boudreau Mill in one of those old buildings they used to house the workers. There was a bullet through his head. An apparent suicide."

"Suicide? No way, Mama. Whitey would never kill himself." Morgan was in shock and felt tears forming in the corners of her eyes. She could only imagine how devastated Pam felt upon hearing the news.

"Arthur Lee DuPont said he was behaving rather strangely for the past several weeks and then he simply disappeared," Marie reported what she'd read in the evening paper. "It doesn't make sense. Why would Whitey kill himself? He just called me last week to say he and Pam were getting married and he'd accepted a position with the Dade County Sheriff's Department in Florida. He was leaving St. Vincent in a couple of weeks. Mama, somebody killed Whitey." Morgan's voice cracked with emotion as tears slid down her face."

"Lisa, please do not start all that again," Marie snapped. She quickly became irritated. "I was right about Winn." Morgan insisted. "Mama, I know this has something to do with Alexander Franklin." The silence on the other end was louder than any argument she and Marie could ever have had.

"I just wanted you to know about Whitey. I know you were classmates and you were fond of him. I thought if you knew the damage your meddling has caused you would end all this foolishness. Russell Morgan was your father, Lisa. I'd think that would be enough for you." Marie's voice was colder and more distant than usual.

"Mama, it was enough. This is not about Daddy. It's about Alexander Franklin. Mama, you have to talk about him now. Don't you see that you may have information that could shed some light on these murders?" Morgan said through her tears.

"Lisa, there is nothing to talk about," Marie snapped and bit her lower lip. The throbbing just above her eyes signaled the approach of a headache.

"I think there is, Mama. Did you know Alexander Franklin had another daughter by a woman named Geneva Hastings? Both of them were murdered. Mama, people are dying and you are keeping secrets about some lover you had almost thirty years ago. Mama!" Morgan cursed as the dial tone buzzed in her ear.

C. J. knew it was Lisa on the other end of the phone as soon as it rang. He took a deep breath before answering.

"I know," he said before Morgan could say a word.

"C. J., please tell me what's going on. Please tell me you understand what's happening. God, C. J. They killed Whitey." Morgan's sobs almost made her words unintelligible.

"Lisa, you've got to calm down. We don't know anything for sure yet." C. J. didn't even believe his own words. He hoped Lisa, in her grief, would.

"You cannot honestly tell me you don't think there is some connection between Whitey trying to help us and his disappearance and death. Suicide my ass, C. J. Someone is killing people and I know this is connected to Alexander Franklin and so do you. Have you had any luck getting Irene to talk about him?" Morgan's tears, now replaced by anger, calmed her.

"None. I don't know what's going on with her."

"Will you call your friend in the FBI and ask him to work his contacts within the state police to investigate?"

"Already done. Now, try and get some rest," C. J. cautioned. The last thing he needed was Lisa getting herself hurt, or worse.

"You too, C. J. You too." Morgan pushed the **END** button and wept until she fell asleep.

CHAPTER EIGHTEEN

Morgan stood in the middle of the room, the faint smell of wet paint was in the air. She looked at the soft, pale blue walls. The woman who helped her select from hundreds of shades of blue had called it Iconic Sky. The ceiling was barely a shade lighter. She'd used the stencils

Rhonda's artist friend had designed for her to paint fluffy, white clouds across the ceiling. The day was brisk and cool and the air coming through the open window would dry the room quickly. She had already taken off her paint spattered clothing, showered, and slipped into her favorite pair of jeans and an ivory lightweight wool v-neck sweater when the doorbell rang. Morgan walked quickly to the door and smiled as she saw Maurice's peep-hole distorted face.

Morgan opened the door, took shopping bags from his arms, and placed them on the wooden hallway bench as he reached for her. She let herself relax in his arms and felt a sense of protection she didn't realize she needed. Morgan inhaled the scent of his cologne before she gave him a kiss that let him know how glad she was to see him.

Maurice knew she was hurt by the death of her friend and could see the pain in the smoldering gray of her eyes. He would do anything he could to take her grief away. He asked, "How are you really, Morgan?"

"Maurice, I don't even know how to put what I feel right now into words. If you knew Whitey, you'd know there is no way he would commit suicide. I know his and my brother's deaths are linked to Alexander Franklin," Morgan said. Tears clouded her eyes. "Enough of that for now." Maurice could see the change in her posture as she took a deep breath and steeled herself not to cry.

"Come on, you've got to see Penny's room. I finished the clouds last night. The ceiling looks like a real sky." She kissed him again, this time quickly and pulled him down the hallway.

"Impressive," Maurice said while he walked slowly around the room and admired Morgan's handiwork. She'd done an incredible job. The sky she'd painted on the ceiling made him feel as if he were standing outside on a clear spring day.

"Not as impressive as it will be after we get all this furniture assembled." Morgan pointed to several large cardboard boxes in the corners of the room. The words **"Assembly Required"** were marked in bold, black block letters written across the side of each of box.

"Just how many babies are you planning to bring home, Morgan?" Maurice hoped he was as handy with a screwdriver as he had presented himself to be.

"I took Rhonda with me. There was no stopping her," Morgan answered then laughed. The sound brought a smile to Maurice's face because he knew Morgan was going to be okay despite the recent bad news.

"One of those bags I brought in contains the ingredients for my world-famous spaghetti sauce." Maurice turned off the light and headed toward the door. "I think we could both use a good meal before we start on this project. What do you say, counselor?" "I'd never go against your orders, doctor." Morgan followed him from the room. "I'll boil the water and make a salad."

"Wine. We'll need wine." Maurice retrieved the bags from the hallway and headed toward the kitchen.

"Doctor, I'm going to have to object." Morgan filled a large pot with water. "Did you see those boxes? They're marked 'assembly required.'"

"Objection sustained." Maurice laughed as he pulled fresh basil from the bag and placed the wine aside for after assembly.

"Do your hands do everything this well?" Morgan asked. She stood next to him later that evening while he admired his work. He had assembled a solid oak crib and the matching changing table while Morgan had tackled the swing and the play pen. She was glad she'd paid extra to have the dressers assembled. It was already late and she was hoping to spend some time with Maurice without a hammer and screwdriver in her hands.

"Give me a couple hours and you'll be able to answer that question yourself." Maurice took her in his arms.

"You think Penny will like her room?" Morgan closed her eyes as Maurice kissed first her ear and then her neck. She felt her head spin slightly as he pressed his body against hers and stated his intention without words.

"Um huh," Maurice uttered, his voice deepened with passion. "Let's take this to another room."

"Good idea," Morgan whispered as she led him down the hall toward her bedroom.

The light from the full moon gave Morgan's bedroom a soft, delicate glow. She blinked and wondered if she were dreaming. Maurice's eyes met Morgan's gaze. His kiss was gentle; his tongue was wet and sweet. Morgan sighed softly.

"That's a good sign." Maurice kissed her again and enjoyed the texture of her welcoming tongue.

"What?" Morgan propped herself up on her elbow and turned her body toward him. "Your smile." Maurice pulled her closer. Her body felt warm and soft
against his.

"Will you stay with me tonight?" Morgan asked. She never wanted to move from this spot. Something felt so right about this moment and this man that she could not imagine herself anywhere else.

"If you ask me *nicely*." Maurice replied. It was not long before she began to ask him
nicely.

"Surprise!" A loud chorus of voices greeted Morgan as she walked into the expensively furnished executive conference room at McDouglas, Bradshaw & Newman. It took her a moment to reconcile what she saw–the forty smiling faces of her colleagues and lots of pink and white decorations. Her smile lit up her face as everyone began to clap. The far corner of the conference room was filled with a mountain of beautifully wrapped packages. Penny would be home in three days.

"You all are incredible," Morgan said. She took a glass of punch from her secretary and looked at the table filled with food catered from one of her favorite restaurants. In the center of the table was a pink and white cake in the shape of a baby bootie.

"We did not want you to think you were not loved," said Damon Edgewater. He had been her co-counsel on several cases when she first joined the firm.

"We had no idea you were adopting a baby, Morgan. You certainly kept that quiet. I do not know how you did it while orchestrating that merger between Bagby Investments and that firm in the Philippines. Girl, you are certainly 'every woman'," said Corliss Evans, one of the firm's top litigators, who then laughed. She led Morgan to a chair near the mountain of gifts.

"Thank you all so much. I did not expect anything like this." It was almost one hour later when Morgan finished opening gifts.

"Duh!" Rhonda said while she poured Morgan a glass of champagne. "That is why they call it a 'surprise.' You will never get another one, if I have anything to do with it. You are too nosy."

They all laughed, teased her, and shared the many times when the inquisitiveness that made her an excellent attorney had almost ruined the party. Parents shared stories of what her first days with her new daughter would be like and offered her advice that didn't make any sense right now. She made mental notes and knew before long she'd be glad for the tips. Those single and without children vowed to remain single and without children for the rest of their lives.

"A toast," Rhonda said. She held her champagne glass high. She paused a moment as others filled their glasses and held them high. "To L. Morgan Franklin. My best friend. The *second* most talented attorney I know and soon to be the best damn mommy any little girl could ever dream of having."

"Here. Here." Glasses clinked in merriment.

"I cannot believe she is really coming home," Morgan said as she and Rhonda made their last trip to Morgan's car with packages from the shower. Rhonda had driven her Range Rover and would follow Morgan home with the gifts filling her vehicle.

"Well, she better or I'm going to move into that nursery myself. Morgan, you really outdid yourself, honey. Martha Stewart would turn green with envy if she saw that room. I saw an ad for a baby room contest in one of those mommy magazines you've been reading by the truckload. Penny's room looks better than anything I've seen in those magazines. The first-place prize is $5,000. I could invest it for her and make my goddaughter a millionaire by the time she gets to kindergarten. I'll take some pictures tomorrow." Rhonda gave two finger snaps above her head as she finished loading packages onto the backseat.

"Well, I had some help." A sly grin curled the corners of Morgan's mouth.

"If you smile like that thinking about The Doctor one more time, I'm going to slap you," Rhonda teased. She could not have been happier for her friend.

"Don't hate, darling. What can I say?" Morgan gave Rhonda a high five. "Let's get out of here. We're both due in court at eight tomorrow morning."

<u>CHAPTER NINETEEN</u>

"What's not the look I expected to see on your face today. You been waiting six months for this day. What's the matter, Morgan?" Elaine asked. She placed a stuffed pink elephant into one of the many bags packed for Penny Lyons to leave Rivers C. Frederick Medical Center. It had been nearly six months since she had arrived there, near death. Elaine hardly recognized the healthy, smiling baby girl in Morgan's arms.

"It just dawned on me that we have never spent the night together alone," Morgan said as she looked into Penny's sparkling gray eyes. "Elaine, what if something happens tonight that I can't handle?"

"It won't," Elaine assured her. "Penny is fine. And you are going to do just fine taking care of her, Morgan. Every mother feels like this when she takes her baby home for the first time. Relax. You're luckier than most. You had almost six supervised months of parenting. Most moms get two or three days and we put them out." Her laughter immediately stopped the tension increasing in Morgan's neck.

"I have never been so nervous in my life. This feels so big." Morgan held Penny close and sniffed her hair.

"Because it is big." Elaine placed her hands on her hips. "And as long as you feel that way, Penny will have the best Mama ever. You two just take care of each other." Penny's first two caregivers hugged each other warmly. Elaine would be returning to St. Vincent in the morning. She had turned down Maurice's offer to stay in New Orleans. She said she was needed back in L'Ouverture. Although she'd miss her, Morgan had to agree that what Elaine had observed and learned in the past six months would probably save the lives of hundreds of infants at St. Vincent's General Hospital. She would be working closely with Lonnie Jean who welcomed the help. Elaine made Morgan promise to bring Penny by General to see her when she was in town visiting.

After Penny was settled in her new car seat and bags were packed in the trunk of the car, Morgan waved goodbye to the staff who had accompanied her and Penny outside.

Elaine handed her a note from Maurice as she started the engine. He was in surgery and would stop by on his way home tonight. Morgan wished he was in the car going home with them.

"It's me and you, baby girl. Are you ready for this?" Morgan took a quick look at Penny and a long look in the rearview mirror. More concerned about safety than she thought possible, she turned on her signal light and pulled carefully away from the curb. She and Penny were headed home.

"I was in town yesterday and heard they got a suspect in Whitey Peters' murder. Last name Ledeaux," Raymond said. He nodded at the waiter as he filled his coffee cup.

Marie dropped two sugar cubes into her tea and stirred without looking at Raymond. She bit her lower lip, something she rarely did anymore. "A lot of people in Louisiana are named Ledeaux, Raymond."

"Heard he had kinfolks in La Fitte." Raymond poured maple syrup on the stack of pancakes the waiter had just placed in front of him.

"That's your problem, Raymond. You live too much in the past." Marie sprinkled pepper on her spinach and mushroom omelet.

"Past always got a way of coming back on you, if you don't put it to rest. What them boys done." Raymond looked at his sister.

"Are you going to eat breakfast or bother me with ancient history?" Marie snapped. "Just wanted you to know before you seen the boy on the television. The resemblance is uncanny." Raymond took a sip of his coffee.

"You know what, Raymond. This was a bad idea."
Marie took $20 from her wallet and threw it on the table. She left
the restaurant before Raymond could say another word.

Marie stopped at a small newsstand on campus and
grabbed a copy of the *L'Ouverture Gazette*. She walked quickly
toward her office, nodded as students and faculty said good
morning. Once at her desk she opened the newspaper. Raymond
had been right about the resemblance. Even as she looked at the
name Davis Andre Ledeaux printed under the picture of the
pock-marked face of the young white man police suspected in
the murder of Whitey Peters, it was the face of another Ledeaux
that caused chills to run up and down her spine.

*"Cain't you keep this little nigger bitch from wigglin' so
damn much, Newell? Fourteen-year-old Matthew Ledeaux had
cursed under his breath and wished he had brought more rope.*

*"Hell, I'm holdin' her tight as I can. Just hurry up and
get that shit on her," said Newell Lawson, Matthew's sixteen-
year old co-conspirator. He had forced his balled- up fist into
Marie's screaming mouth. Her mouth was not visible through
the burlap sack he had pulled over her head, but he had known it
was her mouth because he had felt her teeth against his knuckles
as he had punched repeatedly. The squirming had stopped as a
blood stain spread slowly across the front of the sack.*

"This'll teach this white nigger bitch not to talk shit to my cousin Mattie," Matthew said. He had laughed as he smeared the dark, sticky substance on Marie's arms. "Damn, what you put in this? It stinks worse than my pa's hog pens." Newell asked.

"Chicken shit. Burns like hell. Put some of that sticky stuff my pa used to put up that paneling in my grandma's kitchen in with the axel grease. She'll look like yo' everyday nigger when we finish with her uppity ass." Newell had been careful not to get any of the gunk on his already dirty overalls.

"Wish I coulda got my hands on some tar. Heard they tarred and feathered one of them uppity yella niggers from over in Rockhurst just last week. Damn near took all the skin off the bastard trying to get that shit off his ass," Matthew said. His laughter had sounded like the cackling of a wild hyena. "Help me get some of this on her legs 'fore she come to."

"Damn sure hate to say it, but she gone be a looker in a couple years," Newell said. His coarse hands had rubbed the disgusting substance on her legs. His eyes had lingered on her simple cotton drawers. "We might have to come back for this one."

"You damn right about that." Matthew removed the sack from her face. Marie was unconscious, her mouth was bloody *and swollen. "She out cold. When it dries, they say it'll burn like hell. Let's get somma this on her face."*

"Now she looks and smells like a nigger. Too bad Mattie cain't see her now," Newell said. On his face was a devilish smirk. He stood up and admired his work.

"Let's get outta here 'fore she come to," Matthew said. He had unzipped his pants and started to piss on her. "That's for calling Mattie a stankin' pig ass." Newell had laughed hysterically and added his own yellow stream to his friend's before they ran off deeper into the woods.

"If Marie out here playin' games again, I swear I'm gone skin her alive," Raymond, Jr. had fussed as he and his friend moved slowly through the woods.

"Told you to let her go on and have some ice cream," twelve-year-old Coretta Granger complained as she had moved aside the brush. "Miss Essie gone do more than skin us alive if we don't find that girl before dark."

"Wait. Corrie did you hear something?" Raymond asked. He had held her arm to keep her from moving. "Sounds like it's coming from over near the old Colored school house."

"Probably just a coon caught in somebody's trap. Maybe we better go get, Mistah Ray," Corrie said. She had inched slowly behind Raymond who was headed toward the school house.

"Over here." Raymond's heart had pounded as he ran toward the sound. He'd recognize that whimpering anywhere. "Marie! Marie! Come on out girl. I'll let you have my ice cream for a week. This ain't funny."

"Oh, God!" Corrie said just before the scream left her mouth. She had pointed toward the school's outhouse.

"Marie." Raymond had run and fell to his knees before her. "Corrie, give me your sweater. I can't take her home to my mama like this."

Marie unconsciously rubbed the dime-sized, puckered flesh on her right wrist. It was the only evidence of that horrible day. She folded the newspaper and put it in her desk drawer and glanced at the clock over her desk. She would have to hurry. Her morning lecture was across campus.

CHAPTER TWENTY

Penny has an appointment with her pediatrician and cardiologist in a week. After that, we'll come for a visit. We'll have to stay with you and Uncle Raymond. Mama is tripping big time. She hung the phone up in my face last night," Morgan said into the telephone's headset.

She balanced Penny on her hip and poured formula into a bottle.

"Yeah, I know. She had another pretty big argument with Daddy yesterday. He asked her point blank how all this was connected to Alexander Franklin. Said you deserved to know, in case you were in danger. Aunt Marie nearly blew a gasket when Daddy mentioned the man's name. It's really bad between them this time, Lisa. I wish Mama Essie was here," Lonnie Jean said as she handed Anthony a signed permission slip for a field trip next week.

"That makes two of us." Morgan carried Penny into the living room and placed her into her swing.

"Whitey's funeral is tomorrow. The preliminary autopsy report was negative for gunpowder residue on his fingers. C. J. was able to find out there was a partial fingerprint on the gun that did not belong to Whitey. Thanks to C. J., the suicide has been changed to homicide and L'Ouverture is crawling with state police and media folks again. St. Vincent has been on all the local news stations from here to Baton Rouge and Anthony saw C. J. on CNN this evening. The Louisiana State Attorney General held a press conference this morning. He wants answers from Sheriff La Fontaine."

"There seems to be no end to all of this." Morgan wound a musical bear for Penny and placed it in her outstretched arms. "I wish I could be there tomorrow. Whitey didn't deserve to die like this, Lonnie Jean. I can't help but feel like this is all my fault. How's Pam?"

"Lisa, this is not your fault and everybody knows you just brought Penny home from the hospital. Nobody would expect you to be here. I know Whitey would understand." Lonnie Jean hated the sadness she heard in her cousin's voice. "Pam's taking it really hard. She's been sedated pretty much since they found Whitey. Her sister came from Little Rock to be with her. She's taking Pam back with her after the funeral. Scared to leave her here with all the talk about Whitey getting killed."

"I swear I did not know anything like this was going to happen. I just can't stop thinking that if it hadn't been for me,

Whitey would still be alive." All too familiar tears of sorrow and regret filled Morgan's eyes.

"Lisa, you didn't kill Whitey. Now, I don't know how all this mess is connected, but I know you're doing everything you can to find out. You can't blame yourself for this." Lonnie Jean's rebuff was gentle but firm. She remembered Morgan mentioned Maurice was out of town. She would go to New Orleans after the service tomorrow and spend a couple days with her cousin. Lonnie Jean knew her cousin would appreciate the company, although she'd never ask her to come. "The guys they picked up for Winn's murder are going to trial in a week or so. Now they saying they just did what they were told to do, but they won't say who told them to do it."

"Do they know anything about Whitey's murder?" Morgan lifted a sleeping Penny from the swing. Penny snuggled close to her chest as Morgan walked toward the nursery.

"They picked up some white boy in La Fitte. Of course, he says he's innocent." Lonnie Jean looked at the clock over the stove. "Look, you kiss that pretty baby girl of yours and call Maurice. I'll be up there tomorrow after the funeral. Please try and rest tonight. You hear me, Lisa?"

"Yes, Lonnie Jean. Good night." Morgan laid Penny in her crib, covered her with a pink, satin comforter, and wondered if she'd ever rest peacefully again.

CHAPTER TWENTY-ONE

Stephanie Arceneaux took a deep breath and quickly patted the tight curls at the back of her head before reaching out to ring the buzzer next to the name: M. Franklin. "Stephanie Louise Arceneaux calm down," she whispered to herself just before a voice spoke from the intercom.

"Yes, may I help you?" The voice sounded professional, yet pleasant.

"I'm here for a 1:30 p.m. meeting with Ms. Franklin. My name is Stephanie Arceneaux." Stephanie hoped she sounded as calm as she wanted the voice to believe she was.

"Yes, Mrs. Arceneaux. Please come in. Use the bank of elevators to the left of the water wall." The voice disappeared with a gentle click.

"Don't let the woman hear your heart beating like the second line at Mardi Gras," Stephanie said aloud when she pressed the golden button with eighteen written in an Old English script. The elegance of the place was unmistakable. Stephanie was able to take in everything as she looked at her reflection in the smoked mirrors of the elevator walls. She was fifty-three years old, but she didn't feel it. Stephanie was glad she'd gotten her hair done yesterday even though her stylist, Marion, had thought her crazy since her last visit had only been four days before.

"You'd think you was goin' to meet the Queen of England or some damn body, Steph," Marion said. She had spun Stephanie around in the black leather chair and brought her to a stop in front of the leopard-print framed mirror.

"This is important, Marion. I don't just need this job, I want it," Stephanie said and had placed an extra $10 in her hand.

"Told you not to sign that damn prenup." Marion had put the money into the pocket of her zebra print smock. "You let that bastard off too easy. But we're not going there again."

"Thank you. This is my second meeting with Ms. Franklin. It's at her home this time. That must be a good sign." Stephanie had let Marion help her into her jacket. The first meeting with Morgan Franklin had been over a week ago at a restaurant in downtown New Orleans. After being the wife of a very successful surgeon for thirteen years, Stephanie had been used to nice things, but the opulence of Restaurant August had even impressed her. She had been equally impressed with the young, attractive attorney with her ready smile and Halle Berry haircut.

"Did you at least ask your doctor friend to put in a good word for you?" Marion had known the answer before she even asked the question. Stephanie was determined to rearrange her life on her own terms.

"He was good enough to refer me, Marion. That's enough." Stephanie had kissed Marion's cheek. *"Wish me luck."*

Marion had shaken her head and beckoned for her next customer to come to her chair from under the dryer. *"The last time I wished you luck, you married an asshole."* God let this go well for her, she had thought to herself as she watched her friend drive away.

Stephanie smiled at the young woman who opened the dark mahogany double doors. She shook her hand and couldn't help but notice the diamond and black pearl ring on the middle finger of her well-manicured right hand.

"I'm Rhonda Lattier. Ms. Franklin will be right with you," Rhonda said and stepped aside to allow her into the entryway. Stephanie quickly noted the ebony marble floors and custom-designed silk wallpaper with small African symbols that looked hand painted. As Stephanie looked quickly around the room, Rhonda sized her up with the quickness and accuracy she used on opposing counsel. "May I get you something to drink, Mrs. Arceneaux?" Rhonda offered her no choices. She wanted to include whatever the woman chose as a beverage to the list of the information she was gathering on her.

"Some ice water would be just fine. Thank you, Ms. Lattier." Stephanie followed Rhonda into the living room.

"Water it is. Please have a seat." Rhonda turned toward the kitchen.

Stephanie sat on the edge of a beautiful ultra-suede sofa and enjoyed the feel of the fabric against the backs of her stockinged legs. Despite the exquisite décor and furnishings in the room, it had a warm, lived-in feeling.

"It will be just a few more minutes, Mrs. Arceneaux. Ms. Franklin is just finishing up her notes from the last interview, which ran a little longer than expected." Rhonda handed her a glass of water and took the seat across from her. "I hope you didn't have any trouble finding the place. Some of the construction in the surrounding areas can make it a little confusing."

"No, no trouble at all. The directions Ms. Franklin's secretary gave me brought me right to the front door. But you are right about the construction. This area has really changed since I was here last. You can already tell how beautiful it will be when everything is finished."

"I understand you've recently just moved back to New Orleans from Virginia." "Yes, I've been back home almost one year now. I lived in Virginia Beach for thirteen years. That's where I met Dr. LaShurr. I was a surgical pediatric nurse when he completed his neonatal residency." The interview had clearly begun.

"What brings you back to New Orleans?" Rhonda heard Morgan's office door open down the hallway.

"Virginia was my ex-husband's home. The marriage ended. There was no reason for me to stay. New Orleans is home to me, Ms. Lattier, and I'm glad to be back." Stephanie finished the water and omitted telling her she'd lost most of the friends she'd made in Virginia Beach before the ink on her divorce papers was dry.

"Virginia Beach is a beautiful place. It must've been difficult to leave." Rhonda remembered some summer vacations along the coast.

"I've found the most beautiful place is where you can lie down in peace and wake up looking forward to the day." Stephanie stood as Morgan entered the room.

"Mrs. Arceneaux. Good to see you again. Thanks for your patience," Morgan greeted. She extended her hand toward the woman dressed in the neatly tailored navy suit. "From the sounds of it, the interview has started without me." She glanced quickly at Rhonda.

"Not at all, Ms. Franklin." Stephanie followed Morgan down the hallway. Rhonda remained seated in the living room. "Ms. Lattier was just extending that southern hospitality you can only get in New Orleans."

"I looked up her address while you were with her. She lived in an estate in Ashville Park," Rhonda said. She placed a bowl of Caesar salad and a platter of plump garlic, honey-roasted prawns on the kitchen table. That's a very upscale area."

"Her ex-husband was the head of neurology at the medical center there; a brain surgeon, believe it or not," Morgan said then spooned steaming rice into a bowl and passed it to Rhonda.

"I called downstairs and talked to Antoine while she was coming up in the elevator. He said he saw her parking a white 1997 Lexus GS 300." Rhonda bit into a prawn. "Why is the ex-wife of a brain surgeon driving a 1997 Lexus?"

As if on cue, they both sang out, "prenup."

"Damn," Rhonda said. She shook her head in disgust and poured each of them a glass of Chardonnay. "She put up with thirteen years of a surgeon's bullshit and walks away driving an old car and looking for a job."

"She and the doctor didn't have any children. She had a son from a previous marriage. He died of leukemia about three years ago. He was a junior at the University of Virginia." Morgan retold the story told to her hours earlier. "She's been living off of a small divorce settlement that ends in about six months. She wants to get her life back on track."

"Well, her references are stellar. Of course, I talked to The Doctor and he had only good things to say about her." Rhonda took a sip from her wine glass before she focused her attention on the folder on the table containing everything that had been gathered on Stephanie Arceneaux. "If she passes the 'Penny test,' I think your search for the 'World's Greatest Nanny' may have just come to an end."

"She's going to meet me at the hospital in the morning at 8:00 a.m. Even though I've explained Penny's medical condition, I want her to talk with Penny's doctors. I also arranged a conference call with Elaine for this evening since she can probably share things the doctors won't know. That will really give her a feel for what she's signing up for. I want her to be sure." Morgan put another prawn in her mouth. "You like her?"

"Of course. If I didn't like her, she never would have gotten past Antoine," Rhonda smirked and tipped her glass to Morgan.

Stephanie slipped off her jacket and shoes and pulled a spaghetti and meatball Lean Cuisine dinner out of the freezer and popped it into the microwave on the small cart next to the refrigerator. She felt very confident about the interview process so far and even though Marion had told her to just "claim it," Stephanie decided to ask God for the job one more time as she bowed her head over the steaming spaghetti dinner. Ms. Franklin seemed nice and she even liked the way Ms. Lattier had poked around in her life. That showed Ms. Franklin had someone who cared enough about her to have her back. She'd gone over the medical reports Ms. Franklin had given her on Penny's condition between interviews one and two and had been given some updates and additional information during today's meeting. She had a call with Penny's nurse in one hour. She was certainly a sick little girl and Stephanie said an extra prayer for her before she finished her dinner.

As she showered that night, Stephanie wondered if maybe this job might be too much. What if the baby didn't make it? Could she handle that kind of pain again? She'd nearly lost her mind after Daniel's death to leukemia and she certainly never wanted to get that close to insanity again.

"This baby needs you, Stephanie. And I think you need her too," she whispered to herself as she turned off the bedside lamp.

CHAPTER TWENTY-TWO

The fog and heavy rain turned the usual hour and a half drive to L'Ouverture into a slow moving three hours. The bridge that led into St. Vincent from the highway was washed out and the detour through La Fitte added almost twenty miles to Morgan's trip to her Uncle Raymond's house. The pouring rains had turned the front yards of many of the homes she passed into small lakes. Penny slept peacefully in her car seat; her breathing was strong and steady. Morgan skillfully maneuvered around standing water and floating debris in the roadway and hummed to herself. She was looking forward to her time with Uncle Raymond and couldn't wait for Carl and Irene to see how much Penny had improved since they'd seen her last.

It was a little past noon when Morgan pulled into her uncle's driveway. She looked for a path to the front steps as she turned off the engine. The front yard was one big, muddy puddle. She pulled around to the back of the house, honked revelry on her car horn, and pulled on her hooded raincoat. Covered in a yellow rain slicker, rain hat, and rubber boots that would easily fit him three years from now, Anthony made his way to the car. He reached for the bags Morgan handed him as she took Penny, now wide awake from her car seat. Morgan walked carefully and held Penny tightly under her oversized umbrella as she sloshed along behind Anthony up the back steps.

"You had me worried, Little Girl. I was just about to come out to meet you," Uncle Raymond said. He took her wet umbrella and put it in a basket near the door. He hugged Morgan and took Penny from her arms as she pulled off her dripping raincoat and muddy boots. Penny smiled and squealed with pleasure as Raymond held her above his head. "This rain been going nonstop since yesterday morning. Lonnie Jean called about a half hour ago and said she won't be able to make it home tonight. There was a bad accident out on Surrey Road."

"Sorry to worry you, Uncle Raymond. The bridge is washed out. I had to come through La Fitte and then use the old mill road behind the Dulaine place. I tried to call but I couldn't get a signal on my cell because of the storm."

"Well, y'all made it. That's all that matters. This girl looking good, Lisa. When she get a little more meat on her bones, she's going to be mighty pretty." Raymond gently bounced Penny on his knee.

"Auntie Lisa, she looks just like that baby picture of you Aunt Marie keeps on the piano at her house." Anthony observed as Penny held onto his finger.

"He right. Think you was about Penny's age when Doc took that picture. He loved to take pictures of you. Drove Marie crazy." Raymond remembered.

"I'm just so thankful that she's going to be all right." Morgan followed Raymond and Anthony into the front room and sat on the couch. "Maurice and the other doctors are pretty amazed at her progress. There's something special about this little lady. Ain't that right?" Morgan playfully kissed Penny's cheeks which caused her to laugh.

"Carl and Irene been calling all morning checking to see if y'all made it. You better give them a call. Said they'll be over tomorrow if this rain lets up some. Roads bad out their way."

"How're they doing?" Morgan handed Anthony a small cloth doll for Penny to hold so he could get his finger back. Penny grabbed the doll with her left hand and continued to hold onto Anthony's finger with her right hand. Anthony shrugged his shoulders and smiled.

"They seem to be managing. Carl picked up a part-time janitor job at one of the office buildings over in Rockhurst. Blue Jeffries got him doing some handyman work on the weekends for his mama and he do a delivery every now and then for old lady Malveaux at Lawson Eddie's Fish Market. That damn Sam Austin tried to cheat him out what little money he had in that pension fund. Took C. J. to help him get it all figured out. It's a damn shame after all them years Carl give him. Had Carl still making delivery's when some of his drivers didn't show up for work and he knew how bad Carl's back was."

"Can it get any worse, Uncle Raymond?" Morgan sighed. She put Penny on Anthony's lap as soon as he sat down next to her on the couch.

"Sure it can. But most of the time, it don't."

"Oh, yeah. I almost forgot. Aunt Marie called. She said she would appreciate it if you would call her when you got here," Anthony said as he engaged Penny in a game of Peek-A-Boo.

"Then again, sometimes it does." Raymond laughed. "Might as well get it over with."

Morgan shook her head and got up from the couch. She walked toward the kitchen to use the phone, took her uncle's advice, and dialed her mother's number.

"Lisa, it is ridiculous for you to have come down here in this storm." Morgan held the receiver of the wall phone away from her ear as Marie droned on and on about how unnecessary it was for Morgan to have made the trip to L'Ouverture. "I hope those people realize you have a life of your own. They've already saddled you with a sick baby. I hope they don't expect you to bring her here every weekend."

"Mama, no one saddled me with anybody. Penny is my niece and she's doing very well." Morgan bit her tongue to keep from saying more. "Anyway, I promised Carl and Irene a visit with Penny this weekend. It's easier for me to make the trip than it is for them to come to New Orleans."

"Well promises are made to be broken," Marie snapped. "I hope you won't try to get out there to see them today. I'm sure all the roads back there are a mess and I heard on the radio there's a fatal accident on Surrey."

"I'm not going anywhere today, Mama." Morgan rolled her eyes as Raymond came into the kitchen to check on what smelled like his famous chili. He had a knowing smirk on his face. "I need to put Penny down for her nap. I've got to go. Bye, Mama." Morgan didn't wait to hear Marie say goodbye before she placed the receiver back in its cradle.

"She makes me…" Morgan began and grit her teeth.

"Go put Penny down for her nap and come on back and get some of your Uncle Raymond's chili. It'll…"

"…make it all better," they finished together in unison.

Morgan was up early the next morning. She made her way quietly to the kitchen to make herself a cup of tea and put on the coffee for her uncle. Moments later, wrapped in a soft multicolored afghan her Tee-Tee Corrie had crocheted before either Morgan or Lonnie Jean was born, she settled onto the porch swing, tea cup in hand. Moisture was still heavy in the air, even though the rain had stopped. The patchy fog placed everything under what looked like a light veil. She had always enjoyed the stillness of early morning in St. Vincent. It was as if the day was waiting for some formal invitation before it began. Morgan sipped her tea and looked out into her uncle's front yard. The huge magnolia tree sagged and dripped with yesterday's rains and lent its fragrance and beauty to the camellia bushes that ran along the inside of the fence. She inhaled deeply and enjoyed the soft symphony of the wind chimes hanging out of sight on the back porch.

It was during quiet times like this that Morgan thought most of her father, Russell Morgan. Growing up, she had always felt closer to him than Marie. Even though he had a busy medical practice and spent several months during the year traveling to national and international conferences, he had always made her feel as if she was the most important thing in his life. No matter what, he never missed a dance recital or school event. He had even canceled a lecture at Yale School of Medicine to visit her during her freshman year in college because she sounded homesick on one of their weekly calls. Morgan was glad Maurice had known her father, even if only through his work. She was sure her father would have approved of her relationship with The Doctor, as Rhonda liked to call him and would have probably even found it somewhat amusing that his lawyer daughter was 'carrying on' with a physician.

"Well, look who's up," Raymond said as his 6'4" sturdy frame walked onto the front porch with a coffee mug and newspaper in his hands. His work boots thudded across the worn wooden planks of the front porch. Things hadn't changed much. Uncle Raymond never lounged around in a robe and pajamas. His charcoal gray work pants had a razor-sharp crease. The gray and black plaid flannel shirt complimented the silver- gray hair mingling with the thick mass of black hair he wore closely cropped. Uncle Raymond's light brown eyes sparkled and his caramel complexion shone with the look of health from good old country living.

"I think I like this time of day because it always reminds me of Mama Essie. She used to say, getting up early guarantees you'll have a part of the day just for yourself. She said it was like watching God unveil His latest work just for you. Since Penny came home, early mornings have become my guarantee I'll have some time for myself. She's an early bird. Once she wakes up I don't have a free moment." Morgan tucked her feet under her and made room on the swing for her uncle.

"You doing a fine job with her, Little Girl." Raymond winked at her and handed her the comic strip section. They both remembered when she couldn't wait for that section of the newspaper. "I'm proud of you, Lisa. I know Doc would be, too."

"Thanks, Uncle Raymond." Morgan quickly kissed his cheek. "I wish Mama shared your sentiment."

"For all of her accomplishments, there's a lot of things your mama cain't do," Raymond turned his attention to Morgan. "Marie always had some kind of picture in her head about how the world was supposed to look. Never seemed satisfied with what was. No matter how much she gets, she always wanting something she don't have. When things don't turn out the way she planned, she just ignores everything that ain't in her picture. Those are her demons, not yours. Don't you worry about Marie. You just keep taking care of that little girl of yours."

"How did you get so smart?" Morgan put her head on his shoulder, grateful her uncle always seemed to understand her.

"I was born this way," Raymond teased, a twinkle in his eyes. "Carl and Irene called after you went to bed last night. Said they'll be here around noon. They can't wait to see y'all."

"You think Mary Joyce will come with them? I called her before we left home to let her know we were coming. She didn't have much to say, even when I told her how well Penny was doing. She acts like she's mad at me for something." Morgan sipped her tea; her eyes grew sad.

"What Mary Joyce do 'bout this baby ain't your worry, Lisa. Everybody do what they have to do. You did and one day so will she." Raymond said and stood. "You hungry, Little Girl?"

"You cooking?" Morgan rose from the swing. She wondered if she could coax him into making some of his famous buttermilk biscuits. She followed Raymond into the house for a breakfast she knew would keep her full until dinner.

CHAPTER TWENTY-THREE

Carl parked the car in the driveway beside Raymond's old pickup truck and looked at his wife. To him, she was still as beautiful as she was when he first saw her. He took her hand in his and kissed her palm like he did all those years ago when they were courting. "You gone have to talk to somebody about all this, Irene. Let this thing out. It's caused enough pain. Cain't nobody blame you now for what you did then." Irene reached over and kissed him softly on the mouth, his mustache tickled her nose like it always did, then said, "Let's get on in here before Raymond come out after us. You know he don't like his food to wait."

"Will you just look at her, Carl? Hard to believe she was ever sick at all," Irene gushed as she held Penny on her lap. They had all settled in the living room after a meal that had caused them all to eat a little past full.

"Her doctors are very pleased with her progress. They don't anticipate any more problems with her heart, but they will be watching her for the next 12 to 18 months. Her lungs are another matter. Penny was born too early and that puts her at a little higher risk than other babies for asthma and pneumonia. So far, there haven't been any signs of either," Morgan said, grateful for favors large and small.

"We gone keep her lifted in prayer. His grace is sufficient and His many wonders have yet to be unveiled," Irene stated in a voice that almost sounded like a prayer as Penny pulled at the buttons on her blouse.

"We give Mary Joyce the pictures you sent. Said she'd try to make it out here to see you before you leave. She may not show it right now, Lisa. But she glad about what you doing for Penny. She love her kids no matter how it seem sometime," Carl said.

"I know that, Carl. That's why I want her to spend some time with Penny."

"Penny got you, baby. That's what she need right now. Mary Joyce cain't help this child none right now, no way," Irene said. Penny began to fuss and reach for Morgan.

"Is she still staying with Darrell's mother?" Morgan took Penny who began to rub her eyes. "She doesn't stay too far from here. I can take Penny over to see her tomorrow." "She done moved in with his sister Lynette over in St. Augustine. Them boys was too much for his mama, I think. Mary Joyce let 'em run wild half the time. I know his mother would enjoy seeing the baby. Tried to get her to come back home, but she still put out with us about Darrell goin' to jail. Been almost two weeks since we seen her or the boys," Carl explained. There was no missing the disappointment in his eyes. "Mary Joyce'll find her way back," Raymond reassured them. He handed Carl a beer. "I think somebody needs a nap. I'll be right back," Morgan said. Penny's head was now on her shoulder.

"I'll put her down for her nap, Lisa. You go ahead and finish visiting," Lonnie Jean said and took the baby from her cousin.

"I'll cut us some of that pecan pie. Coffee?" Raymond said as he rose from his chair. Carl held up his beer bottle indicating he was fine. Irene nodded as Morgan shook her head no. Raymond headed toward the kitchen.

"Tanya will be leaving with her other sister for Chicago pretty soon. Sho' do hate to see her and William go so far away. That boy lookin' more and more like Winn every day. He got his daddy's eyes and that old goofy way of laughing, but I understand. She need a chance to start over new. Hard to see past her pain here," Irene said.

"I know Tanya will make sure William gets down here to see you as often as possible. And Chicago's not a bad place to visit. It's time you and Carl did some traveling," Morgan said and winked at Carl. Raymond came back into the dining room with pie and coffee.

"Her and William comin' by Sunday after church, for dinner. Y'all come on over. I know they'll both be glad to see you, Lisa. And Raymond, you can come too if you promise to bring one of these pies," Carl said as Raymond sat down at the table.

"I ought to be able to manage that." Raymond poured himself and Irene a cup of coffee.

"Folks sayin' they gone give them boys the death penalty for killin' Winn. I was glad they found them, but killin' them don't set right with me. Won't none of it bring Winn back to us," Irene said. Lonnie Jean walked back into the room and sat next to her father.

"The prosecutor went to law school with one of my colleagues at the firm. I'll see if I can't talk to him for you," Morgan said and passed around dessert plates with generous pieces of Raymond's pecan pie.

"I'd like that," Irene said and nodded.

"Can take 'em out and shoot 'em both in the head for all I care. What they done to my boy was wrong," Carl said while he emptied his beer bottle.

"Carl. All that hate ain't good. You got to leave it in the hands of the Lord," Irene scolded.

"Um, huh. You handle it your way, Irene. I'll handle it mine."

"I read in the *Gazette*, they let the guy go they picked up for killing Whitey. Not enough evidence," Morgan said. She wanted to move the subject away from Winn to avoid further upsetting Carl and Irene. She took a bite of the pie and enjoyed the sensation of it melting in her mouth.

"Who would want to kill that boy? Whitey ain't never hurt nobody in his life. It's a shame what happened to him," Carl said. He smacked his lips and rubbed his belly. "My compliments to the chef."

"Can I get anyone more coffee?" Morgan asked. She rubbed her thumb across her right eyebrow. "Lonnie Jean?"

"None for me. I'm stuffed." Lonnie Jean recognized their childhood signal immediately. Morgan wanted them to clear out so she could talk to Carl and Irene alone. "Daddy, I'll help you get started on the dishes." She gave her father a look that stopped him from saying they had plenty of time for dishes.

"Good idea. We got to pick Anthony up from his tutor pretty soon. I'll put a fresh pot of coffee on before we leave, in case anybody wants more," Raymond headed toward the kitchen. They quickly left the room.

Morgan felt the muscles in her jaws tighten as she cleared her throat. She wondered if it was a mistake to have Lonnie Jean and her Uncle Raymond leave the room. Now she wished she had Uncle Raymond's always reassuring look to drive away the sick feeling making its way to the pit of her stomach.

"Irene, has anyone ever tried to contact Mary Joyce? About any of this?" Morgan paused. She knew any mention of Alexander Franklin could upset her. She and Carl had been through enough already and she didn't want to make it any worse.

Carl gave Irene a nod and reached for her hand. Morgan noticed the tears forming in Irene's eyes.

"You mean 'bout y'all father?" Irene looked intensely into Morgan's eyes. The eyes that refused to let her forget.

Morgan was stunned, not only at Irene's words but the look of resolve on her face. She responded with a quick nod.

"It was 1975 when he come to town with smooth talk and his pockets full of money. In St. Vincent, we used to call it long money. It was right around the time Junior turned three. Me and Carl had been married about the same length of time and I was finding out being married wasn't like they made it out to be in the movies. Lisa, I had a itch down inside of me that not even Carl's love and kindness could scratch. Said he'd take me away from here. I'd only been out of St. Vincent district a few times. Alex took me to places I didn't even know existed," Irene spoke, no longer sitting in Raymond Baptiste's dining room in 2004, but somewhere in her distant past. She continued, "And he did make it better for a while. He was a gentleman and handsome as sin. Shoot, I wasn't surprised he had other women. A man like that always did. I didn't care. Wasn't much I coulda said anyway; I was married to Carl. When I got pregnant with Winn, Alex changed. Seen a side of him I didn't like. He got real mean and hateful. He stopped coming around soon after that. He sent me money for a while. After Winn was born, I went to the address on the envelope. It was a fancy roomin' house way over on St. Augustine's north end. I wanted him to see his son. I guess I thought if he just saw Winn, he'd want us; want me again. He'd already moved on when I got there."

"When did you see him again, Irene?" Morgan asked gently. She understood how hard this must be for her. Carl looked as if he were in physical pain. His face was drawn, his eyes squinted, and his jaws clinched. Morgan realized how difficult hearing all of this must be for him. Even with that, he never let go of Irene's hand.

"A couple a years later. Carl and me had been havin' some real bad times. I couldn't get Alex out my system. Threw it up in Carl's face every chance I'd get. How Alex could do things he couldn't. How Alex had been places he couldn't dream of going. Naturally, that was hard on Carl. We started to argue a lot after Winn was born. Carl left for a while." Irene paused and wiped the tears from her eyes with a crumbled napkin from dinner.

"Go on, darlin'. Tell her everything. It's all right now," Carl spoke softly.

"Alex came to town while me and Carl was split up. Acted like he didn't know me when I saw him on the street. I got my sister Grace Ann to watch Junior and Winn for me one night. I got myself all dolled up and got me a ride to N'Orleans. Wanted some fun, I told myself; I knew I was lookin' for Alex. I'm 'shamed to say all this to you, Lisa. I ain't always been a God-fearin' woman. Done some things I had to repent for later." Irene paused again and wiped away a stray tear. She took a sip of water from a glass Carl handed her before she continued.

"I saw Alex as soon as I walked into that nightclub. Something inside me said, Irene get yourself out of here, but I kept right on walkin'. I walked right past him and over to the bar. After I'd had a couple of drinks, he come up behind me. Started talkin' about how good I looked and how much he missed bein' with me. I let him buy me another drink. We danced. We went to one of them fancy hotels in the French Quarter. When I woke up the next morning, he was gone. Mary Joyce come nine months later."

Morgan turned away as Carl took Irene in his arms. She wept bitterly for a few moments before she responded to Carl's tender whispers. Morgan knew she had never seen love so pure, so honest than what she witnessed at this very moment.

"I come back home a few months after that. Irene told me she was havin' another baby. Another one of his babies. It hurt like hell; but she was my world, Lisa. Sure, my pride was hurt, but I never stopped lovin' her. So, I stayed. Right before Mary Joyce was born, we got a letter from some lawyer in New York City. It had some money in it for Irene and the kids, and a note saying there would be no more contact from Mr. Franklin," Carl finished the story while Irene recovered in his arms.

"Do you have any idea where he might be now?" Morgan asked and felt no closer to the answers she wanted. She felt immense respect and appreciation for the courage Irene had shown in breaking the silence that surrounded Alexander Franklin. Courage she doubted she would ever see in Marie.

"No, sweetheart," Irene said and shook her head. "We didn't want another word from him or about him. It was time for me and Carl to fix some things, if we was ever gonna have any kind of life together. Time for me to start lovin' Carl the way he deserved. I don't think he would've ever come up again if Winn hadn't got in that accident and Carl found out about you."

"Knew the first time I saw you, you was Alexander Franklin's child. All of you got eyes just like him. The color, the shape, everything. I wasn't never gonna say nothin' about it though. I know the kind of trouble that can bring to a house and I didn't want no trouble for Doc. He was always good to me. Didn't put on airs and do things to make me feel less than a man just 'cause I didn't have no fancy education or live over in Rockhurst." Carl paused and wiped his face with a handkerchief he pulled from his shirt pocket.

"Like my mother," Morgan finished the statement for him.

Carl simply nodded. "When Winn got in that accident, I didn't know what to do. I couldn't let my boy die. I didn't care who his father was, he was my son. One of the hardest things I ever had to do in my life was drive over to Doc's that day. Your mother was fit to be tied when I came in there asking for your blood to save Winn. Left up to her she woulda let Winn die, but Doc wouldn't have it. He come to the hospital with me and stayed to make sure Winn was goin' to be all right. Checked up on him every day 'til Winn was well enough to come home. The only thing he asked of me was that you never be told why your blood saved Winn. He didn't want you to know nothin' 'bout Alexander Franklin and I didn't blame him. I woulda promised him anything for doin' what he done for Winn. After that, he started bringin' you over to play with the kids when he was seeing to his patients over our way. Even sat and played some cribbage with me a time or two. He was a good man, Lisa. Your daddy was a real good man."

"At Christmas and on their birthdays, he'd send y'all housekeeper, Naomi, over to our place with presents for Winn and Mary Joyce. Always with a note saying they were from you. I know your mama didn't know nothin' about that," Irene said.

"I remember she was home one Saturday when Daddy and I came back from your house. Daddy rushed me upstairs for my bath. I was filthy and of course she wanted to know how I had gotten so dirty. I heard them arguing. Naomi said she was just mad because I had ruined my dress, but I heard her say something about "playing with his kids." It was something about the way she said the word "his" that made me wonder who she was talking about."

"When you come to us that day with your birth certificate, I didn't know what to say. I had promised Doc I'd never tell you, but you was standin' right in front of me with the proof in your hands. When you told me you had already spoke with your folks, wasn't nothin' else to do but tell you that Winn and Mary Joyce was your brother and sister," Carl explained.

Morgan remembered. "I already loved Winn and Mary Joyce, so finding out they were my brother and sister was the easy part. Even though Alexander Franklin wasn't his father, C. J. was the greatest big brother a girl could wish for. He still is."

"Oh, them children loved you so much. Junior used to act like you was a bother to him, but he always made sure to be around the house when he thought you was comin' out our way with Doc," Irene said. She smiled for the first time since their conversation began. "We could hardly get Mary Joyce to sleep after she got through playin' with you. She'd go on and on and on 'bout all the things her friend from Rockhurst told her. Used to make all the other little girls so jealous. She looked up to you, Lisa. Still does." "Once Winn found out you was his sister, you couldn't get him to shut up about his 'big sis.' How his big sister went to college and he was going to do the same. If anybody had said they saw you walking on the water, he'd a believed them," Carl said. He laughed at the memory.

Morgan smiled remembering. "Irene, why did you go so long without talking about Alexander Franklin? It's not like things like this don't happen."

"Oh, Lisa. I was so ashamed and it was a different time then. People wasn't open about things like that like they are now. 'Specially 'bout relationships between people like me and people like Alex." Irene picked up her forgotten coffee cup and took a sip. She patted Carl's knee and found more warmth in the reassuring expression on his face than the lukewarm coffee.

"I can only imagine how much worse the class issues were then. It would've been harder for you, being married, than him. From what I've been able to figure out, he was pretty wealthy. I'm sure it would have been more acceptable for him to have his pick of Rockhurst's debutantes. I guess it would have been quite a scandal for the colored bourgeoisie." Morgan shook her head.

"Colored?" Irene asked, her eyes narrowed in confusion. She and Carl exchanged a quick look that Morgan did not miss. "Lisa, Alexander Franklin is a white man." Irene reached for her purse, rummaged through her wallet, and pulled out a photograph. She handed it to Morgan.

It was a black and white photograph of a young Alexander Franklin that Irene kept in a shoebox of old family photographs. She had convinced herself the reason she kept the photograph was in case Winn or Mary Joyce ever wanted to know what their real father looked like; but that wasn't the complete truth. This morning as she was getting dressed for her visit with Lisa and Penny something told her to take the photograph with her.

In the photograph, Alex's hat was pushed back off his face; his sharp, tailored suit made his wealth apparent. He was standing in front of a shiny black Lincoln with large white wall tires. Morgan stared at the picture in her hands. There was something very familiar about the face of the man–the white man–who stared back at her.

CHAPTER TWENTY-FOUR

G randpa, you think Aunt Marie's going to be nice to Auntie Lisa tonight?" Anthony asked. He placed an Allen wrench in Raymond's greasy hand near the right front fender of the blue Chevy truck. "She's always telling me to mind my manners and treat people with respect. She's been yelling at Auntie Lisa and calling her names. I heard her when I was over there with Auntie Lisa yesterday."

"I'll see to it that your aunt Marie is on her best behavior tonight. After all, I'm her big brother. She has to do what I say." Raymond's voice came from underneath the front end of his truck. Anthony could tell his grandfather was smiling even though he couldn't see his face.

"I heard Auntie Lisa crying after she got off the phone with her once. I could hear Aunt Marie yelling and I was all the way in the hall," Anthony reported.

"Sometimes tears help wash away sadness or say things that don't fit into words. You don't worry about you're Auntie Lisa. She's made of tough stuff." Raymond rolled from underneath the front end of the truck and sat up to look at his grandson. "What else is on your mind, son?" He knew without asking that something was troubling his grandson.

"Some kids at school said Uncle Winn was shot. Was he really shot, Grandpa?" Anthony asked as Raymond stood to his feet and took the rag Anthony held out toward him to wipe some of the grease off his hands.

"Yes, Anthony. Winston was shot and killed." Raymond stuck the now greasy rag in the back pocket of his even greasier overalls.

"Why doesn't the sheriff catch who did it, Grandpa? That would make Auntie Lisa happy. That's what detective Bobby Simone on *NYPD Blue* would do," Anthony blurted out before he realized he may have just confessed to staying up past his bedtime.

"How about you let the grownups worry about all that and you just worry about getting to bed when your mama says." Raymond's stern look told Anthony his grandpa, who often sided with him, would take his mother's side on this one.

"Grandpa, do you think somebody might shoot Auntie Lisa? I heard Mama tell Auntie Lisa to be careful snooping around," Anthony asked despite the stern look his grandfather had just given him. His eyes grew large as he looked up into the face of his grandfather. Anthony was tall for his age and

Raymond realized it wouldn't be long before he'd be able to look him in the eyes.

"You staying up past your bedtime *and* listening in on grown folks' conversations?" Raymond patted his grandson's shoulder and hoped to wipe the look of worry off his young face. "Anthony, you don't have to worry. Nobody's gonna hurt you're Auntie Lisa. Don't know if I can say the same for you, if your mama catches you watching *NYPD Blue* and eavesdropping. Now you get your mind on getting cleaned up before you're Aunt Marie comes. You know how she hates dirty fingernails."

Raymond wiped the sweat from his brow as Anthony flashed a smile revealing teeth that would soon need braces. He took off up the driveway toward the back door. Raymond looked up into the blue of the afternoon sky. "God, I hope I ain't just lied to my only grandson."

"Are you going to be okay?" Lonnie Jean asked as she and Morgan set the dining room table. Marie was coming to dinner and both knew eating in the kitchen where Morgan had been having her meals during her visit was not Marie's style.

"I need to have a hard conversation with Mama. To be honest, I am not looking forward to it."

"It might go better than you think." Lonnie Jean placed a vase filled with violets, lilies, and daisies in the center of the ivory lace tablecloth Mama Essie had always used for holidays and special occasions. "It wasn't as bad as you thought it would be with Irene."

"Lonnie Jean, you know Marie Baptiste Morgan is no Irene." Morgan laughed. Anthony came into the room. Penny crawled quickly behind him. They had become inseparable in the last week.

Marie was polite during dinner. She made small conversation, complimented Lonnie Jean on what she'd heard of her work at General, and reminded Anthony how important it was to stay focused and keep good grades at Mercer. She complained about the extra time she would have to spend at the gym while helping herself to a second helping of Raymond's famous honey and garlic grilled shrimp and grits. She even managed to smile at Penny as Morgan fed her grits from her plate and commented on how well she looked.

After a dessert of fresh blackberry cobbler and homemade vanilla ice cream, Raymond, Lonnie Jean, and Anthony decided to go see *Spider-Man 2* and left Morgan alone with her mother. Morgan felt it might be easier to talk to Marie alone, but when she saw her Uncle Raymond's truck back out of the driveway, she wished she could change places with Anthony who was waving goodbye from the back window.

Morgan put on water for tea before she excused herself to get Penny ready for bed. She could hear Marie moving around in the living room. Penny had fallen asleep quickly, exhausted from all the day's activity. Morgan continued to rock her to delay the conversation. She shook her head as she heard Mozart's Piano Concerto no. 21 replace the voice of Dinah Washington singing "Long John Silver." Marie didn't share her brother's taste in music.

"That did not take long. It seemed it used to take your nurse hours to get you to sleep," Marie commented as Morgan rejoined her in the living room. Morgan placed the blue flowered tea service she'd purchased in Venice for Lonnie Jean's birthday last year on top of the coffee table. She poured Marie a cup and added cream.

"She was pretty worn out." Morgan sat in an overstuffed arm chair near the living room's front window.

"I never will be able to understand why Raymond does not move out of this big, old, drafty house. I guess he is waiting for it to fall down around his thick head," Marie complained from her seat on the couch across from Morgan. She took a sip of her tea and reached for the silk shawl she'd placed on the back of the sofa.

"Uncle Raymond is happy here, Mama. There are a lot of happy memories in this house. Mama Essie was always so proud of it. I would think you would be glad it is still in the family," Morgan said in her uncle's defense.

The house had been built by Morgan's great-grandfather, Jean Baptiste, in the late 1880s. Both Raymond and Marie were born in this house—in the room at the top of the stairs. Morgan would always think of it as "Mama Essie's room" although it had been Raymond's den for years. Raymond and Corrie moved back into the house when Mama Essie became ill. When Lonnie Jean divorced Anthony's father, she moved back in with her toddler son. After Corrie passed, Lonnie Jean did not want to leave her father alone. Soon it seemed right she and Anthony stay with him. Together, the three of them made it a home again.

"Raymond could get a fortune for this land. Developers have had their eyes on this area for some time. They want to bring a golf course and resort here. I would think the money a deal like that would put in his pocket would make up for any 'happy memories' he would lose when they tear this place down. It's a good thing he bought my share many years ago or I would have the developers out here in a heartbeat," Marie quipped.

"Mama, Uncle Raymond understands that a home is more valuable than money. Everyone's not like you," Morgan snapped, frustrated with Marie's attitude. She had not meant to antagonize Marie with meaningless conversation. That would only make the conversation she hoped to have about Alexander Franklin all the more difficult. "Lisa Morgan, what you know about having a home is the result of the sacrifices made by your father and me. This house you and your Uncle Raymond are so sentimental about does not hold warm and wonderful memories for everyone." Marie's voice drifted as her memories took their place in the room and sat down between her and Morgan......

"Cain't believe how she holding up and she just a child." "Look like she gone be the backbone of this family." "She a tough one. Just like Mistuh Ray."

"Her pa would be proud of her and how she carryin' herself." "The Lord will have to hold them all in His mighty hands now."

The words, whispered behind paper napkins and muffled behind mouthfuls of crawfish, red beans, and dirty rice, had found their way to Marie's ears.
Marie Esther Baptiste had sipped her sweet tea, now watery from the melted ice cubes, and wished these people would leave. She had wondered how her mother could breathe in the stuffy living room with all the women from the church huddled around

her. She could hear eighteen-year old-Raymond, Jr. and some of the older boys in the dining room, their voices had been hushed and respectful.

"Raymond sho' was a good man."

"God make a way for Essie Mae and these children, if you will." "Essie and these kids gonna have to hold to God's unchangin' hand."

Marie had known she wouldn't be able to stop the scream that was fighting to leave her throat, if she had heard one more word about how "good" Raymond Baptiste, Sr. was or about the "keeping powers" of Jesus. It would be years before she could hear the word "stroke" and not hear the screams of her mother and the sobbing of her brother ringing in her ears.

"Marie Esther, your daddy was a good man," said a woman stuffed into a black knit dress. The black straw hat on her head had shaken slightly as she let a fresh batch of tears fall. Marie had looked for an escape, found none with the small group now encircling her, and placed her glass on the small table next to her chair. She had gritted her teeth and stood.

"My daddy, Raymond Baptiste, Sr., was a colored man in St. Vincent and ain't nothing all that good about that," Marie said coolly. Her voice had sounded more like a woman betrayed by the world than that of a thirteen-year-old girl who had just lost her father.

Marie had not noticed her mother had come into the room. The sting of the slap on her cheek was unmistakably from Essie's hand.

"Don't you never open your mouth again to say a disrespectful thing about your father," Essie had hissed as the woman in the black knit dress had taken hold of her hand to stop Essie from slapping Marie again. The reddened print of her hand had taken shape and spread quickly across Marie's left cheek.

Marie had clinched her jaws tightly to keep from grabbing her cheek, which felt as if it were on fire. The room had gone silent. Under different circumstances, her mother would have said it was quiet enough "to hear a rat piss on cotton." Marie's anger had raged inside of her as she held back the tears that burned behind her eyes. She had willed the tears not to fall. Marie would not give her mother the satisfaction of seeing her cry. The crowd had parted and left just enough room for her to pass through. She had walked slowly from the room, but not before she turned to glare at her mother. Essie had met her gaze. What Marie had seen in it cooled her boiling blood. Years later, they both realized it had been that look that separated them forever.

Marie shook herself slightly to return to the room with her daughter, the memory slowly faded with the day's light.

"I took Penny out to visit with Mary Joyce and the boys yesterday," Morgan said to change the subject for now. "She said she would stop by tomorrow on her way home from work."

"It seems to me Penny would be better off not knowing that poor, pitiful girl or her jailbird father." Marie's eyes were cold.

"That's easy for you to say. You grew up knowing your father."

Marie flinched slightly and wished her cup was filled with bourbon instead of tea. "What were you protecting me from? What kind of man was my father? What kind of man was Alexander Franklin?"

"Lisa, I will not have this conversation with you." Marie looked away. "Why is it not possible for you to leave things you do not understand alone? None of it can do anyone any good now."

"You are wrong, Mama," Morgan insisted. "It just might help find out who killed Winn and Whitey. Or maybe, I would be able to tell a woman named Gloria Jones who killed the little girl who became her daughter. The little girl who was his daughter. She said Andrea Jones had our father's eyes."

"It seems you picked the wrong area of law, Lisa. You should have been a criminal attorney. Or perhaps, with your imagination and flare for the dramatic, you would have made a better mystery writer. Your interest in murder and mayhem is becoming terribly annoying, Lisa," Marie spat the words at Morgan.

"I know he was white." Morgan moved to where Marie was now standing near the front window. Morgan's words hit Marie with such impact that Morgan saw her flinch for the second time that evening. "I know he was a good-looking smooth talker. He promised to take Irene away from St. Vincent. What did he promise you, Mama? What made the grand Marie Esther Baptiste fall in love with Alexander Franklin?" Morgan tasted the blood in her mouth before she realized she had been slapped.

"You don't know anything about him, Lisa. Don't you ever mention him to me again." Marie's body trembled with anger and her eyes blazed.

"Did you think he would take you away too?" Morgan cried. Her cheek burned and she could feel a welt rising under her eye. "Did he send you checks in the mail after I was born like he did Irene? Did you go looking for him only to find out he had left without you? Did you think he loved you?!" Morgan's last question came as Marie slammed the front door. The windows framing the door shook so hard that Morgan held her breath and waited for them to shatter. The loud noise woke Penny and she screamed. Morgan went to her and wept along with the baby she loved so much. She held Penny close as she rocked her and hoped to soothe them both.

CHAPTER TWENTY-FIVE

The activity in the office of the St. Vincent Sheriff's Department came to a complete standstill as Morgan walked through the front door. Deputy Henry Prioleaux was the first to recover from her entrance. He looked as if he had slept in his uniform. The rank odor that accompanied him as he moved toward the counter proved the appearance to be true.

"What can I do for you?" he asked. His belly fell onto the counter that separated them and his balding pate shined under the rows of fluorescent lights.

"I would like to speak with Sheriff La Fontaine," Morgan stated.

"What business you got with the Chief?" Deputy Prioleaux tucked in his shirt as he spoke.

"Excuse me, Deputy Prioleaux," Morgan said reading his badge. "That is between the sheriff and me."

"Damnit, Henry, step aside," Arthur DuPont said and pushed himself into what little space remained at the counter. "Chief's out right now. Can I help you?"

"No. My business is with Sheriff La Fontaine. When do you expect him to return?" "Ain't you Doc Morgan's girl?"

Arthur Lee took a good look at Morgan. He hadn't seen her in years, but there was no mistaking those eyes.

"I am." Morgan did not recognize the deputy and preferred to not spend time on idle conversation.

"Never can tell. Could be a few minutes. Could be a few hours," Arthur Lee answered her question.

"Thank you. I will wait." Morgan walked to a row of laminated wooden chairs. "Could be a while," Arthur Lee repeated.

Morgan picked up one of the outdated magazines from the metal table next to the chair, sat down, and crossed her legs. "I know. A few minutes or a few hours."

Morgan had gone through each of the waiting room's six outdated magazines when Sheriff Claude La Fontaine walked into the room. He was laughing loudly with a man in a dark brown suit. He looked in Morgan's direction when Henry Prioleaux rushed up to him and whispered something in his ear. He put the gentleman in the brown suit in the capable hands of a young deputy and turned his attention to Morgan. He straightened his tie and walked toward her. She stood as he approached and noticed for the first time there were several of St. Vincent's deputy sheriffs between her and the only apparent exit. Morgan breathed deeply. She was glad she had worn her comfortable rubber-soled shoes with her simple gray pantsuit and not her usual heels.

"Well good afternoon," Sheriff La Fontaine said. He smiled and extended his right hand. "I'm Sheriff Claude La Fontaine. How can I help you?"

"My name is Morgan Franklin." Morgan did not take his outstretched hand. "I think it would be better if we spoke in private."

Claude La Fontaine appeared taken aback as he glanced over his shoulder. The visitor had drawn quite an audience. He led the way to his office and barked orders to get back to work. After he closed the door and Morgan sat, he asked again, "Now, how may I help you?"

"I want to follow up on some information I received from the state police in the murder investigation of my brother, Winston Banks."

"Brother?" Claude feigned ignorance. "Thought you said your name was Franklin?" "The difference in our last names is irrelevant. Winston was my brother."

"Well then, Miss Franklin." Claude leaned back in his chair. "You will be happy to know we assisted the state police in catching the two men who are suspected of killing your brother. They will no doubt get the death penalty. Seems a shame to kill those two boys seeing how they was merely protecting themselves."

"Excuse me?" Morgan knew she must have misunderstood what the sheriff just said. "Did you say they were protecting themselves?"

"Well, Winston was trying to kill them," Sheriff La Fontaine stated this as if he had just proclaimed grass green. "I guess you didn't know your brother very well, Miss Franklin." He went to a much-used file cabinet and pulled out a worn manila folder. He handed the file to Morgan.

"There must be some mistake." Morgan grabbed the folder with Winston's name written on the tab and read through its contents. It was full of police reports documenting crimes from juvenile offenses to a recent arrest for the sale of drugs just two days prior to Winn's murder.

"Them state police didn't seem to think this was important enough to let them poor boys off." Sheriff La Fontaine shook his head. He enjoyed the look of discomfort that was apparent on Morgan's face. "They lawyer was glad to get it, though. Gave him a copy of the entire file just yesterday. He said it was just what he needed to stop that jury from killing them poor boys."

"Sheriff La Fontaine, I am afraid there is some mistake. Winn was never in trouble." "Family members, especially them that don't stay around here, are usually the last to know about these things. I'm afraid your brother, Winston Banks, was what we call around here a bad actor, Miss Franklin." Sheriff La Fontaine hoped she would mistake his disgust for sympathy.

"Well this family member also happens to be an attorney, sheriff. You will need much more to prove that statement than the contents of this folder. This will never stand up in a court of law without corroboration." Morgan locked eyes with him. He looked away as she placed the folder on his desk and stood up. She took a deep breath and was about to say more when she saw a pair of coal black eyes looking at her through the window behind the sheriff's chair. Something in those eyes stopped her from saying another word.

"It's all right there, in black and white. Is there anything else I can do to help you?" Sheriff La Fontaine had a smug look of satisfaction on his face.

She looked toward the window again. The eyes were gone. "No, sheriff. You have done enough. Thank you for your time."

Claude felt the all too familiar burning sensation make its way down the back of his throat and into his stomach as soon as Morgan left his office. He watched her car pull away from the curb before he started cursing. Claude slammed the door to his office and cursed again as a picture of him and the Governor of

Louisiana crashed to the floor. He searched for his Rolodex in the mess that was his desk and knocked over a forgotten mug of coffee with just enough coffee to make a puddle in the middle of paperwork he had yet to sign. He pushed the sodden papers to the floor and reached for the telephone.

"Goddamnit, we tried it your way! I'm not going to wait around and let this shit blow up in my face. I'm getting calls from the state attorney general. There was a news truck outside my house when I got home last night, for Christ sakes!" Claude yelled into the receiver. He took a deep breath and lowered his voice. "I just got a visit from Morgan Franklin and she's asking questions I don't have answers for. We fix this and now." He slammed the receiver down and reached for the unopened bottle of Tums now standing in the coffee puddle in the middle of his desk.

Claude reached for the Rolodex again and dumped the bottle of Tums into his mouth. He chewed as he dialed the phone. "We got more business. You get your lanky ass out to Queenie's tonight or them gun charges that disappeared will reappear. I'll have your Black ass shipped off to Angola faster than you can say crawfish." He slammed down the phone and cursed again.

Outside on the sidewalk several yards from the sheriff's office, Morgan saw the eyes again. They stared at her from the window of a small café at the end of the block where she parked her car. She went quickly into the dimly lit café; the smell of fresh seafood and Cajun spices stung her nose when she entered. She walked toward a table in the corner as if she had been drawn there.

"Had to come see you, since you not come to see me. It is time," Celeste said. She did not look up. Her attention remained on the soft-shell crab leg in her hand. Morgan sat down.

Morgan had been twelve years old when she first met Celeste DuMaurier. She had been with her father, on his weekly rounds, when a young boy met them just outside a farmer's house. He had begged him to come and see about his father. The boy had been going on and on about "The Witch" putting some kind of hex on his father. A shadow had passed across her father's face as he told her to wait at Irene and Carl's for him. Morgan could not imagine missing an opportunity to see a real live witch. She had known how hard it was for her father to say no to her and begged to go with him. As she and her father had followed the boy to a small clapboard house on the edge of the swamp, Morgan's eyes were wide in search of "The Witch." She could already see the looks of amazement on her friends' faces

at recess on Monday when she told them she had met a real live
witch who lived in the swamp.

 "You too late, good doctor," a voice had whispered
behind Morgan and her father as they left the small house.
Morgan had turned to see a woman, a thick black braid wrapped
around her head, looking at her father. "His sickness is his evil
ways catching up to him. None of my doin'." When he had
turned toward the voice, the woman was gone.

 Morgan looked at the woman sitting across from her and
thought this is what was meant by the term ageless. Celeste
looked no older than she had that day in the swamp. Legend had
it she was 100 years old or close to it. Celeste was dressed in a
loose fitting, purple and gold African dress. Her hair, now a
shining silver-gray, wound around her head in a large, thick
braid. The small gold hoops in her ears flashed as they caught
the glow from the small tealight candle on the table.

 "You stopped me from saying anything more to Sheriff
La Fontaine. Why?" Morgan asked. She had never felt so
strongly about anything being true in her life.

 "The baby will be fine," Celeste commented and ignored
Morgan's question. "She'll grow strong and make you proud.
Give her a strong, proud name. Penny's a name given to her in
her father's regret and shame. It is full of pain and worthlessness.

Give her a strong name so she will be strong. Always tell her the truth. Only the truth will allow her to grow."

"I will." Morgan felt strength leave the old woman and seep into her.

"You are close. Too close for them." Celeste's words sounded as if they were coming from far away.

"Madame Celeste, who do you mean?" Morgan searched her face for answers.

"The boys got too close," Celeste stated in a trance-like tone. Her coal black eyes locked on a place just above Morgan's head.

"The boys? Winn and Whitey? Do you mean Winn and Whitey?" Morgan gasped. She felt beads of sweat running down her back even in the coolness of the restaurant. "Madame Celeste, do you know who killed them?"

"Take this," Celeste said, the trance broken. She pushed a flat, smooth, purplish stone across the table toward Morgan.

"What is this?" Morgan touched the stone without picking it up. It felt warm. She placed her hand over it.

"It's been covered too long. It can't help but smell bad. Bring light to it." Celeste looked at Morgan as if for the first time. "Your eyes are like his. All of you had eyes like his."

"Madame Celeste, did you know Alexander Franklin?" Morgan swallowed hard, her eyes wide as she took in Celeste's entire face.

"She thought she was better than the others. She thought she would be his wife," Celeste mumbled as she went back to her crab leg. "Russell Morgan begged her not to leave him even though he knew he would never win her heart. Never. He loved her, more than she deserved. He loved you more than his own life. But Marie could only hate when that man walked away. The others got over him. But, never Marie. She tries to hide him under all her high and fancy living, but he is still there. In you."

"Do you know where Alexander Franklin is?" Morgan felt weary from the strange, rambling conversation. "Please, Madame Celeste. If you know where he is, please tell me."

"You are close," Celeste repeated and sucked the meat from the crab leg with a loud slurp. She placed her hand over Morgan's and smiled. "No more of this talk. Talk to me of my beloved N'Orleans. We've been parted too long she and I." Morgan sighed, her fist tight around the purplish stone.

CHAPTER TWENTY-SIX

Morgan turned the lights out in the living room and checked to make sure the alarm system was set before she peeked in on Penny. She walked down the hallway to her bedroom and hoped her excitement about tomorrow would not keep her awake too long. She wanted to be well rested for Penny's baptism and naming ceremony in the morning. Rhonda had agreed to be her godmother. She had purchased a beautiful white satin gown and matching shoes and bonnet for her eight-month-old goddaughter. The tiniest of pearl earrings, a small pearl necklace, and pearl bracelet had been purchased to accessorize her outfit. Rhonda had insisted on paying for a catered gathering at her home following the baptism and had also had the paperwork drawn up for Penny's new name: Imani. Morgan could think of no other name that suited the little girl better than the Kiswahili word for "faith."

Not wanting to disrespect Mary Joyce, Morgan called her to get her approval of the name change. She also invited Mary Joyce and the boys to come up for the weekend to attend the baptism. Mary Joyce said she had a visit scheduled with Darrell and wouldn't be able to make it. She used Christmas being only two weeks away as her excuse for not wanting to miss her visit with him. As far as the name was concerned, she had never heard of Kiswahili but liked that the name Morgan picked meant faith. She then said she had to pick one of the boys up from Irene's and rushed to end the conversation.

As Morgan stood looking out at the lights of the city from her bedroom window, she felt something warm under her foot and looked down. The purple stone Celeste DuMaurier had given her laid in the deep piles of the carpet. She bent down to pick it up; her mind quickly replayed the day over one month ago when Celeste had given her the stone. Morgan had not seen it since that day. She thought she must have lost it before she returned home from her visit. She looked at the stone and turned it over and over. At first, she thought her eyes were playing tricks on her. Were those words delicately etched in the stone? She turned on the light and read the words: **Euclid Rose**.

"Oh, Celeste," Morgan said aloud. She was sorry she hadn't pushed the old woman for answers. "Who is Euclid Rose?"

"Rhonda really out did herself," Maurice said. Morgan handed him a hand-blown crystal champagne flute filled with an expensive sparkling wine from one of Rhonda's favorite California vineyards. She had insisted on having it for Imani's baptism reception and stated there would be nothing but the best for her goddaughter's special day. Morgan had wasted her breath reminding Rhonda Imani preferred her formula to the $250 bottle of bubbly. Rhonda had clicked the "Submit Order" button for her online purchase of a case and said, "Part of my job as godmother will be to show her the finer things in life. I might as well start now."

Maurice had slipped away from the celebration for a moment. Morgan found him on one of the three garden terraces surrounding the second floor of Rhonda's home. Actually, it had taken Morgan twenty minutes to find him. Rhonda's 4,000 square foot tri-level home sat on three and a half acres of the most beautiful land in Louisiana, just outside of New Orleans. Morgan had spent many an enjoyable afternoon on this terrace. They all paled in comparison to this day.

"Rhonda Lattier spares no expense when it comes to giving parties and she has informed me she plans on sparing none when it comes to her goddaughter either. She's already building an investment portfolio and has established a trust fund to pay for Imani's college education. Complete with a year in Europe immediately following high school, of course." Morgan said. She smiled thinking about her friend's extravagant generosity. "Now I have to spend the next eighteen years trying to keep her from spoiling Imani rotten."

"I'd wish you luck with that if I thought it would do you any good." Maurice laughed and sipped from his glass of champagne. "You've done well yourself, counselor."

Maurice's last comment earned him a quick kiss and one of Morgan's smiles that always made him think that somewhere at some time he must have gained favor with the gods.

"Thanks. I wish you didn't have to leave in the morning." Morgan sat down next to him on one of two wicker love seats.

"I wish you didn't have house guests tonight." Maurice gave her a look that said he wished fifty people weren't less than five yards away from them right now.

"How about I pick you up and take you to the airport?" Morgan asked. "Carl and Irene will be with Imani."

A smile spread over Maurice's face. "How about you come early?" "Yeah." Morgan took a slow sip from her champagne flute. "Really early."

"Flowers again? You better go on and marry The Doctor before he spends all his money sending you flowers." Rhonda kicked off her suede, burnt orange pumps that perfectly matched her burnt orange pantsuit. She took a bite of her tuna salad sandwich. This was as close to lunch as either of them would get today. They would be in court all afternoon. The beautiful bouquet of tiger lilies, roses, and gardenias filled the office with a delicate, sweet fragrance.

"It's his way of keeping in touch. We haven't been able to spend much time together in the last month. He's in the midst of the final interview process for the director position. I haven't had a minute to catch my breath since I was named second chair on the Hudson and Barnes case." Morgan sipped some sparkling mineral water and took a forkful of her Caesar salad. "Imani was asleep when I came home last night. It was the first night since she's been home that I didn't get to rock her to sleep." Tears welled slightly in the corners of Morgan's eyes.

"I'm sure she thought about you right before she dozed off, sweetie. Don't worry." Rhonda hoped her statement would lift Morgan's spirits. "So, how much longer before we close this thing with Hudson and Barnes? I have other clients who are paying dearly for my attention."

"This afternoon ought to do it." Morgan confidently passed Rhonda a folder with the latest draft of the contract. She was lead counsel on the merger of two Houston based oil companies and was already being praised for the exceptional job she was doing on the case.

"Good. Let me visit the ladies room and then I will meet you at the car. You drive." Rhonda wiped her mouth and slipped back into her shoes.

Walking to the car, Rhonda and Morgan talked in the tones attorneys often used when discussing strategies. The conversation ended when Rhonda screamed. Morgan dropped her brief case at her feet as she started to move closer to her car.

"Don't go any closer," Rhonda said. She pulled out her cell phone to call the police with one hand and grabbed Morgan's arm with the other.

"Oh, my God," Morgan gasped. Her car windows had been smashed, shattered glass covered the ground. The hood, roof, and sides had been bashed in with what must have been a very heavy object. Morgan turned to Rhonda; her calm exterior belied the terror slowly creeping up her spine. "Guess you *will* have to drive."

Rhonda dropped Morgan off at home, despite her offer she and Imani spend the night with her. It was after eight o'clock in the evening. Morgan had filed a police report and given a statement to the building's chief security officer after returning to the office from the courthouse. She and Rhonda had closed the case. All that was left to do was file the appropriate paperwork to the court and submit the billing. Rhonda agreed to handle everything first thing in the morning, so Morgan could follow up with the police about the vandalism to her car. After a closer look at the car, a young officer, with hair the color of boiled lobster and what could easily have been a million freckles sprinkled over his face, found a note in the car's glove compartment. The note, printed in bold, black block letters on a crumpled piece of notebook paper stated the message clearly: **STOP LOOKING.**

Morgan decided not to call and mention any of this to Maurice. He had enough on his mind. She spoke briefly with Imani's nanny, Stephanie Arceneaux. Morgan was happy Maurice had recommended the pediatric nurse as a nanny for Imani. Imani had suffered her first asthma attack several weeks ago, and Morgan hated to think what might have happened if Stephanie hadn't been present. Morgan had come to rely on Stephanie's expertise and Imani adored her.

"Miss Franklin. I hope you don't mind," Stephanie said while she put on her sweater. "I had the urge to cook today, so I fixed some crab cakes, yams, and greens. Rice and black eyed peas are in there too. And I brought you a slice or two of my custard pie. It's detrimental to my hips to keep it at home any longer."

Morgan smiled. She knew Stephanie was mothering her and tonight it was particularly welcomed. "Thank you, Mrs. Arceneaux."

"You're welcome. You have yourself a pleasant evening." Stephanie closed the door behind her. Morgan walked to the nursery to peek in on Imani. To her surprise, Imani was sitting up in her crib as if she had been waiting on Morgan.

"Hi there, pretty girl," Morgan cooed. She kissed her and reveled in the fact Imani kissed her back. "How is my baby girl? I missed you. You're Auntie Morgan had quite a day, but it's okay now." Morgan lifted Imani from the crib and sat with her by the window in the huge mahogany rocker Maurice had given them as a baptism gift. Soon Imani was fast asleep.

Morgan was still too wound up to sleep. She made a cup of chamomile tea to go with a slice of Stephanie's custard pie and went into her home office to look through the mail that had been piling up on her desk over the last week. She had just started to flip through a month-old *Essence* magazine when the telephone rang.

"Lisa, I found Euclid Rose." C. J. skipped his usual, "What's up, sis?" greeting; his tone was urgent.

"Who is she? Another one of Alexander Franklin's lovers or do I have another sister?" Morgan was not sure how much more she would be able to handle in one day.

"Neither. It's a cemetery." "Did you say a cemetery?"

"It's in a little place right outside L'Ouverture called Hammond Bluff. I remember riding out there with Daddy on deliveries when I was little. I got to St. Vincent this afternoon. I'm going to ride out there in the morning."

"Do you think Alexander Franklin is dead, C. J.? I always imagined he was alive somewhere," It was the first time she considered the fact she might be chasing a ghost.

"I'll know tomorrow. Are you all right?"

"Something happened today." The thought of it caused Morgan's stomach to tighten. "My car was vandalized. Whoever did it, wants me to stop looking. At least that's what the note said."

"What?!" C. J. exclaimed. His voice was filled with concern. He paused and took a quick sip of a forgotten cup of coffee before speaking again. "I know you well enough to know that asking you to stop would be a waste of breath. I also know this is bigger than either of us imagined and is obviously dangerous. Lisa, you have to be careful."

"I know." It seemed the violence surrounding Alexander Franklin was moving closer, maybe too close. "The police dusted for finger prints. They assigned a detective to the case, a woman named Kim Davis. She said she would call me tomorrow."

"Lisa, you shouldn't be alone. Why don't you go to Rhonda's or at least take Imani and check into a hotel? Can you stay at home tomorrow?"

"I could do all those things, but I won't. I will not hide from cowards, C. J. I'll be fine and please don't mention any of this to Carl and Irene. I don't want them to worry."

"No need. I'll be worrying enough for all of us." C. J. was glad she could not see the somber expression spreading over his face. "Try and get some sleep. I'll call you after my visit to Euclid Rose."

Morgan hung up the phone and prayed silently. As she reached to turn off the desk light, she eyed the small purplish stone Celeste had given her that day in the café. She had placed it on the corner of her desk. It seemed to glow in the darkened room.

CHAPTER TWENTY-SEVEN

The lamp fell to the floor and barely made a sound on the thick, soft carpet. Marie thrashed about on the sweat-soaked linens of her queen-sized bed, her arm swung across the nightstand. The impact of the lamp's porcelain base on her forearm woke her from her nightmare. In the darkened room, she sat up in the bed. Her gown, drenched with sweat, clung to her body. Her throat felt dry and raw. The screams she thought had been a part of the dream had been real. She swung her legs from the bed and reached for the lamp on the floor near the bed. Her breathing came in quick gasps. She struggled to push air in and out of her lungs. It took a while for them to settle back into a recognizable rhythm. She returned the lamp to the nightstand, pulled the delicate woven tassel, and brought the lamp's soft light into the dark room. Marie wiped tears from her face and ran her shaking hands through her damp, soft curls now plastered to her forehead. She pulled the wet satin nightgown over her head, let it drop to the floor, and stood on wobbly legs. Marie's nose wrinkled involuntarily at the scent of her bitter perspiration in the gown. This is what hatred must smell like, she thought. Her

dark, elongated shadow cast itself against the pale yellow walls
as if it were mocking her.

"Damn you, Alex. Damn you," Marie cursed. She
walked nude to her shower. She turned on the cold nozzle and
adjusted the showerheads to their highest intensity level. The
force of the cold water pounded her body. Even though she was
now awake, the dream seemed to remain just behind her eyes.
She allowed the water to cascade over her head as the dream and
its effect on her swirled with the water at her feet before going
down the drain.

She could never remember the dreams once she woke,
but she knew they had to do with Alex. She could *feel* him in the
dreams. Lisa and all her damn questions were to blame, she
thought as goose bumps rose on her arms. They started about a
month after the dinner at Raymond's house; the night Lisa had
tried to get her to talk about Alex.

They hadn't spoken about it again or much of anything
else over the last several months. She'd returned her invitation to
Imani's baptism with her response card marked *"Unable to
attend"* and had not called Lisa even after she received a
program from the baptism and naming ceremony with pictures of
her and the baby enclosed. She had accepted the department
chair position she had long coveted and had allowed her new
responsibilities to fill her schedule. Hoping to avoid another

argument with Raymond, she hadn't taken a call from him for weeks and she had given her secretary strict instructions to take messages and not to send his calls through to her office. She was grateful he hadn't forced the issue by coming to the house or campus.

Marie wrapped her shivering body in a huge, plush bath towel and looked at herself in the lighted mirror above the sink. She blinked. Lisa's face seemed to appear in the mirror and blocked the reflection of her own face. "What the hell do you want?" she asked Lisa's face as it faded and left her looking into her own red-rimmed eyes. Marie hurled a glass tumbler at the mirror shattering it. Shards of glass crashed into the sink, against the wall, and onto the floor. "What do you want?"

CHAPTER TWENTY-EIGHT

Morgan could not keep the look of satisfaction off her face as she waited for her office door to open. Her secretary had just buzzed her to let her know Maurice was waiting to see her. Morgan rushed to the door to be closer. When he closed the door behind him, she greeted him with a kiss that showed him how glad she was to be in his arms. His lips responded with a similar message.

"Now, let me tell you how upset I am with you," Maurice said. His arm was around her as they sat on the navy leather sofa in her office. "Rhonda called me this morning to tell me you had some 'car trouble' yesterday." He couldn't get their *conversation out of his head.*

"This stuff with Morgan and her family is out of control." Rhonda had found herself pacing her kitchen floor as she talked. A clear sign her nerves were now involved. "Somebody vandalized her car yesterday and left some note about her backing off."

"What! Rhonda is she hurt?" For a moment it had seemed as if Maurice's heart had stopped. "Rhonda is she, all right?"

"Thank God, she wasn't hurt," Rhonda had taken a deep breath. "She's stubborn as a mule, but she and Imani are all right. I'm scared for her, Maurice. Please talk to her."

"What the hell is going on?" Maurice had known Rhonda didn't have any more answers to that question than he did.

"I don't know, Doc. But whatever it is, it's dangerous."

"Please explain why you didn't call me?" Maurice had cleared the conversation from his head for the moment.

"Maurice, you have a lot going on right now. I didn't want to be a distraction." Morgan looked into his eyes. She relaxed as she saw the anger being replaced by concern.

"As smart as you are, attorney Franklin, somehow you missed it." Maurice held her hands in his. "I am in love with you. You and Imani are the two most important people in my life right now. You both come first. Do you understand me now?"

"I think you have made yourself very clear, Dr. LaShurr." Morgan's eyes filled with tears. "And for the record; I'm in love with you too."

"You don't know how happy I am to hear you say that." Maurice gently kissed her tears away and released the breath he didn't realize he had been holding. "Now, what did the police say?"

"Detective Davis called while I was in a meeting. I haven't had a chance to return her call." Morgan wiped her face with the handkerchief he handed her.

"This has to do with the murders of your brother and that deputy sheriff who was a friend of yours, doesn't it?" Maurice asked. Morgan nodded. "So, I guess it wouldn't do any good to ask you to leave whatever it is the hell alone, would it?"

Morgan shook her head no. Maurice sighed and held her close.

"Carl Jr.?" The question came from between full lips the color of deep purple ripe plums.

"Yes ma'am, Miss Mavis. It's me." C. J. walked toward the worn, red Formica counter top and took a seat on the chrome and black vinyl stool. He spun around and smiled.

"You better hope Reenie don't come through that door and see you spinning 'round like that." Mavis winked. Her inch-long false eyelashes almost covered the smooth wrinkles beneath her eyes. She placed a large red mug in front of him and poured steaming black coffee to the rim.

Mavis Freed was all of seventy years old but still strutted around the café like the teenage girl she had been when her mother ran the place. The sign outside the door, in blinking red neon lights whether it was day or night, read *Café Free*. The "d" in Freed had blown out before C. J. was born and one day when one of the customers commented on how he liked coming into a place where a colored man was "free," Mavis' mother had decided not to replace the "d."

"I was so very sorry to hear about Winston. He was the sweetest lil' ole thing. Every time I make up some pralines, I think about him. He did love my pralines. Never saw a boy could eat that many pralines without his belly aching. I been praying for your mama and daddy and lighting a candle for them every day since I heard." Mavis lifted the clear plastic top off the pie plate that sat at the end of the counter and eased a large slice of sweet potato pie onto a bright red saucer. She slid the saucer down the countertop toward C. J. "Know they hearts is broke in two. Lord knows you ain't supposed to be burying your child."

"I know they'd appreciate that. They have good days and bad ones." C. J. opened two pink and white packets of C & H Sugar and watched the crystals dissolve into the hot, dark liquid before he took a bite of the pie.

"Carl and Irene strong. They'll come through this, Lord willin'." Mavis wiped what must have been an imaginary spot on the glistening counter top. "What you doin' way out here? I know you ain't come all the way to Hammond Bluff for my pie, good as it is."

"No, ma'am, but it sure makes the trip worth it." C. J. took another bite. "I'm looking for a cemetery named Euclid Rose. My map has it right off Johnson Road, but I've been up and down Johnson three times and can't seem to find it."

"Johnson Road is the closest thing you can put on a map. All them maps is wrong. You'll never find Euclid Rose from no map." Mavis took a small notepad from the pocket of her black apron with Café Free written across her belly in bright red and pulled a pencil from behind her ear. "Johnson Road wasn't even there when the slaves built that place."

"Slaves?" C. J. watched as Mavis drew a map on her pad.

"Hammond Bluff's white and Black folks didn't get along as well as the ones over in L'Ouverture. These white folks out here wasn't fancy Frenchmen looking to take care of their brown women and café au lait babies. These was crackers come down from Alabama, Mississippi, and Arkansas. Most of 'em running from the law and the rest hopin' Jesus would save they evil asses from a hell they surely deserved. They worked

Black folks until they dropped dead and then didn't even want to give them six feet a dirt as a resting place." Mavis poured herself some coffee and continued. "My grandmamma said before the slaves cleared the land for Euclid Rose and started to burying they own out there, these white folks would pile bodies up in somebody's springhouse until they got five or six of 'em and then take them out past the old Guthrie place, dig a hole, throw 'em in, and set the bunch on fire."

"Damn," C. J. muttered and shuddered at the visual as Mavis finished her map. He'd never heard this bit of history before and made a mental note to do some research on Hammond Bluff once he brought some closure to the deaths of his brother and Whitey. "You workin' on a story or something for your New York paper? We all proud of you around here, Junior." Mavis pointed to a framed, yellowed newspaper article behind her head. It was an article and a picture of a smiling C. J. at age twelve just having won first place in an essay contest. She slid the note pad with the map across the counter to him. "Something like that." C. J. looked at the map, and slipped the piece of paper into his pocket. He placed $20 on the counter and reached across it to give Mavis a kiss on her smooth, barely wrinkled cheek. "Thanks, Miss Mavis. You're the best."

"I always have been. Junior, you be careful now," she called after him. "Hope that boy got enough daylight left to find his way out from back there." Mavis sipped her coffee in the quiet of the café as she watched C. J. steer his car back onto the road in the direction of Euclid Rose.

C. J. entered the office of Mrs. Jewel Langston. She had been Euclid Rose's administrator and caretaker for the past thirty-five years. She was what one would call a handsome woman and had a forehead most would consider too broad for a woman of her petite stature. She greeted him and invited C. J. to sit In the chair opposite her desk.

"How may I help you, Mr. Banks?"

"Do you have an Alexander Franklin buried here at Euclid Rose?" "May I inquire why you're asking, Mr. Banks?"

"Yes, ma'am. I'm an investigative journalist working on a story and a source led me here," C. J. reached into his satchel and showed her his press credentials.

"Thank you, Mr. Banks. You understand I can't divulge our decedents' information to anyone without ensuring a request is legitimate."

"Of course, Mrs. Langston."

Mrs. Langston stood and walked toward a large file cabinet in the corner of her office. She opened the middle drawer. C. J. watched her from his seat as she flipped through files; something she must've done thousands of times before.

"Here we are." She clicked her tongue in a sound that indicated she was pleased with her discovery and removed her glasses. She handed C. J. the folder as she took her seat. He scanned Alexander Franklin's burial paperwork and looked up only long enough not to appear rude. The space between his eyebrows wrinkled as he tried to make out the signature scrawled across the bottom of the form.

"Mrs. Langston, can you make out this signature?" C. J. slid the paper across the desk.

"Don't need to," she said barely glancing at the paper before responding. "I remember him like it was yesterday. His name is Mr. La Fontaine. Claude La Fontaine. Few come to bury their loved ones in such a remote place. He explained Mr. Franklin had been a loyal *employee* with no family and it was the least he could do. I told him loyalty was certainly a treasure when found. Would you like copies, Mr. Banks?" she asked already taking the folder from his hand and moving toward the copier.

C. J. nodded his head in reply as his mind raced and asked, "Are you certain it was Claude La Fontaine?"

"Yes, sir." Mrs. Langston handed C. J. the copies in a new folder she pulled from a shelf over the copier. "Claude La Fontaine."

He thanked her again for her time and rushed to his rental car. As C. J was about to start the car, his cell phone rang. It was his friend, federal agent, Jarvis Dalton.

"Hey, Jarvis. What's up man?"

"Remember that Bingo character you asked me to look into? My contact in L'Ouverture informed me that he got himself arrested around 2:30 a.m. in La Fitte for manslaughter. He tried to steal a car and the owner of the car saw him and tried to stop him. During the scuffle, he shot the guy and killed him. A neighbor saw the two men fighting and called the police. Fortunately, a squad car was nearby and caught him before he could get away."

"That's an interesting story, Jarvis. But why are you telling me this?"

"Seems that when the police brought Bingo in, he offered them information on some murders in St. Vincent If they cut him a deal."

"Okay, now you have my attention. What murders?"
"Your brother and Whitey Peters."

"What did you just say?" C. J. tightly grabbed the steering wheel with his free hand. "Yes. He claims he was hired to kill them." Jarvis told C. J. Bingo's murder-for-hire story. C. J. was rendered speechless. "C. J.? Are you still with me?"

C. J. took a few calming breaths to get himself together and said, "Jarvis, man. Please tell me he's lying."

"I wish I was bro. But, Bingo knows too many details about the murders that only the killer would know."

"Thanks, Jarvis. I owe you," C. J. disconnected the call. He quickly dialed Lisa's number.

He cursed when the call went immediately to voice mail. He started the car and sped along the road that took him off the grounds of Euclid Rose back toward the highway. Lisa was in danger. More danger than he had imagined.

CHAPTER TWENTY-NINE

Pierre La Fontaine, Sr. had been the only one of the six children Celeste Du Marnier bore to live to adulthood. He had also been the only one to take the café au lait complexion of his Creole father, Armande La Fontaine. Armande had been a kind man. Unfortunately, he had been a married man. He insisted. Pierre be educated in Europe and once he went away, Celeste left New Orleans and returned home to L'Ouverture. The beautiful swamp land just outside of St. Vincent, where her grandparents had raised her after her parents had been viciously beaten to death by drunken klansmen looking for sport on a hot and muggy Saturday night, brought her comfort. Her lonely spirit found healing in its safety.

Celeste soon found joy in her quiet life. That joy would be robbed from her again, when Pierre returned from Europe with his high-minded ideas. He had been treated as well as any white man while in Europe and explained to his mother he could not go back to being a colored citizen in New Orleans. While Pierre had changed, New Orleans had not. His plans for success were often stymied by the color of his skin. His illegitimate birth kept him from sharing in the estate of his father. Celeste had hoped marriage and children would erase his bitterness; but as his children grew, the bitterness and anger grew like a malignant tumor.

Alexander Franklin had not been a white man after all. His father, Pierre Sr., and mother, Elise, were Creole. While the Spanish and French blood that raced through his father's veins had done well to hide the blood of his African ancestry in skin the color of warm milk, his mother's skin reminded all who looked upon her beauty of a lightly toasted croissant. Alexander Franklin was the oldest son of parents who lived a very privileged life in the Colored society of Louisiana. His father always resented the second-class status afforded to the "well-to-do" Creole community and felt his sons might do better if no one knew of their mixed heritage. There certainly was no evidence of African ancestry in their creamy, white skin and their gray-colored eyes. Their hair had only the slightest wave.

Pierre Sr. moved his family to Connecticut where they were sometimes mistaken for Italian, other times Jewish. When they were old enough, he placed them in the finest boarding schools where they were accepted and admired among their peers. Elise didn't share her husband's disdain for her African lineage and blood. Her father had been the product of the too often familiar liaison between a privileged white man and a Black woman. Elise had failed in her attempts to have her sons embrace their African ancestors. Their father's approval meant too much to them and to receive it, they were willing to deny the part of themselves that he despised.

It had broken Elise's heart to go along with her husband's ruse. She'd been grateful for the solace she'd found over the years in her friendship with her mother-in-law, Celeste. Her periodic trips to visit Celeste's beloved swamp served as a much-needed balm for a soul that had been weighed down with the lies she lived in Connecticut. Pierre, Sr. encouraged her to visit Celeste, noting how much happier she was upon her return home. Over cups of chamomile tea or bowls of spicy gumbo, Celeste and Elise built a loving bond that helped take away their shared anger, pain, and regret over Pierre Sr.'s choices.

Elise's position in the family was often relegated to nanny when her relationship with her sons came into question. Pierre's threats that he would take the boys away from her entirely left her no choice. The lie was a simple one: his wife had died giving birth to their youngest son. Alexander and his brother became the beloved children of a devoted father and widower. As the boys grew, Alexander's younger brother found their father's idea easy to accept. He had always been amused by how easy it was to pass and took pleasure in the privileges bestowed upon him by being white. White people wanted to believe he was white. So, he let them.

Alexander's brother married a very wealthy, white socialite and eased comfortably into her world. Alexander had married the beautiful, young daughter of a Connecticut bank owner. Together, they were invited into the finest homes and their pictures often appeared in the society pages. While Alexander enjoyed the lifestyle his father had designed, he enjoyed even more the affections he found in the arms of the many women of a darker hue. His wife, soon tired of his affairs and fearing scandal, got a quiet divorce and moved to Europe. Pierre Sr. had been furious with his son's indiscriminate behavior and the loss of Alexander's social status following the divorce.

Alexander estranged himself from his family after a horrible fight with his father. Breaking his mother's heart again, he moved to New York. It was there that his academic and social education paid off. It was so easy to fool the countless white men and women who could not wait to invite him for a weekend at an exclusive lodge or give him access to their villas and yachts. Alexander, fueled by wanting to prove he did not need the protection or assistance his father's wealth afforded him, worked hard. In a matter of several years, he made his fortune in the financial world and became much richer and more successful than even his father.

But Louisiana was in his blood. It seemed to call to him from the cold, industrial environment of New York City. He loved the sights and smells, the food, and women of Louisiana and decided he had enough money to live in both the world his father had wanted for him and the one he truly desired. He traveled easily between his life in New York City and the one he created for himself in the cities and countryside of his birth state. His father had been right about one thing: being white got him things being colored never could. There was no doubt Alexander enjoyed the finer things in life. He soon grew accustomed to summers in the south of France, suits designed by Italy's most talented designers, and weekends spent on the beaches of Brazil. In New York City, he made a new life for himself.

He set his eyes on the daughter of one of the world's wealthiest diamond importers. Six months after an enchanted courtship, they were married. They attended all the right social functions together, posed for the society pages, and hosted large dinner parties for New York City's elite in their upper West Side apartment, a wedding gift from his new father-in-law. In the summer, they entertained at their home on Long Island often hosting the families that made the world turn.

His wife knowingly and graciously looked the other way when Alexander's eyes wandered. Her only request was he never be seen in the company of any of the Colored women he seemed to enjoy so much. Theirs was a marriage of mutual respect, convenience, and comfort. A life that worked well for both of them and gave each of them what they wanted. He had access to a world that only existed in the dreams of those of his *true* race; she had a handsome and rich husband her parents adored and made her the envy of every woman who saw them together. In a way, he did love her and had felt true sorrow when she died from a brain aneurysm only three years after they were married.

Once again, he had to make a new life for himself. Alexander became the grieving widower who was too devastated by the death of his beloved wife to ever think of marrying again. Instead he became the consummate playboy who enjoyed the charms of New York's richest socialites. On the rare evenings he spent alone at home, he enjoyed listening to his rare jazz collection and drinking cognac. It was on these nights he spent time thinking about his ability to recreate himself over and over. His first creation had been the name Alexander Franklin. He had found the name while reading the obituaries shortly after arriving in New York. If his father did not want anything to do with him, he would have nothing to do with his father. He'd found great pleasure in abandoning the name that had brought his father such pride: Pierre La Fontaine II.

CHAPTER THIRTY

Morgan had a bad feeling even before she parked the rental car in front of the abandoned hunting lodge. All day, the events of the past several months ran through her mind like scenes from a horror film: Winston's powdered, death-mask face haunted her from his grave; Marie's voice uttering the words "heart attack" as if they were an incantation to ward off evil; the primal screams of Whitey's fiancée as she told Morgan Whitey was dead; and Madame Celeste's whispered warning that she was close. Why did C. J. want to meet her way out here? Was there something so wrong he did not even want Carl and Irene to be around when he told her? Were her answers here? Had he found Alexander Franklin? She looked at the small piece of paper in her hand and read the message again. She had it right. This was the place. She did not see another car. Morgan hoped C. J. would arrive soon. It was getting dark and she certainly wanted to be as far away from this place before nightfall as possible.

Morgan looked back over her shoulder as she went up the creaking steps to the cabin. She was sure she could hear animals she prayed would remain unseen scurrying underneath the rotted wood of the front porch. Morgan pushed open the door, which hung off its hinges and called out to C. J. Maybe he had parked around back and was already inside waiting for her. She was almost to the middle of the room, when she heard footsteps behind her and heard the door bang shut. "C. J., why did?" Morgan questioned and turned around quickly. Her words hung in the dusty air as her eyes adjusted to the growing shadows. It was not C. J. She could feel that. The bright light of what must have been a very large flashlight blinded her, but she recognized the voice at once.

"Why the hell couldn't you just stay in N'Orleans and leave us alone down here?" The words rushed out in anger. "You and all your damn questions." The light left her face and illuminated the room as it was placed on the splintered mantel of a crumbling stone fireplace. The eyes staring back at her were familiar although distorted with hatred. The gun pointed at her confirmed just how much.

"I worked too damn hard for you to come and mess things up for me, girl. I am too close to lose it all." Claude La Fontaine moved closer. He frowned and looked into her gray eyes. Of all the things they held, none of them was fear. He had counted on her being afraid. "You're worse than Winston or Whitey. A damn lot smarter too. Time for us to get rid of you too."

"What are you going to say happened to me, sheriff? You've already used heart attack and no one will believe another 'suicide.' Maybe a hunting accident?" Morgan sneered. Her words taunted him.

"No." Claude grew angry at her audacity. "You just ran off. Probably because of the money you embezzled from your law firm. Or maybe the pressure of raising a sick baby was just too much for you? Or at least that's what it will look like when I'm finished." He laughed.

"C. J. is on his way here, right now." Morgan hoped she sounded surer than she felt. "You will not get away with this."

"Be sure to give Ms. Franklin the message. I have the information she has been looking for. I'll meet her at the lodge out past the old DuBose place on Grandine Road," he spat into a far corner. Had Sheriff La Fontaine not been standing in front of her, she would have sworn she was listening to C. J. It would have been even easier to fool her secretary. "We'll be so far gone by then it won't matter what people believe. No one will ever find us." This time his statement sounded more like a question and there was no laughter.

"Will you at least tell me why?" The reality of the situation was all too evident now. "Why did you kill my brother? And Whitey?"

"Sadly, I didn't have the pleasure. Bingo killed those boys and at a bargain price." Morgan's mind flashed back to the mugshot of Dwayne "Bingo" Gibbins that C. J. had shown her. Here was another piece of the puzzle. She struggled to put the rest in place. Claude's voice brought her back to the moment.

"Don't you want to know about your other sister, Andrea? Or, what about Alex?"

"You mean Alexander Franklin?" Morgan tried to make sense of it all and struggled to remain calm. "So, he's dead."

"Guess you not as smart as I thought. No, Alexander Franklin is not dead because he does not exist. But Pierre La Fontaine The Second sure as hell is. Our daddy loved calling him by his entire name. He was so damn proud of my big brother. Never noticed a damn thing I ever did. Nothing I did was ever good enough for the old man. When Pierre left town for good, I just knew my daddy would love me the way he'd always loved him. No matter how much Pierre fucked up, he was always Daddy's favorite." Claude moved so close to Morgan she could smell the stale cigarettes and whiskey on his breath. "Pierre *became* Alexander Franklin when he moved to New York City. Changing names seems to run in this family, *Lisa*. He risked everything running around with them nigger *bitches*." A snarl crossed Claude's face when he said the word "bitches." "Sooner or later people would find out we weren't who we appeared to be and then everything would be lost. Everything my daddy had worked for. Hell, everything I'd worked for. Do you know what they did to Colored men for passing? That's right, Lisa. The La Fontaines were Colored. Creole to be exact, but that never mattered to the blue bloods. Our daddy worked hard. Made a fortune but it was a *Colored* fortune. Never would be enough for them. He wanted more for his sons, Pierre and me. We got more too, just like he said we would. Pierre was just greedy. He wanted to have it both ways. I tried to warn him, but he couldn't stay away from his nigger women. I had to stop him before he ruined it for me. I begged him to be careful. He laughed in my face and called me a coward. We owed our daddy. Pierre never understood that. I couldn't let him ruin all our daddy had worked for. There was no other way but to kill him. Can't believe it's been almost ten years. Made it look like one of them nigger women up in Harlem cut him up. Cost me a lot to keep it out the papers. Especially, with Alexander Franklin being such a success and all up there. White folks were glad to hush it up though. Wouldn't look right for one of their own to be murdered like that. Hell, one of Alex's friends used his private jet to fly his body outta there. Didn't want to cause 'any embarrassment,' he said," Claude shouted. He spat at the ground near Morgan's feet.

Morgan's stomach began to churn violently as the confused and hazy picture Claude La Fontaine painted came into focus. "Seems like all your daddy's work came to no good after all. You're no more than a common thug. Do you think becoming a murderer would make your daddy proud of you, Claude?"

"You just watch your mouth. Hell, guess you should be calling me *Uncle* Claude." His deranged laughter echoed off the cabin's stone walls. "That's why they can't find you, Lisa. I'm not losing everything. Not this time. No, this time I'm walking away with what I deserve."

"You're sick," Morgan sneered. He pressed the gun against her chest. She could feel the cold steel through her cashmere sweater. She heard a car door slam shut and the sound of shoes running across the porch. The door opened slowly. The steps were too light to be C. J.'s. Morgan's head began to swim as a faint, familiar fragrance reached her.

"Damn it, Claude! This was supposed to be over by the time I arrived." The anger in the whispered words chilled the room.

"Mama?" Morgan gasped; shock took her breath and much of her voice away.

"Shut up. Don't you ever call me that again," Marie hissed. "Claude finish this. We have a plane to catch."

"I thought you might want to do this one yourself." Claude lowered the gun and remembered how Marie had insisted on killing Andrea. Eric had just been a poor boy in the way.

"Don't be ridiculous." Marie turned away from Morgan's stare. "Goddamn it! Kill her now, Claude."

Claude raised the gun again. Morgan clinched her teeth like that would somehow give her the strength not to beg for her life. All she could think about was Imani and how she had to get back to her. No matter what.

"Why?" Morgan managed in a voice she did not recognize as her own.

"Why?" Marie mimicked Lisa. She turned to face her and stared into Morgan's eyes. The eyes that reminded her of the life she had lost. Alex's eyes.

"Because he owed me. He owed me all of it. He promised me a life. He was my way out of L'Ouverture and away from the stink and dirt-poor poverty of St. Vincent. Alex and I were in love and looking white was the only thing either of us needed in order to have the life we wanted; the life we deserved. He had all the others fooled. The first time I saw him, I *knew*. We would laugh about how we fooled them all. How we could move into their world and take it over if we wanted. Then I found out I was pregnant. I knew the baby was Alex's. Russell was away in Switzerland at the time. I thanked God it wasn't his.

He was so happy when I started to show. He couldn't stop talking about how happy I'd made him.

Russell was such a fool. So in love, he couldn't see that I despised him. Alex told me to stay here until he was able to relocate his business to France. I planned to leave Russell as soon as the baby was born. Alex and I would be married. We were going to live in France. I even started to study French. He promised to take me away from L'Ouverture. He would have married me too if it had not been for you. I took one look at you and knew no one would take you for a white baby. I cursed the day you were born. People went on and on about you and your beautiful skin. Your beloved Mama Essie thanked God you wouldn't have to suffer the way I had, always wanting to be white just because I looked white. Alex was furious. How would we ever explain you? I begged my mother to keep you, but she said you were my responsibility. It was torture looking at you. I hated you every time I looked in your face," Marie declared and slowly closed the space between them. Morgan could feel the rage emanate from Marie's body. She carefully inched away from her and moved farther into the cabin.

"Russell begged me not to leave him. He said it didn't matter you weren't his. You were mine and that made him love you. Every time I looked into your eyes, I saw Alex looking back at me. I wanted you dead from the moment you took your first breath. Dead like every dream I ever had. Every day you reminded me of what I had lost. I read about Alex building a fortune for himself and hated you even more. We were to share that fortune, not those stupid little rich white bitches he loved to show off to the press.

After your grandmother Elise died, I received a letter from Baton Rouge. I'd heard Alex had purchased an old plantation there and was renovating it as a hotel and spa. I thought the letter was from him. After all those years, there was a part of me that still believed he would come back for me. The letter turned out to be from Claude. He needed me to help him get what he thought should have been his. After all, he'd been the one who'd lived the life his father always wanted for his sons. Pierre La Fontaine, Sr. had left a fortune. I'd be generously compensated for my assistance, of course. There was just one problem. Your *grandfather* died and left everything in the hands of your grandmother. *Elise* left Pierre Sr.'s entire fortune to your father and his heirs in *her* will." Marie glared at Morgan.

Marie's eyes brought to mind the eyes of a dead deer Morgan had seen on the side of the road once in St. Vincent. "You will never get away with this," Morgan snapped. Her anger overriding the fear she felt knotted in the pit of her stomach.

"We already have. Once Alex and his heirs are all dead, the fortune would go to Pierre Sr.'s second son, Claude La

Fontaine. The only problem was the codicil to their mother's will made it very clear that her two sons, Pierre and Claude were not white. Claude couldn't claim his fortune without relinquishing his status in the white world. Something he wasn't willing to do. We had to find another option and we did," Marie said with a pleased look on her face. "My cruise to the Greek Isles wasn't all pleasure. There is always an abundance of men on cruise ships who are easily enticed and willing to do anything; even pose as someone else for the right amount of money. I found a willing fool and provided him with a monetary incentive and back story. And, voilà— Claude La Fontaine, the last living relative of Elise La Fontaine lives in Greece. One call to the new estate attorney I bought and the money will be transferred to a bank in Mykonos this time tomorrow. The Claude imposter will be killed shortly after the money is transferred leaving no trace of subterfuge back to me or the real Claude La Fontaine. You're the last one, Lisa."

"Marie, this little history lesson is interesting, but we have a plane to catch," Claude grumbled and looked between his co-conspirator and niece.

"What do you mean the last one? Have you forgotten about Mary Joyce and her sons or William and Imani? There's a long list of La Fontaines between you both and that money." Morgan's voice echoed off the walls of the cabin.

"Please." Marie sneered. "The rest of those people you love so much will all be dead before the wheels are up on our plane. Who will question the explosion of a propane tank in that trailer park where Mary Joyce and the boys are staying? And who knew how easy it is to pass as a mechanic with Chicago Public Schools and tamper with the brake line of a school bus filled with children? William will soon be dead just like his father."

"That one will make the news," Claude laughed. "You spread enough money around, anything is possible."

"Such a shame about Imani. Just when she seemed to be doing so well. Too bad you won't be around to sue the pharmacy for delivering contaminated medication to Stephanie in just about fifteen minutes," Marie said and closed the space between her and Morgan. "You just can't trust anyone these days."

"You can have the money. Just don't do this," Morgan pleaded. She gave into the fear that climbed up the base of her neck and willed herself not to faint.

"Do you know how much money Elise La Fontaine's estate is worth? Over $700 million dollars. It would have been so different, if Alex had just kept his promise and married me. I would have made him a good wife. Instead, I ended up with the pride of L'Ouverture's Rockhurst district, Dr. Russell Morgan. Once you were born, I had no choice but to resign myself to the life of L'Ouverture's Black aristocracy," Marie said through gritted teeth and seemed not to have heard Claude call her name as she moved closer to Morgan.

Tears slowly slid down Morgan's face as all of her questions had been answered. She looked at the woman she had known as her mother for twenty-eight years change into someone unrecognizable.

"Au revoir, niece," Claude said in a sickening sing-song voice as he raised the gun to Morgan's head.

"Hold it right there, Chief!" Arthur Lee DuPont's voice yelled as the rotted door fell in front of him. A rifle was aimed at Claude's head. Claude turned quickly. The bullet intended for Morgan grazed Arthur Lee's arm. The shot Arthur Lee fired into Claude's chest knocked him against the cabin's far wall. Morgan saw the gleam of steel and screamed as Marie removed a gun that was hidden in her coat pocket. A demented grin twisted her face into a grimace. She aimed at Morgan and fired. Morgan ducked and screamed as the bullet meant for her hit the wall just above her head. The second shot fired from Arthur Lee's rifle ripped through Marie's heart and instantly killed her. Her body hit the floor hard making a loud thwacking sound that rang throughout the cabin. The dark red, circular blood stain spread across the blonde mink fur of her coat. Morgan stood trembling; the sound of sirens and voices came through the shack's threadbare walls. Arthur Lee found an old blanket in the corner. He put the musty, heavy wool blanket around her shoulders and led her from the cabin.

CHAPTER THIRTY-ONE

A slow, steady rain fell the day Marie Esther Baptiste Morgan was buried in a vault in Euclid Rose cemetery. There were no flowers or eulogies or dirges to mark her passing. No members of her church, sorority, or colleagues from the university were in attendance. A minister hired by the mortuary said a silent prayer over the simple white casket before it was placed in the stone walls of the mausoleum. At last, she would be with her beloved Alex. An hour later, the body of Claude La Fontaine was cremated. Deputy Sheriff Arthur Lee DuPont looked out the window at the falling rain and packed up the things from his desk. He was amazed at how little he had accumulated after thirty years. He was glad. Arthur Lee did not want to take much away from this place. He was just glad to leave with his sanity. He smiled to himself as he picked up a framed picture of himself on his first day on the job.

Arthur Lee had been nineteen years old when he became a clerk in the L'Ouverture County Courthouse. He'd worked hard and hoped to one day become a deputy sheriff in St. Augustine. He'd almost given up after failing the written exam twice; but on the urging of his mother, he tried again. This time he'd passed with flying colors. Arthur Lee watched several men who joined the department after him move past him in the ranks. St. Augustine had a reputation for advancing the sons of its more prominent and influential white citizens. Arthur Lee did not have a father who was well connected or uncles who donated generously to the department's favorite charities. After six years in St. Augustine, he transferred to St. Vincent and was promoted to deputy sheriff in just six short months. The friends he'd made in St. Augustine made fun of him for having to work on what they called "the darker side" of L'Ouverture. Arthur Lee ignored them. His mother had raised him to be proud of an honest day's work and to treat people, even colored people, the way he wanted to be treated.

The morning Arthur Lee killed Claude La Fontaine and Marie Morgan had started off like any other day. He had joked around with a couple of the deputies about their losses in the previous night's poker game, had a cup of coffee and three glazed donuts, and began to skim the log book for anything that required his attention. He read a poorly written entry by Henry Prioleaux describing a complaint that Bingo Gibbins had been seen lurking around a trailer park in St. Vincent yesterday afternoon. he wasn't picked up because by the time a deputy was dispatched to the location, Bingo was long gone. Arthur Lee had caught him prowling around the university's parking lot two

months ago and had been about to bring him in when Dr.
Morgan had walked up on them and said Bingo was waiting to
talk to her class. Something to do with felons getting a second
chance.

Sheriff La Fontaine had called in sick and the
atmosphere in the station had been relaxed until Carl Banks, Jr.
rushed in demanding the whereabouts of the sheriff. Arthur Lee
had thought him crazy and hoped he would be able to get him to
leave without a physical confrontation; one he was certain to
lose. Arthur Lee could feel the eyes of Henry and the other
deputies on him as C. J. hurled around accusations about the
sheriff and Marie Morgan, shoved pictures and documents in his
face, and pleaded with him to do something. C. J. finally had
uttered the words that made Arthur Lee listen, *"Doc Morgan's
little girl is in trouble."* Arthur Lee had stopped thinking of Lisa
or Morgan as she called herself now and immediately saw her as
"Doc Morgan's little girl."

Doc Morgan. He had been the only one willing to help
when Arthur Lee's mother was dying of stomach cancer. The
"respectable" white doctors would not come to see about her
because the DuPonts were St. Augustine's embarrassment. The
words "white trash" were often whispered behind the backs of
him and his mother. Russell Morgan had come. He had come
and he had saved her life. Arthur Lee had always looked for

ways to repay the doctor without raising the suspicion of his friends and neighbors. He thought he had, by not treating Black folks as harshly as some of the other deputies and by secretly donating toys to the colored churches' toy drives at Christmas.

Arthur Lee had sprung into action after listening to C. J. and receiving a call from federal agent Jarvis Dalton. Moments later he received a fax from the La Fitte Police Department that further corroborated C. J.'s story. There was no time to waste and process what he just learned. Lives were at stake. He sent units to Mary Joyce's house. He had a deputy he trusted contact police in Chicago where Winston's son now lived.

He made the call to the sheriff's department in New Orleans himself requesting units be sent to Morgan's home to make sure her baby girl was safe. Now he had a real chance to repay Doc Morgan.

CHAPTER THIRTY-TWO

Pierre Sr. had cursed the African blood of his mother and it had cursed him back through his sons. They had both been a disappointment to him. While Pierre II always remained his favorite, he could not tolerate his penchant for black women and Claude's greed often made him stupid and careless.

Celeste was sorry he hadn't lived to see Morgan, his granddaughter. Of all of them, she would have made him the proudest. She reached for the worn scrap book on the table next to her candles that held Morgan's achievements. African blood had not stopped her success. Celeste carefully cut out the article in the *L'Ouverture Gazette* and glued it neatly on the last page. She'd read and re-read the article about the deaths of Marie Morgan, Claude La Fontaine, and how Carl Banks, Jr. had provided the answers to the questions for which Winston and Morgan had searched. He'd also uncovered their plot to steal monies from Elise La Fontaine's estate. Now it all rightfully belonged to Alex's remaining heirs.

Celeste knew Morgan would legally do what was necessary to make sure Mary Joyce's portion of the money wouldn't be wasted. Maybe she could set up one of those trust things. She'd overheard a couple discuss setting up one for their wayward daughter the last time she'd eaten in town. Celeste knew Morgan would make sure Winston's son was well taken care of and that Carl and Irene's life became easier as they lived out their last days together. They had all suffered because of the man who called himself Alexander Franklin. Now they would all benefit. Celeste thought of Marie and was sorry for the pain Morgan must feel, but she could not mourn Marie's death. She had always despised her and her mean and hateful ways. Her arrogance and greed had destroyed everything she touched. Marie had gotten what she deserved. She hoped the ancestors would not be too angry with her because the death of Claude La Fontaine, her grandson, left her with no sadness. His heart was always a dark one, she thought as she settled onto her rocker.

Celeste sipped a sweet mint tea as she lit a white candle in the quiet of her cabin. She smiled as she saw Morgan's face appear in the steam from her tea. She would be the one to know true joy. The handsome doctor was good for her. This would all one day be a scar that reminded her of a different time in her life. A scar that would bring her strength and increase her faith. Celeste slipped Elise's will into her last manila envelope and wrote Morgan's name on the front.

Elise had been like a daughter to Celeste and they had talked and visited one another throughout the years. Celeste remained Elise's greatest confidant. Although Alexander lived his life as a white man, he still loved and maintained contact with his mother. She knew of all his children, her grandchildren, and their mothers. Elise was never happy about how he chose to live his life, but he was her son and she loved him.

Fifteen years ago, Elise's will had been delivered to Celeste by courier after her death. Celeste had cried for days and refused to leave the swamp for months after opening the large envelope and discovering that her dear Elise had closed her eyes for the last time. Celeste had planted a pickerel bush on the first anniversary of Elise's death and always called her name each June when the deep blue flowers returned.

The morning sun shone brightly through the thickness of the willow trees. She wrote the name "Johari" on a single piece of pink stationary and put it in the envelope. Morgan and the doctor would have a son. They would name their son Johari which meant "something valuable." They would raise Johari to be a great man who understood true riches were in the love of accepting oneself. He would make them proud.

With this thought, she could almost hear the celebration of the ancestors in the familiar sounds of her swamp. Celeste would wait until the sun was high in the sky before she made her last trip to the post office.

EPILOGUE

Y ou ready?" Rhonda asked. She smiled and handed Morgan a bouquet of white lilies and gardenias. Rhonda had never seen her friend more beautiful than she was standing before her in an ivory, satin, and chiffon Vera Wang bridal gown. Nothing was more brilliant than the sparkle in her eyes; a sparkle that had been absent for nearly two years. "The church is packed Morgan, and The Doctor looks good enough to eat." Rhonda laughed and quickly stuck her head out the door and winked at her boyfriend, Dr. Wayne Pierre who looked equally as handsome as The Doctor.

"Where's Imani?" Morgan asked. She smiled at her friend, and her antics. Rhonda looked splendid in a champagne colored silk bridesmaid gown from the same collection. She took a few deep breaths to still the butterflies in her stomach.

"She's sitting with Carl, Irene, and Stephanie on the front pew looking beautiful and waiting to watch her Auntie Morgan marry the finest man in New Orleans," Lonnie Jean answered. She picked up her own bouquet of orchids, roses, and baby's breath. They smiled at each other; the sound of organ music reached their ears. "Mary Joyce and the boys just arrived with Tanya, William, and C. J. I also saw Arthur Lee DuPont and his wife. I know how important it was to you that he be here today."

Morgan smiled and then said, "Please tell me this is really happening and that I am not dreaming." She adjusted her veil and took one last look at herself in the mirror. Raymond came through the door, his smile almost too large for his face.

"It's both, honey. A real dream come true," Rhonda said. "You just be sure you throw that bouquet in my direction. I have some future plans for yummy Dr. Pierre." She kissed her friend on the cheek, winked at Raymond, and followed Lonnie Jean out of the church's bridal dressing room.

"This is it, Little Girl." Raymond extended his tuxedoed arm as his pride threatened to burst the buttons on his dove gray striped vest.

"Yes, it is, Uncle Raymond." Morgan smiled as she gently took his arm.

Raymond kissed her cheek as they heard the organ strike the first chords of "Here Comes the Bride." Morgan paused and inhaled deeply. She looked upward briefly and prayed silently as she thought of her father, Mama Essie, and even Celeste. Then, she moved forward as the faint fragrance of sweet mint tickled her nose.

ABOUT THE AUTHOR

At the urging of her friend and mentor, Blanche Richardson, La Rhonda attended Tina McElroy Ansa's first Sea Island Writers' Retreat on Sapelo Island in 2004. It was there where she began to "see" herself as a writer.

La Rhonda is a contributor to the award-winning Life Spices from Seasoned Sistahs anthology series and has also published work in Go, Tell Michelle: African American Women Write to the New First Lady; Sassy, Savvy and Bold After 50; The Beauty of Darkness (poetry); and Jubilee's Journey (a serial novel). She is honored to be a part of the anthology All the Women in My Family Sing edited by Deborah Santana.

La Rhonda, a native of Oakland, California, lives in the San Francisco Bay Area with her husband and biggest fan, Ernest Johnson.

Made in United States
Orlando, FL
28 March 2022

16247242R00195